Born in Stirling, Scotland in 1961, Malcolm Lyon was educated at Dollar Academy and the University of St Andrews, where he studied pure mathematics. After a short stint teaching in Kenya, he trained as a maths teacher before going on to work as a research officer for the Scottish Council for Research in Education. In 1990 he and his wife left Scotland to study French in the south of France before heading across the Mediterranean to Tunisia. He spent ten years living in the old city of Tunis, learning Arabic, soaking up local culture, researching local history and teaching English at the University of Tunis. Malcolm now lives in Marseille with his wife and two daughters, where he works in multi-lingual web development.

Malcolm Lyon

THE BRONZE LADDER

Matador
9 De Montfort Mews
Leicester LE1 7FW, UK
Tel: (+44) 116 255 9311 / 9312
Email: books@troubador.co.uk
Web: www.troubador.co.uk/matador

ISBN 1 905237 51 0

Cover illustration: Ian Legge

Typeset in 11pt Stempel Garamond by Troubador Publishing Ltd, Leicester, UK
Printed by The Cromwell Press Ltd, Trowbridge, Wilts, UK

Matador is an imprint of Troubador Publishing Ltd

*To the young people of Tunisia
who stand today between the echoes of the past and the choices
of the future.*

Contents

Foreword   ix

PART 1 THE POTTER'S SON

1	The Roar of the Mob	3
2	Here in Thuburbo Minus	12
3	The Price of Folly	22
4	Flight to Freedom	35
5	In Carthage	45
6	The End of the Road	54

PART 2 THE NOBLEMAN'S DAUGHTER

7	The Refusal	67
8	The Passing of Winter	77
9	A Secret Discovered	86
10	The Dream	97
11	The Evangelist	106
12	Further Encounters	116
13	The Agreement	127

PART 3 THE NEW FAMILY

14	First Impressions	141
15	Brothers in Christ	151
16	The Visitor	161
17	A Family Divided	170
18	The Edict	180

PART 4   THE JOURNEY HOME

19	The Prisoners	193
20	Descent into Hell	203
21	Ascent into Heaven	216
22	The Healing of Hope	226
23	Comfort in Adversity	235
24	The Last Days	245
25	Weaponless Warriors	254

Historical Note   265

Foreword

Modern Tunisia, along with Algeria and Libya, are heirs to an easily-forgotten past which deserves to be richly commemorated and celebrated. Together they were home to the strongest regional movement of Christianity in the world of the Western Mediterranean during the later Roman Empire. From about 200 to 450 CE it was the church of Roman Africa which produced the best minds and ablest leaders of Latin-speaking Christianity. In many respects the Christianity of the lands north of the Mediterranean - which in time would form the new Europe - was permanently influenced by the stellar Christian life and thought of North Africans.

This distinguished heritage is easily forgotten for the simple reason that it is an Islamic identity which dominates present-day Tunisia and its neighbours to the west, south and east. Yet each of these countries in its own way acknowledges and honours the illustrious Christian presence in its ancient past. From a holiday in Tunisia in 2004 I carried home a bottle of red wine from Chateau Saint Augustin. Attached to the neck was a folded gift card which sketched in French Augustine's life, conversion and immense theological and spiritual influence. 'This Augustine, this African, the last great figure of Antiquity, continues to live on sixteen centuries after his death.'

This novel by Malcolm Lyon tells the story of other early North African Christians whose lives belong with equal merit to the noble Christian history of Roman Africa. His source is perhaps the most vividly personal of all the extant records of the early Christian centuries. The Passion of Perpetua and Felicitas has attracted increased attention in recent decades because it includes the earliest known writing by a Christian woman – Perpetua's own prison diary, a text of quite remarkable sensitivity to women's experiences. The story of this group of Christian martyrs put to death at Carthage (near modern Tunis) in the year 203 has not yet been picked up by Hollywood, but this moving and dramatic Passion with its unimpeachable historical authenticity lends itself so naturally to the imaginative genre of a novel (and no doubt equally to that of a film). Malcolm Lyon lived and worked in Tunis for many years and has done his work with scrupulous regard for known historical realities as well as strong historical probabilities. Above all, he has crafted a narrative of compelling human and spiritual interest.

And if readers wonder how an account of the deaths of North African Christians squares with the larger picture of this vigorous and successful regional African church, Tertullian, its liveliest writer, has the answer: 'the blood of the martyrs is seed'. Perhaps the tired declining churches of today's Europe should be learning still from the ancient North African Christians: only Christians who know how to die for their faith (as distinct from socio-political causes) will attract others to live for it.

David Wright
Emeritus Professor of Patristic and Reformed Christianity,
University of Edinburgh
October 2005

Part One

THE POTTER'S SON

1

The Roar of the Mob

"Saturus! Saturus!" The call slowly penetrated the unconscious corridors of my sleeping mind. Through the fog of my awakening it became louder and clearer, recognisable as the voice of Rufus, calling up to me from the street. Suddenly reality flooded my mind and in a rush of excitement I leapt off my bed. In the darkness I began a ridiculous dance about the floor of my room which was the result of my attempts to get my feet into my sandals while simultaneously wrapping my cloak about my body. After some moments of silence from the street, the cries were renewed.

"Saturus, wake up you good for nothing bedbug – we'll miss everything if you don't come quickly!"

"Yes, coming!" I yelled in the direction of the shuttered window through which the cries were to be heard.

"Thank the gods! I thought after last night you were going to chicken out, you lily-livered milksop!"

"Why don't you go and stick your head in the cess trench and wait there till I'm ready?"

We were the best of friends, Rufus and I. We shared everything together, including, as of three days before, our proud membership of the Youth Guild of the town of Thuburbo Minus. And it was in support of our new-found comrades in the Guild that we were headed that morning to the amphitheatre games. The games! For how long had I longed to go and see the games? But, alas, my father had what he called a 'modern' outlook, and never attended the games himself, nor had he ever allowed me to attend. Until today. Despite his misgivings, he had given in to my pleas to let me join the Guild, and now how could he stop me going to support my companions, who were putting on a performance of their own that morning?

"That's it! If you're not out here in one minute I'm going without you!" came the voice from the street.

"Don't you dare! I told you, I'm coming."

The dance was over, and I was dressed and clattering down the wooden stairs. I glanced around at the dim shadows of the deserted pottery workshop on the ground floor of our house. This room was normally a hive of industry with a score of slaves busily mixing clay, turning it on wheels, decorating and dipping it, and stoking the fires beneath the kilns which turned it into the finished product. However, today was a public holiday, and most of the slaves would be at the games as well. Out in the street I was dazzled by the morning sunshine, and there was no sign of Rufus anywhere. A few other passers-by were mostly headed in the direction of the amphitheatre.

I silently cursed Rufus for his impatience, for, excited as I was about attending the games, I had no desire to go there alone. Then, just as I was setting off down the street, there was a shriek from around a corner and Rufus bounded out at me, brandishing one of the urinal jars from outside the fuller's workshop.

"Here," he cried, "I've brought you something from the cess trench!"

I ducked as he upturned it over my head. Of course, it was empty.

"Why don't you grow up?" I said. "I remember you doing that when we were still at primary school."

"Still gets you every time!" he laughed. "Hey, guess what? I saw old Flavius heading for the games – better make sure we stay well clear of him."

Flavius was our grammarian, who had been attempting for the last two years to teach us the Greek and Latin classics. This was no easy task for him, but he was a man of immense fortitude who seemed to thrive on such a challenge, and he laboured at it day after day in the hope that one day he might see some fruit.

"I still can't get over that gladiator – where was he from again?"

"The Crow, you mean? He's from Utica. Been at it for five years now I heard someone say, and he's still alive to tell the tale. Must've killed hundreds of opponents."

We had gone along with other members of the Guild the night before to the *cena libera* or free banquet, a lavish meal laid on for all the combatants who were going to take part the following day. Anyone who wanted could go and watch this event, and we had found it well worth a visit. With morbid curiosity we had walked among the tables, wondering which of those bodies filling themselves so nonchalantly now with meat and wine would be bloody corpses before the following evening. The largest group of onlookers had been crowded around the man nicknamed the Crow, who had risen to fame in Africa as a formidable Samnite gladiator. He always appeared in the arena dressed entirely in black, including his shield and visored helmet, hence his nickname. He had been sitting in his familiar black attire, making lewd remarks to the young women who draped themselves around him, and boasting now and then to no-one in particular.

"Six times they awarded me the wooden sword. Six times I came back to fight again. The Crow will always be back – have no fear!" And he laughed out loud at this, for he could see plenty of fear in the faces of some of the less experienced gladiators sitting nearby, who were clearly praying to the Fates not to pair them with the Crow the following day.

"Is he never going to retire?" I said to Rufus. "He must have a death-wish or something."

"Probably can't do anything else but fight, drink and bed women." Rufus' explanation seemed more likely.

We would have to wait till the afternoon, however, to see the Crow in action. As was the usual custom, the morning would be devoted to combats involving animals, while the afternoon was reserved for the even more popular contests between gladiators. In the morning most of the blood spilled was animals' blood. In the afternoon it was one hundred per cent human.

"And that runaway slave!" Rufus was referring to a condemned prisoner who had also been eating at the banquet alongside the gladiators, and who was due to be executed during the midday interval. "What a cretin he looked. Imagine trying to escape and then getting caught."

"It'll be his guts that'll do the escaping today," I remarked, and we both cackled at my wondrous wit.

As we approached the amphitheatre, the noise of the crowd, and the accompanying music, grew gradually louder. Our amphitheatre in Thuburbo Minus is not like those grand edifices that you see in cities like Carthage or Thysdrus. It is actually a natural bowl in the hill on which the town is built, with the arena at the bottom and the seats built up on terraces around the sides. It is thus an unimposing structure when viewed from the street, since all that can be seen is a ten foot high wall, topped by the masts for the awning, but the noise which was coming from the other side of the wall betrayed the fact that today there were several thousand people in there. Having never been through the gates in this wall before, I was taken aback by the sight that met my eyes when we went in. We entered at the top of the highest terrace and had an immediate view of the whole bowl, across the crowded terraces and down into the arena. I stopped and stared, rooted to the spot in amazement, until Rufus jerked me forward.

"Get a move on, you sloucher! What are you standing there for?" I was suddenly aware that I was partially blocking the entrance way, and that people were beginning to shout and push past me in annoyance.

"Look," said Rufus, "down there's the area that's been reserved for the Guild. You won't usually get to sit that near the arena, but they've given us good seats today. Aren't we the lucky ones?"

In the centre of the sandy arena was a lion tamer with a large whip, making a troupe of three lions do tricks like climbing onto stools and jumping through hoops. As we threaded our way slowly down through the crowds, my gaze wandered from the performance in the arena to the terraces all around, which by now were about three quarters filled. As we came lower we were rubbing shoulders with higher and higher ranks of society. At the top, near the entrances, stood the slaves and other non-citizens, then there was a tier especially for women, and lower down the various classes of citizens of the town. On the podium just above the arena sat the town's dignitaries and visiting officials, as well as a small band of musicians who intermittently struck up a tune on horns, trumpets, flutes and a water organ. We were positioned just above the podium, not far from the band, with a superb view of all that was happening.

Around us were thirty or forty other members of the Youth Guild, those who had not been selected to take part in the performance. The performance was a mock hunt, in which the participants would pit themselves against ever more difficult and dangerous beasts. As a finale the most skilled huntsman of the Guild, a fellow by the name of Archaeus, was going to face a leopard single-handed.

Despite the fact that Rufus had claimed that we were in danger of missing the whole show due to our late arrival, we were actually in plenty of time. Various performances, often with musical accompaniment, were following one another in the arena now, but these were just openers. Almost anyone, it seemed, who could juggle a few balls or do a few somersaults, was allowed to step into the arena and display his skills, or lack thereof in many cases.

After about half an hour the arena was suddenly empty, the band played a rousing fanfare, and the crowd became noticeably quieter as people who had been paying scant attention to the proceedings now looked to see what was happening. Our performance was first on the bill, and the Guild members around us grew especially quiet and tense, waiting to see our comrades appear. Then from the main opening into the arena four figures emerged. I recognised all of them as having been at the banquet the night before. As they appeared a great cheer erupted from the crowd, and the Guild members around us went wild, shouting and whistling and waving their arms in the air. Rufus and I joined in, swept away by the elation around us.

The four huntsmen were armed with hunting spears and

daggers, and they strode proudly to the centre of the arena where they took up position. Immediately, from four gates in the arena wall, four bulls were released, and began to trot back and forth in the sandy space, pawing the ground with their hooves, evidently suspicious of the group at the centre. The crowd, hungry for blood, roared all around them. Thus the first battle of the day began. It did not take a genius to see that the bulls had drawn the short straw. There was little chance of them coming out of the affair alive, but the question was, would they manage to shed any of the huntsmen's blood before they succumbed to their weapons?

The first bull was dispatched by a carefully aimed spear which went straight into its neck and brought it down, to a tumultuous roar from the terraces – blood was flowing at last! The beast was finished off with the spear-thrower's dagger, and the four huntsmen remained unscathed. However, before the other three had claimed their victims, one had been knocked over, though apparently unhurt, and another had been caught in the thigh by one of the bull's horns. This development sent the crowd to a new pitch of excitement. We cheered madly as he picked himself up and staggered away from the bull, with blood flowing freely from the wound in his leg, while his companions threatened the animal with their spears. In the end, wounded as he was, the injured huntsman still managed to claim his bull, and all four left the arena, to redoubled cheers and whistles from the crowd.

Someone sitting next to Rufus was shouting something in his ear, but I couldn't hear what it was. I leant over and shouted amid the din.

"What's he saying?"

"That's Marcus Sunnius who got it in the leg – his first time in the arena, apparently."

"Will he be all right?"

"Should be. It didn't look too bad – a lot of blood, but that's what everyone comes to see isn't it?"

And a lot of blood was certainly spilled before our eyes during the remainder of the performance. After the bulls' blood we were treated to buffalo's blood, bear's blood, lion's blood, and finally Archaeus, the hero of the Youth Guild, was out there alone in the arena, face to face with the leopard. In the combats leading up to this finale the participants had been armed with various weapons, most of the killing being done with spear and bow, but several huntsmen had also wielded burning firebrands. Archaeus was carrying a spear as he walked out into the arena, but the first thing he did was to throw it away, and draw a short dagger, provoking an awed response from the crowd – a collective gasp of amazement arising from the terraces, as he flourished the dagger in the air, turning around to take in the whole crowd at once.

Now the leopard was out too, circling around him. I felt a sudden chill, wondering if it would really be possible for him to kill the creature with only a short dagger. I was shouting, with all those around me, "Archaeus! Archaeus!" as he advanced towards the leopard, dagger at the ready. Exactly what happened next I was never very sure about when I tried later to picture the incident once more in my mind. All I can recall is the magnificent creature suddenly bounding at Archaeus, and a glint of metal as the dagger rose then flew into the air to fall several yards away on the sand. There was a roar from the crowd as the hunter fell heavily and then a scream, audible even above the din of the spectators as the leopard tugged at something violently and blood flowed out from where its jaws were. Almost immediately the beast fell on its side, and I could not understand what had happened until I noticed an arrow protruding from its flank. Then several attendants ran out from a gateway and quickly crossed to the prone forms of Archaeus and the leopard.

Excited voices could be heard all around us.

"What happened?"

"What was the fool playing at, trying to fight with only a dagger?"

"Is he still alive?"

The answer to this last question soon became evident, as the attendants finished their inspection then gestured to some other attendants who came out in their turn, carrying a stretcher, lifted the body of Archaeus onto it, and began to carry it towards one of the arena's two main gateways.

"The *Porta Libitinensis*," said Rufus, "That means he's dead."

I stared in shock at the body of the leopard and the red stain in the sand beside it. I had just witnessed a man being killed before my very eyes. Most of the crowd seemed to take it in their stride, although several of the Guild members were leaving the terraces, with looks of dismay on their faces. I guessed that they were personal friends of Archaeus. I wondered if I was going to be sick, but then I told myself to act like a man. What would Rufus and the other Guild members around me think if they knew how shaken I had been at the sight of violent death? It happened all the time in the amphitheatre, and the crowd seemed to love it.

And indeed, by the time we climbed the steps that afternoon to make our way out to the street at the end of the games, I was surprised when I recalled how that first death had affected me. I had seen a lot more during the course of the day, and each time I had grown more accustomed to the sight, until in the end I was as eager as anyone in the crowd for more. First there had been the condemned slave, torn to pieces by a bear during the midday interval, a rather gruesome sight as his arm had ended up detached from his body while he was still alive. This I found particularly nauseating, mainly because Rufus and I were eating lunch at the time – some bread and cheese which Rufus had bought from a vendor. At least, he said he had bought it, although many of Rufus' 'purchases' did not actually involve money changing hands. Then most of the gladiatorial contests had ended with the death of one of the participants. The Crow had, of course, done away with one more opponent, to the delight of the crowd, and had strutted arrogantly out of the *Porta Sanavivaria*, the Gate of Life, as he had done so many times before.

"You're a weed, Saturus," said Rufus as we made our way along the crowded street, heading back towards the forum. "I thought we were going to see your lunch spewed all over the terrace."

"It was the cheese," I replied. "It tasted rancid."

"You're a hopeless liar," he laughed. "Still, I suppose it was your first time. Even I got a shock when Archaeus got himself chomped. That was pretty horrible."

"He died quicker than most," I said. "That wretch of a slave, for example."

"But that was different. I mean, Archaeus wasn't meant to die. You know what I mean? The prisoners and the gladiators – they know what they're in for. But Archaeus – he was just showing off..."

I pondered this opinion for some moments as we walked along, wondering if it was possible to distinguish between different kinds of death in this way. Then Rufus suddenly stopped in the street, staring ahead of him in horror.

"What is it?" I asked.

"Weren't we supposed to have learned that passage of Virgil for tomorrow?"

"Come now," I began, "and I shall tell you of the glory that lies in store for the sons of Dardanus, for the men of..."

"Oh, you make me sick, you really do!"

"Me?" I said innocently. "Are you sure it's not that rancid cheese we had for lunch?"

We were at the forum by this time, standing amid the huge temples and other public buildings that formed a focus for the life of Thuburbo Minus. There was still about half an hour before the time of the evening meal, and Rufus stopped me beside the steps of the temple of Saturn.

"You've really learned the passage?" he asked me.

"I think so – more or less."

"Right. You'd better teach it to me." He sat down on the steps, and I leapt onto the pedestal at the side and began, putting on an exaggerated impression of our grammarian Flavius during a lesson.

"Gnaeus Speratus, repeat after me: 'Come now, and I shall tell you...'"

Half an hour later he had, like me, learned it – more or less. And by that time, I knew it perfectly.

2

Here in Thuburbo Minus

It was a bright morning in April, the weather was turning warmer and the sun promised some heat later in the day. Rufus came into the schoolroom late, which was quite usual, but this time he was obviously seized with emotion. His face was flushed, and he had been running.

"The emperor! The emperor!", he cried waving his arms around wildly. We all turned away from Flavius, who had been in the middle of reading a passage from Livy, and stared at him in astonishment.

"What? Here in Thuburbo Minus?" asked Flavius, raising his eyebrows in mock astonishment. Such a visit was unheard of, but our tutor was not being serious. In any case, we all knew that Marcus Aurelius was campaigning thousands of miles away in Pannonia on the Danube frontier, and had been for most of the last five years.

"He's dead! I heard it in the forum – on the northern frontier – two weeks ago!" Flavius was on his feet in an instant sending his chair crashing backwards against the wall.

"Is this true? If this is one of your misguided pranks..." It was the sort of thing Rufus had indeed made up in the past, hence the added difficulty he now had in trying to persuade us that he was serious.

"I swear it! Go out and see for yourself – the whole town will be talking of it soon enough." Flavius strode to the doorway and looked out, but, finding the street deserted, he turned back in to question Rufus further.

"What exactly is the news, boy?"

"Just what I told you, sir – the announcement was being posted in the forum when I came through it just now. Marcus Aurelius died at Sirmium two weeks ago – Commodus is now sole emperor." Three years previously the emperor had named his own son Commodus co-emperor with him, to rule after his own death.

"How did he die? In battle?"

"He fell ill of a stomach ailment and died soon after – that's all it said."

"Anything else?"

"No. Oh, yes – he's been deified."

"Of course."

Flavius straightened his chair and sank slowly back into it, staring at the floor. A ripple of excited whispers spread around the room, to which the tutor paid no attention. After sitting in silence for some moments, he looked up.

"So", he said, and a hush fell immediately. "We are left with the emperor's son to rule alone. We must pray to the gods that Commodus will be found man enough to follow in his father's footsteps of wise and courageous government. We have been blessed these past hundred years, you know." Here he looked round at us with a keen and solemn glance. "It is not something to take for granted – to have a man on the throne who knows how to govern an empire the size of Rome's." He was brandishing the scroll of Livy from which he had been reading, as if it was evidence for what he was saying.

I remember thinking at the time that these words sounded rather grand, but I did not take them too seriously. Flavius was, after all, a rhetorician, and what better moment for a little self-indulgence than the occasion of hearing of an emperor's death? But much later, having seen what became of Commodus during the fifteen years of his subsequent reign culminating in his assassination, I realised that our tutor had seen what few others saw then. Did he even then have some inkling of the near anarchy into which the life and death of Commodus would plunge the Empire? I do not know. Perhaps if some in Rome had seen the future more clearly a great deal of turmoil could have been avoided, but then again, perhaps not. There was a sort of dreadful inexorability about the events of those years, as if the world was watching some terrible accident slowly unfolding, but we were rooted to the spot unable to do anything to prevent it. Meanwhile, following the deification of Marcus Aurelius, endless sacrifices had to be offered for him at the temple of Fortuna Augusta over the next few weeks.

Months after we received the news of Marcus Aurelius' death far away on the Danube frontier, the rumours began to circulate in the province that his "stomach ailment" was more likely attributable to poison administered by someone in the pay of his son. With hindsight the story seems not improbable, but such rumours are easily fed by discontent, and hard to prove one way or the other. Suffice it to say that, at the time, stories like this filled our young and over-active minds with a morbid fascination.

*

There were plenty of other events to feed our insatiable appetite for the gruesome and the grotesque. It was I who got to tell Rufus about the twelve Christians from Scillium torn to pieces by the beasts in the great amphitheatre at Carthage that same summer. I thought for once I had got one up on him by hearing about this before he did, but although he had not heard of the execution, his background knowledge about this strange sect appeared to be far in excess of my own.

"They came from among the Jews," he told me, as if he were an expert on the subject, "but not even the Jews can stomach their revolting practices."

"You seem to know a lot about them," I said nonchalantly. Inwardly quite curious, I was, nevertheless, too proud to rise so quickly to his bait. We were sitting under an olive tree just outside the town by the road to Bulla Regia, looking across the Bagradas valley, and my gaze drifted away into the distance, watching the shimmering heat haze above the serried ranks of olive trees that stretched as far as the eye could see.

"Some self-styled prophet from the province of Syria – got himself crucified for stirring up trouble among the masses. Then

14

his followers start going around claiming he came out of his tomb alive – ever heard anything so ridiculous?" He cackled at the joke, and I joined in. There were many strange sects and religions around, with all sorts of bizarre beliefs, but the doctrines of this group sounded particularly improbable.

"I suppose they had really stolen the body?"

"Oh – who knows? Spirited away by sorcery more likely. That's what they dabble in, anyway. Mystic rites and dark rituals behind closed doors. You know, we've actually got some here in Thuburbo – that's what I heard at any rate." He lowered his voice for the coup de grace: "They eat babies, you know."

I have to admit that even I was a little shocked, and more than a little dubious, at this accusation. I had heard of mystic cults that performed who knew what vile practices at their secret gatherings, but here in Thuburbo Minus? It seemed incredible.

"Where did you hear all this?" I asked.

"Oh, everyone's heard of it," he answered vaguely. "I mean, they obviously must be involved in some pretty sordid activities, or else why would they be condemned to death just for being Christians?"

This argument seemed reasonably convincing.

"Do you know any of them?"

"Not personally. But you know Appius Venturius? I think he said one of their slaves has joined them. Oh, and incest – that's another thing they're into. They have these feasts, see – lots of food and even more wine, and then they have this huge orgy – people grabbing anyone they want, even their own mothers or brothers."

"I'm surprised you haven't rushed off to join them yourself," I remarked. "It sounds right up your street."

Rufus laughed. "Not likely. I haven't told you what happens to someone who wants to join them."

"Let me in on the secret – I'm already thinking of putting myself forward for membership. It sounds even more fun than the Youth Guild!"

"I'll come and watch you getting your head chewed off by the beasts – and I'll cheer as loud as anyone, and that's a promise. You can't say I'm not a loyal friend."

"I'm touched," I said. "I really didn't know you felt that way. So what do I have to do to join?"

"Well, first of all they present you with this thing that looks like a cake coated in wheat, then they hand you a knife and tell you to stick it in the cake. You do it, and that's when you discover it's not a cake, it's a live baby. Not alive for long, of course, since you've just stuck it with this carving knife. Then everyone gets a piece of bread and dips it in the blood and eats it. Those with a bigger appetite get some of the flesh as well. So there you are – why don't you go along to their next meeting and tell them you're eager to join?"

"And where *do* they meet, tell me?"

"I'm beginning to think you're serious – you always were a bit soft in the head."

I gave him a pitying look. "I'm just wondering why someone doesn't stop all these goings on. We're supposed to be a civilised society after all."

"They're very secretive – I suppose that's the difficulty with trying to stamp them out. I've heard they own a cemetery on the edge of town where they hold secret meetings at the crack of dawn. Just the place for a bit of sorcery I've no doubt."

"Let's go there."

Rufus looked at me as if I was mad. Then he looked slightly worried as he began to realise that I might be serious. He was no doubt mentally assessing the reliability of his sources and finding it to be less than he might have wished for in this situation.

"What for?" he said, somewhat uneasily.

"To spy on them. I want to see all this stuff for myself."

"Well, you know, I never said I'd actually seen any of this with my own eyes. I'm only passing on what I've heard in the forum." Rufus had become decidedly defensive.

"Listen, I'm not saying you're lying or anything. I just think it would be a laugh to go and see if we can see anything interesting. Or maybe you're too scared." Rufus looked at me levelly, evaluating the proposal. Then his face suddenly broke into a grin.

"All right. We'll go. They usually meet on Sunday – that's tomorrow. But we can go and scout out the ground right now. Find out where this cemetery is exactly for a start, and check out if there's anywhere we could hide to get a good view of what's going on. Come on."

After this we spent a frustrating couple of hours wandering about the outskirts of the town exploring various neighbourhoods where Rufus had imagined the cemetery might be. I was beginning to express my doubts about the veracity of his whole story. Rufus was beginning snap back about the whole hare-brained scheme being my idea in the first place. Then suddenly I noticed a garden, just visible through the bars of a wooden gate set in a wall that ran along the side of the road for a distance of about fifty metres. I stopped to peer through and Rufus joined me.

"What's that?" I said. After a few moments, Rufus announced:

"I think we've found them!" He began to scramble over the gate. After glancing furtively up and down the roadway, which at that moment was quite deserted, I followed him. We found ourselves in the neatly laid out grounds of a private garden, with a number of tombs scattered around. The tombs were of various shapes and sizes, some modest affairs marked only with a wooden plaque, a few more ornate, and there were at least two that looked like miniature buildings, with marble inscriptions. All of them, curiously enough seemed to be oriented in the same direction and many were inscribed with a cross or some other strange symbols. In the middle of the garden there was another wall, higher than the one which bounded the roadway, apparently surrounding a small enclosure. Throwing cautious glances around us as we went, we made our way up to a wooden gate in this wall.

"Locked." said Rufus, after trying to open it. "Here, climb up on my shoulders and see if you can get a peek over the top."

This way round made sense as I was a good bit lighter than Rufus. He bent down and I clambered up his back and onto his shoulders. After he had risen rather unsteadily back to a standing position, it was just possible for me to see over the wall. I was looking down into a high-walled enclosure, and in the centre there was what looked like another tomb, as ornate as any of those outside the enclosure. Around this the ground was mostly paved, with narrow shrubbery beds running along just inside the walls.

"Well, you great elephant," came Rufus' voice from below, "what can you see?"

I described the scene briefly, then jumped down. We looked at each other.

"I'll bet that's where they hold their meetings, then." said Rufus. "Probably keep the door locked while they're doing it as well."

"Well, we could hide behind that big tomb over there." I suggested, indicating one of the miniature house structures positioned not far from the door. "We'd be able to hear what was going on, I bet. And if they were all locked inside, I could even climb on your back again and see over the wall."

Rufus went over to examine the tomb.

"Perfect." he said. "Tomorrow morning then. We'd better be here before it's light."

We set off back towards the gateway, but Rufus kept stopping to examine the pathway and the tombs.

"What are you looking for?" I asked.

He gave me a lurid grin. "Bones and bloodstains."

I snorted. "I think they're too tidy to leave that sort of thing lying around."

We climbed back over the gate and looked at each other. It seemed too early to be heading back home.

"It's a pleasant evening, my friend," said Rufus. "There's an inn near here with good beer and some hot-blooded women in the rooms upstairs. We need something to while away the hours. In fact, why bother to go home at all? If we stay here for the night we won't have to come far in the morning."

"I haven't any money," I said. It was true – I got little enough of an allowance as it was, and it was all spent for that week.

"It's all right, I've got some. You can pay next time."

And so, with that settled, we set off down the road again, in eager anticipation of an evening of abandon.

The following morning we left the inn early, in a rather dishevelled state, and feeling somewhat the worse for our activities of the night before. The sky was still dark, and the stars were still out, and we both could have happily slept much longer. We made our way quickly to the cemetery, without any difficulty this time. The garden appeared to be deserted as before, but I found it's appearance now rather unnerving, with the vague silhouettes of tombs just visible in the gloomy pre-dawn light. No doubt Rufus was thinking the same, but of course, neither of us said a thing about it. Instead we clambered boldly over the gate and went over to take up our watch behind the tomb that we had singled out the day before. It was rather chilly and we both shivered as we crouched beside the cold stone. An occasional bat fluttered by above our heads.

"You think they'll come?" I asked in a low voice. Rufus shrugged.

"I keep telling you – I'm only repeating what I've heard. They meet on Sunday mornings. This is their meeting place. So we wait here and see what happens."

After half an hour, the sky had grown light and the sun was about to come up. We were still waiting for something to happen, and were on the point of giving up and going home, when suddenly there was a sound of rattling from the gate. We both stiffened and peered nervously round the side of the tomb. It was now quite light, and we could clearly see a group of figures in the roadway outside the gate.

"It's them!" whispered Rufus, with a mixture of fear and triumph. "They're coming in!"

We could now hear low voices drifting across the clear morning air. The gate opened and five people came in and walked towards the door in the inner enclosure. They were chatting as they walked along.

"Jocundus and Livia should be here later," said one of them. "They'll have the baby with them."

Rufus and I stared at each other in horror. Up till that moment neither of us had really believed the gruesome tales which Rufus had been telling. Now however, had we not just heard proof with our own ears? Two of the faithful had evidently been assigned to provide the baby for the sacrifice. Where would they get it from? I wondered. The most chilling thing was that the people seemed quite normal, and acted in a perfectly relaxed and friendly way with one another. To chat so casually when one was about to witness, or perhaps even perform, the ritual murder of a baby, one would have to be inhumanly cruel. My heart was now beating wildly as we watched them unlock the door and disappear within the high wall. We could still hear their voices talking, but could not make out what they were saying.

It was not long before others arrived, in twos and threes, and made their way through the garden and into the inner enclosure. We were well hidden and no-one even glanced in our direction. There were men and women, young and old. Quite a number were obviously slaves, to judge from their dress. All of them appeared to be normal, law-abiding citizens, and I was beginning to wonder once more about the tales Rufus had recounted. Then all of a sudden we watched in horror as two people walked past us, one of them carrying a bundle which looked very much like a baby wrapped in cloths. Rufus gestured towards them silently then drew his finger across his throat. His face looked deathly white in the dawn light. Once they were inside the door was shut and no-one else arrived.

The hum of conversation died down and one voice alone could be heard, reciting or reading something, though it was still too low for us to hear the words. Then all the voices joined together in singing. The style was rather unusual, but I caught myself thinking that it had a certain charm, even beauty about it. Then I remembered that the singers were even now preparing to slaughter an infant in cold blood. With that thought the solemn singing seemed to take on a nightmarish quality.

Before the singing was over we heard a sound rising above it which froze our blood – the sudden cry of a baby. I grabbed Rufus' shoulder.

"Shouldn't we do something?" I said.

"You want to walk in there?" he replied, staring at me

wide-eyed. "Those people are devils – they'll kill you. Or turn you into something."

"But we can't just sit here while they..." My words trailed off. I stared at the doorway, trying to picture the scene – the raised knife, the struggling infant. What could I do if I suddenly strode across to the door and broke into their meeting? "Come on. Let's take a look over the wall at least."

Rufus gave his assent, and we were halfway across to the wall when the singing stopped, and, horror of horrors, the door in the wall suddenly opened. We both stood, rooted to the spot in terror. A face appeared just inside the doorway and someone said, "Look there's someone out here!"

We both turned and fled in panic, racing to the gateway. There was a shout from behind us, but we didn't look round. The gate had been left ajar, and we were outside in an instant, sprinting down the street as if we had the Harpies at our heels. We didn't stop till we were several streets from the cemetery. At last we came to a halt beside a doorway and looked behind us. There was no sign of any pursuit. Rufus looked at me.

"Well, now do you believe it?" he asked breathlessly.

"This time," I panted, "I have to hand it to you. But here – in Thuburbo Minus..."

"I tell you, they're everywhere these days. It's a menace to society – that's why they get rounded up and fed to the beasts."

"So – what do we do now?" I asked.

"We leave them to it," he said. "Unless you want to go back there?"

"No fear," I replied. "I've seen enough, thanks."

And so we both returned home, to face the usual ruckus over where we had been all night. It was a tedious business sometimes, being a teenager.

3

The Price of Folly

We didn't go back to the cemetery, though we did visit the nearby tavern again once or twice in the weeks that followed. We were the flower of Thuburbo's youth, or at least that is how we saw ourselves, and we considered it our right to be able to indulge in whatever pleasures were on offer. The only problem was paying for them. Although I came from a reasonably well-to-do family, I had very little money to spend myself. On my father's death I would inherit the family business – a respectable pottery with nearly thirty slaves working it. Meanwhile I had nothing but a meagre weekly allowance. This was the common status of my companions. I loved my father dearly, but I have to confide that I occasionally reflected on the day of his death, thinking that, sad though it be, it would not be devoid of material compensation. It was Rufus who, some time later, initiated me into the manner by which the rewards of that day could be brought forward while the pain of its accompanying grief could be kept at a comfortably unknown distance in the future.

"Cheer up, old fellow," he told me one day, when I had been bemoaning once more our chronic shortage of ready cash. "I believe I have found the answer to all our problems."

"Tell me," I said. "For I don't think I can stand going on like this a single day longer. And even if your scheme involves some form of criminality, which I don't doubt, I hereby declare myself ready and willing to join you in it!"

"Criminality, indeed! What sort of a lowborn son of a Sardinian harlot do you take me for? Listen, my friend, this is entirely legal, and there is nothing at all about it that will besmirch your snow-white character or reputation."

"I'm astounded that you should feel the need to be so law-abiding," I said. "It's entirely out of character for you, you know. Well then, I'm all ears. Tell me what this wonderful scheme is that you've dreamed up."

"I'll go one better, my dear Saturus. I'll take you and show you. Come on," he slapped me on the back, "we're going to take a trip to an interesting part of town."

So we set off, threading our way through the crowded streets, past temples and shrines and market stalls, down quieter alleys, gradually moving away from the regions of the town I was familiar with. All the while I pressed Rufus to tell me where exactly we were going, but he only grinned and gave such replies as "A little patience, my friend", and "You'll see when we get there."

Eventually we found ourselves in a decidedly unwholesome neighbourhood. There was a great deal of rubbish lying about the unpaved streets, and an unpleasant smell to go with it. The houses were mostly small and primitive-looking, and the streets were populated for the most part by cats and dirty children playing amongst the refuse.

"We're going to strike it rich *here*?" I asked Rufus incredulously.

"Trust me, my friend – you'll be stinking rich!" and he howled with laughter, drawing some curious stares from a group of children nearby.

Halfway along one of these dingy backstreets, Rufus suddenly stopped outside a door which, though not particularly pretty to look at, nevertheless gave an impression of solidity, as if whoever lived on the other side of it was concerned about keeping out unwelcome visitors. I stepped distastefully over a dead cat that lay in the roadway near the entrance, but Rufus seemed in high spirits, giving me a conspiratorial glance as he knocked on the door and pushed it open.

The interior was not much more inspiring than the street outside. We were in a small office, lit rather inadequately by the daylight coming in through one high tiny window. There were rush mats on the earthen floor, and the only furniture was a rough wooden table and chair. At the table was seated a small man of about forty, balding with greyish hair, dressed in a grubby tunic, who looked up from the papers on the table before him and peered at us suspiciously. The impression of a scrawny chicken was impossible to ignore.

"Yes?" he said, in a thin, irritated voice. "What is it?"

"Saturus," Rufus put one hand on my shoulder and indicated the seated figure with the other, "I'd like you to meet an acquaintance of mine – Simeon the money-lender! My friend would like to have a little money."

The man's eyes still showed caution and mistrust as he examined me more closely, but now the glint of greed also showed in them.

"What's your name, boy?" he said, rather abruptly, it seemed to me.

"Marcus Saturus." I said, then added "Sir", though I wasn't sure if this was necessary.

"Father?"

"My father? Aulus Saturus, the potter."

Simeon seemed to search his mind for any information he might already have in this connection, then said, somewhat to my surprise, "Owns a workshop on the Cardo II East. Is that the one?"

"Yes, sir," I replied. "We have nearly thirty slaves."

"Yes, yes. Of course." he muttered, more to himself than to me. He scrabbled around among a pile of papyrus sheets on his desk for a few moments while we waited in silence. Rufus grinned at me cheerfully, and I replied by raising my eyebrows, trying to convey that I was still dubious about how I could benefit from this man's services. Finally the money-lender looked up at me again, with a fearful grimace that I realised was actually meant to be a smile.

"So, Marcus Saturus," he said, "you want some of your father's estate a little early, is that it? Well you've come to the right place. Old Simeon can help you out there, don't you worry. How much would you like to begin with?" And he fixed me with a beady eye.

So that was what the business was all about, I thought to

myself. We were going to borrow what we needed from this man, a rather off-putting specimen of humanity, I have to say, but then, I told myself, beggars can't be choosers. In any case, the money-lender himself clearly did not consider it important to try to impress would-be clients with a suave appearance or an engaging manner. The loan would not need to be repaid until I inherited the family fortune. I later learned that young men such as ourselves were his preferred clients. His business depended almost entirely of raking back debts when sons of families such as ours came into their inheritance. In fact, contrary to what Rufus had assured me, the matter was not strictly legal. It was forbidden to lend to anyone under twenty-five years of age, in order to prevent just such invidious practices as Simeon was now engaging in. This was why the money-lender was content to keep his business hidden away in this seedy neighbourhood, where the authorities would not notice what he was up to. I was rather unsure about how much was a reasonable sum to ask for on this first visit, and I looked at Rufus helplessly.

"Why don't you take a hundred denarii for the moment?" Rufus suggested, clearly enjoying himself.

"A hundred denarii?" I asked, unable to keep the surprise out of my voice. It seemed like too much to ask for all at once. But Simeon had already pulled out a large purse from somewhere in the folds of his robe and was counting out eight gold coins, each a quinarius – twelve and a half denarii.

The affair was conducted quickly and without ceremony, and I got ready to leave the office richer than I had ever been before in my life, with instructions to return whenever I needed more. My name was now entered in his books. At that moment Simeon signalled to us with a gesture to come closer. He spoke in a low voice.

"Just one thing," he said. "Not a word to anyone about where the money came from. Or else..." and he drew his finger across his throat.

I nodded nervously, unable to say a word, and was bundled out the door by Rufus.

"There." said Rufus, as we made our way back out of the maze of dirty streets, "You're one of Simeon's boys now! From this point on, money is no object."

I felt the weight of the gold coins that I now had safely hidden away in my money pouch.

"A hundred denarii!" I said in awe.

"You'll find ways to spend it, I'm sure," laughed Rufus, "But we can come back again for more."

*

Thus began my new life. One, as it seemed to me, of unimpeded pleasure. I said nothing of this, of course, to any of my family, even my brother Lucius, and my activities became of necessity somewhat secretive with regard to them. Naturally, my father often questioned me about where I went in the evenings and what I did, and I often argued with him, asserting that I was of age and could do what I wanted. The money I borrowed never seemed to last very long though. As soon as I had it, I felt a compulsion to go and find some way of parting with it. Wine and women were favourites, of course, but I also soon discovered the compulsive thrill of dice games in the gambling house, and the betting agent in a colonnade of the forum, where I could place bets on gladiatorial contests. And of course, the chariot races offered even more excitement for betting, but we did not have a circus in Thuburbo Minus. Rufus and I therefore would often take a trip to Carthage, where we would spend the morning at the huge baths complex down by the sea, before placing our bets and howling with the crowds all afternoon at the circus. I occasionally made some money out of this, but most often I lost. However, after several more visits to Simeon, I began to feel carefree about such things. Why should I worry about losing money, when I could always go and pick up some more whenever I wanted?

Rufus began to notice that the money I borrowed never lasted long. He joked about this, but he was a good friend, and would often pay for me out of his own pocket. It was not long, however, before he began to worry about me. He was much better than I was at managing his finances, and he knew when to stop in the gambling house.

"Lost it all on the greens again, didn't you?" said Rufus as we were searching for a ride on a cart back home to Thuburbo after a couple of days spent in Carthage. He looked at me pitifully. "Well, if we have to pay for the ride I've got enough for you, but just this once."

"It wasn't my day, that's all," I replied. "You have to admit that the races I lost most on were pretty close finishes. Look, there's a cart that could be heading our way. Any chance of a ride, my friend?"

It was a carrier from Thuburbo with a load of amphorae full of fish sauce, and he agreed to take us, but he was clearly an opportunist, and demanded a ridiculous fee, which put Rufus in a sour mood.

"How did I get saddled with the likes of you?" he complained to me as we bumped along the road. "It's bad enough having to line the pockets of this old skinflint, but to have to pay for a waster like you on top..."

"I told you, it's just this once. Remind me that it's my turn to pay next time."

"You're turn to pay!" Rufus snorted. "That'll be a day of celebration. When was the last time that it was your turn to pay, as a matter of fact, my good friend?"

"Some friend you are," I snapped back. "Perhaps you should just ask for my payment back from the good gentleman and I'll get off and walk."

"Perhaps I should." he replied. He didn't, however – twenty-five miles was a little far to go on foot, though I could perhaps have begged a free ride on another vehicle. Instead we lapsed into silence. If I had been honest with myself, I would have admitted that I was being foolish, but I chose to ignore the obvious and drift along in my dream world, pretending that nothing was wrong and that one day I would be rich.

*

It was around this time that my father announced that my education was finished. There were a number of reasons for this. One was that the grammarian Flavius' fees were fairly high, and we were not nobility who could pay for such luxuries without feeling the pinch. Another reason was not given explicitly, but my relationship with my father by this time made it obvious. He was growing gradually more exasperated with my lifestyle. Of course, he knew very little about what I was up to, but he had extensive general knowledge of what I *might* be doing when I was away from home. Since this was most of the time, and since I never talked to my family about anything I was doing, they naturally assumed the worst. My father had begun to accuse me of being an idler, and to hint that the time was coming soon when I would have to start earning my keep. He clearly saw my education as a bad influence in this respect, since it had no short-term benefit for the family business, and even the long-term benefits were now dubious, since it involved more and more study of obscure points of grammar and training in useless rhetoric. The third reason was directly related to our family pottery business. One day he brought an unusual pot to show me. It was not one from our kilns, I could see that immediately from its superior quality and shiny red finish.

"What is it?" I asked.

"This, Marcus, is terra sigillata," he replied. "I hear that they're making it in Carthage now – that's where this came from – and I have a mind to start production of it here in Thuburbo."

My father had always been something of an innovator in his own way. It was he who had built up the family business from lowly beginnings, and now he was evidently dreaming of going even further.

"What does that mean exactly?" I asked him.

"It means learning new techniques and buying new equipment – well-made moulds instead of these old wheels, and specialised kilns. It means money, of course, and it means using all the expertise that we have. It means that you can be put to work doing something useful for a change."

"But why all this change?" I asked, my heart sinking at what this new plan would apparently entail for me. "I mean, it's a very nice pot, I can see that, but isn't it simpler just to continue doing what we're doing?"

"My dear boy, what we are doing is simply supplying the

common people with the necessities of life. That is not the way to make money. This," he brandished the finely-made pot, "is luxury. This is what the rich want to spend their money on, and they will pay well for it. And not just the rich of Thuburbo Minus – oh no, if we can build up a name for ourselves they will come all the way from Rome itself to buy our wares. That is how to make money in this business!"

Thus my fate was sealed. By taking me out of Flavius' schoolroom, and putting me to work in the family business, my father both saved a good bit of money, and, he hoped, gained an assistant with a good education, able to learn about and supervise the new procedures.

The news that my studies were over did not come as a surprise to me, but even so I did not take it well. Not that I had greatly enjoyed the hours spent teasing out every nuance of the Latin language and listening to, and occasionally delivering, bizarre speeches about nonsensical topics, just to illustrate particular styles of rhetoric. At least the thought that that was all behind me was some consolation. It was the hours which I was now expected to spend in the workshop below our home which I resented. And the fact that I would now see Rufus less and less. He was going to continue his education for only a few more months himself, and then he hoped to get a clerical post in the civil service, which might eventually lead to greater things. Although he was sorry for me, I thought I detected a certain measure of relief on his part that we would not be together so much. Again, if I had been honest with myself, I would have admitted that my foolish ways were clearly beginning to annoy and embarrass him, and the truth was that he was in some ways glad to be rid of me. Instead though, I blamed him in my mind for being disloyal and heartless, and began in my turn to avoid his company. I still found ways of spending money, however, but I was usually alone, and although I pretended to be enjoying myself, I was aware that under the surface, I was far from happy.

It was at this point that I began for the first time to think seriously about the debts that I was running up with Simeon, and the interest due at the usurious rates he charged. I tried to estimate the total estate to which I would be the heir on my father's death, and no matter how optimistic I was in taking into account my father's ambitious plans for the business, I realised that I would barely have enough to pay back the money-lender. And there was always the possibility that his plans would come to nothing, that we would be left worse off than we were at present. What, then would become of our family? What if my mother were still living – how could I face her with the awful truth?

My first instinct was to go on a wild gambling spree. One day I went to Simeon and procured a fairly large sum from him, though he was beginning to get suspicious of me. He knew a fair amount about my father's business, and he too had obviously been making calculations. I then blew the whole lot on some pretty unlikely bets which, if I had been extraordinarily lucky, would have alleviated my situation considerably. Of course, I won absolutely nothing on them. Moreover, from that time on Simeon placed a strict limit on how much he would lend me per month. This at least had the advantage that I was now sliding rather more slowly towards financial ruin.

*

By now I was missing Rufus. He had now actually gone to Carthage, where he was an apprentice clerk in the provincial government offices. I saw him only once more, quite by chance one day, in Carthage. My father had taken me along on a trip to do some business with a big pottery merchant in the city, hoping to win some export contracts from him. I had excused myself after a while to make my way to the Antonine Baths – for old time's sake, I told myself. As I approached the complex, and gazed up at its hugeness and the grace of its architecture, which had never failed to impress me anew on each visit, old memories flooded back. I had always been here with Rufus before, and now I was alone. I wondered where he was and what he was doing. I made my way into the changing rooms, and headed for the familiar corner where he and I had always been in the habit of leaving our things. It was almost no surprise when I heard a familiar voice coming from behind one of the marble pillars.

"You're wasting your breath Calenus. I can get all the cleansing I need right here."

I stuck my head around the pillar, and there he was, sitting with another man about our age.

"Rufus!" I said. He looked up in surprise from unlacing his sandals.

"By all the gods! Saturus! What on earth brings you here?"

"I'm here with father on business, but I managed to get away for a while. I had no idea I would find you here!"

"It's the ninth hour isn't it? Where do you expect to find me? Calenus and I come here every day. Calenus is a colleague of mine. Calenus – this is Saturus, my best friend from school days in Thuburbo." He looked me over in an approving sort of way. "And you're looking very well, I must say. A bit of honest work hasn't done you any harm, I'll bet."

"Things are not bad," I said, as we made our way through to sit down in the warmth of the tepidarium, though it felt like I was lying to him. "How about you?"

"The job isn't bad, I suppose, though I'm impatient to get up the ladder a bit. But living here in Carthage – that's wonderful! Like I said, we come here to the baths every day, then there's the circus and the amphitheatre, and I don't think there's anything you can't buy in the markets here – goods from all over the Empire! I tell you, once you'd lived here for a couple of months you wouldn't dream of going back to Thuburbo Minus."

"Lucky you!" I said, regarding him with envy. "And you, my friend," I said, addressing Calenus, "Have you always lived in Carthage?"

"Oh, no," he said laughing. "I'm even more of a rustic than you two. I grew up in Simitthu, a full four days journey from here, but my father sent me to school here. I've lived in the city for six years now, but I must say, I still miss the pleasures of small town life and the peace of the countryside."

"It's true we found plenty of pleasures in Thuburbo, didn't we Saturus?" Rufus grinned at me, and I nodded, grinning in turn.

"They seem so long ago, those days." I said. "It was only a couple of years ago, I suppose. Remember the time we went to the cemetery to spy on those Christians!" I laughed, letting my mind wander freely through my memories of those seemingly carefree days. I suddenly noticed, however, that Rufus was strangely quiet, and that Calenus was giving him an odd look.

"Er... There's something I should mention," said Rufus, when he looked up to find me also staring at him. "My friend Calenus here is a Christian."

There was an awkward pause. I looked at Calenus, but he merely gave a sort of shrug and nodded.

"Oh." I didn't know what to say, but a hundred questions suddenly filled my mind. Had this young man I was sitting talking with been involved in murdering children? Had he shared his dark secrets with Rufus? Had Rufus also been poisoned by this strange superstition?

"I know what you're thinking," said Rufus, "but I can tell you now, I really think it's all lies. Calenus has described what they do in their meetings, and it's all completely innocent."

"But the baby we heard screaming..." I said, remembering once again the horror of that chill morning among the tombstones.

"What did we hear?" replied Rufus. "We saw a couple with a sleeping baby go into the Christians' meeting. We heard it crying out a little later – it had probably just woken up and wanted fed."

"I know the rumours that get passed around concerning our practices," put in Calenus. "It's true that we talk about eating the flesh of Christ, and drinking his blood, but what we are actually eating and drinking is just simple, everyday bread and wine. It's a way that Jesus Christ instructed his followers to remember his death and what it means for us. There are no murdered babies, of that you can be sure."

I looked first at him, then at Rufus. As I went over everything in my mind I had to confess that I could come up with no real evidence for believing the stories that Rufus had told me in the past.

"Well then," I said, not ready to give in without some kind

of an argument, "why do the authorities treat you as criminals? How can someone be condemned to death if they've done nothing wrong?"

Rufus sighed and shrugged his shoulders. "Well, technically they *are* enemies of the state." he said. "You see, they refuse to make the required sacrifice for the welfare of the emperor. Don't ask me why it's such an issue for them. You'd think that amid all the rest of their hocus pocus they could fit in one little sacrifice to keep the authorities happy. But they're a stubborn lot, and it's useless to try to reason with them."

"The emperor is just a man, like you and me," said Calenus. "To make the sacrifice is an act of worship. So what is the object of the worship? That is the question. Is it the emperor – a mere human? Or is it a spirit? That too is blasphemous, for the only one we worship is God himself, the maker of heaven and earth and all that is in them. We say prayers for the emperor, certainly, as we are instructed in our Scriptures, but to make the sacrifice – no, that is impossible."

"But isn't that like the Jews, as well?" I asked. "And yet they aren't hounded out like criminals. They're simply exempted on the basis of their religion, aren't they?"

"But they are not trying to spread their superstitions all over the world," said Rufus. "Haven't you noticed how fast this movement is spreading? That's what the authorities are really worried about. It's a simple question of maintaining the peace and stability of the Empire."

"There's more to it than that," said Calenus. "Our Lord Jesus was a good man who never did anything wrong – I mean not a single thing ever in his life. And yet he was tried and executed on a Roman cross. And he warned those who listened to his teaching that if they chose to follow him they could expect the same."

"And aren't you afraid?" I asked, my scepticism giving way to curiosity.

He smiled an honest smile. "Yes, sometimes."

"But he's completely crazy," put in Rufus. "Won't give it up for anything. I've tried to make him see reason, but he's completely caught up in this whole thing."

"I think Saturus should be allowed to hear the story for himself, before he decides if I'm crazy or not," said Calenus.

"No you don't!" said Rufus in mock rebuke. "He'll take any opportunity to start telling you all about the 'good news', as he calls it. Good news that can get you thrown to the bears – no thanks!"

Rufus successfully thwarted Calenus' gentle efforts to enlighten me further, and the conversation passed on to my affairs and the family business. This was a painful subject for me, of course, and Rufus detected the worry in my voice as I skirted around the main issue on my mind – the debts I still owed.

"You're worried about Simeon, eh?" he said at last. I nodded, and Calenus looked at us enquiringly, but neither of us offered any explanation as to who Simeon was. Rufus simply said: "I'm sorry, old friend, but I can't help you with that."

"It's all right," I lied once again, "I'm sure everything will be fine."

And we left it at that. We went and did some exercise in the palaestra – something I wasn't used to, which left me in quite a sweat – then went through the hot and cold baths, chatting all the while about inconsequential issues, until finally we parted company. I never saw Rufus again, but as I made my way back to the pottery merchant's office, I decided that I had to do something drastic. As soon as we got back to Thuburbo I would go to see Simeon and find out exactly how things stood.

4

Flight to Freedom

"Two hundred denarii? What kind of a fool do you take me for?" Simeon had leapt to his feet and was eyeing me with distaste.

"I tell you it's just this once. I'm going on a business trip with my father and I want to have enough spending money along with me." I was lying through my teeth, and I was afraid that Simeon could see this all too clearly. In despair I had finally made my decision. I was going to get as much as I could out of Simeon and then run away. Away from my home and family, away from Thuburbo Minus, perhaps even away from the province of Africa. The idea had come to me quite suddenly, but once it was in my head I couldn't understand why I hadn't thought of it earlier. All my problems would disappear overnight. No more worry about the debts hanging over me. No more suspicious nagging from my father. No more tedious hours spent in the workshop. I would be free. I had resolved to mend my ways, of course. I would find an honest job and settle down to make a living from it. Yes, I would miss my family, there was no doubt about that. But I considered this a necessary price to pay for the freedom I would gain. If only I could get hold of enough money to pay my way to get well away from Thuburbo, and set myself up in a completely different place. But Simeon was not playing along.

"I'll give you twenty, and not an as more," he snapped in his thin croaking voice. "You can take it, or you can leave."

Twenty denarii. What good would that be? I asked myself. Still, it was better than nothing, which is what I had at that moment. I took it, with as much of a show of injured feelings as I could manage, though I don't think the old crook even noticed. But as I made my way back home, I realised that I would have to do something to get hold of some more. I resolved to keep the twenty denarii aside for a week, without spending it – a feat which would require a superhuman effort on my part – then go back and try again.

*

The following week I was threading my way through the now familiar maze of streets which led to Simeon's office, when I heard shouting and crashing. This was not a particularly unusual noise in that part of the town, but what drew my attention was that it appeared to be coming from Simeon's door. As I walked hesitantly down the dirty street, the door was suddenly yanked open and a young man was thrown bodily out of it into the roadway. A voice was shrieking from inside:

"And if I ever set eyes on you again, I'll kill you! D'you hear that? I'll kill you!"

A pile of clothes came flying out of the door and landed beside the young man, and the door slammed shut. There was the sound of a key being turned in the lock.

I cautiously approached the figure lying in the dirt, glancing fearfully at the closed doorway as I came nearer. He was younger than me, I guessed, and had a shock of dark curly hair. From his dress I guessed that he was Jewish, like Simeon. He was weeping, but he started in surprise when he saw me bending over him.

"Are you all right?" I asked. His face was bruised, and I guessed that he had just suffered a beating.

He eyed me a little suspiciously, through his tears – a look that reminded me of Simeon. It suddenly struck me that he was probably related.

"Er... It looks like he's shut up shop for today," I said, nodding at the door. The young man pulled himself to a sitting position, and gingerly touched his bruised face.

"Who are you?" he asked.

"My name is Saturus," I replied. I had already decided that

anyone who had got on the wrong side of Simeon was a friend of mine, and I was anxious to appear as friendly as possible. "Marcus Saturus. I'm one of Simeon's – er... clients."

The description sounded somewhat ridiculous, but it conveyed the message. The young man gave a sardonic grunt. "One of those poor devils."

"And you – are you one of the family?"

Another grunt. "Not any more I'm not."

"Oh," I said, somewhat at a loss for words. I looked around and my eye fell upon the jumbled heap of clothes. "Are these yours?"

He looked at them forlornly and nodded. "I suppose I should be grateful he's letting me have them," he remarked.

"Where do you live?" I said. He turned and stared at me.

"I don't live anywhere," he announced. "My father has just thrown me out of his house."

"Your father? You mean Simeon?"

He nodded. "Though I don't think he's considering himself as that any longer."

"Listen," I said, "I'd like to help you if I can, though I don't know if there's anything I can do. Can we go somewhere to talk that isn't right on his doorstep?"

He looked at me, and for the first time I detected a glimmer of warmth in his face. He managed a smile.

"There's a cheap tavern nearby – got any money?"

"Um – no," I answered. "That's why I'm here, really."

He was rummaging through the pile of clothing, evidently searching for something. After clearly failing to find whatever he was looking for, he glanced bitterly at the closed door.

"Me neither," he said.

"Your father took it?" I asked.

"It wasn't much anyway. Come on," he said. He gathered the clothes into a bundle with an old cloak as the outer layer and slung this over his shoulder. "Let's get out of here, at any rate."

"Let's head for the forum. I live on the Cardo II East – my father owns the big pottery there."

"Suits me," he said, and we set off together.

"So – do you want to tell me why your father's just thrown

you out of his house?" I asked as we made our way out of the neighbourhood.

"He's just found out. Mind you, I was going to tell him soon, anyway."

I glanced at him, and he gave that slight glimmer of a smile once again.

"I've become a Christian."

I stopped in my tracks and stared at him. It seemed something of a coincidence that I should meet two of this strange breed in the space of a week.

"What's the matter?" he asked. Then an excited look came over his face. "You're not one too, are you?"

I laughed at this. "No fear," I said. "But I met another one just last week. It seems I can't get away from you."

"Who did you meet? Someone from the church here?"

"No, no. In Carthage – a man called Calenus. He works in the provincial government."

"Never heard of him."

"And you? You haven't told me your name."

"Matthias. Matthias Bar-Simeon. Though, as I say, I don't know if that's particularly accurate any longer."

"So you're in the church here – those people that meet in the cemetery out towards Thubba?"

He looked surprised. "You seem to know all about it. I've only been to one meeting there. Most meetings I've been to were at the bishop's house – a big villa near the amphitheatre. That's where I should go now. I'll probably be able to stay with a family for the time being – his or someone else's."

"How many of you Christians are there in Thuburbo?"

"About twenty. It's a small church, but growing."

"That's what gets me. Why should anyone want to join you? Aren't you putting your life in danger?"

"From the authorities, you mean? Personally I think I've got more to worry about from my father and the rest of the Jews in the town."

"That's another thing I can't understand. Isn't the whole thing just a Jewish sect? What's so awful about a Jew becoming a Christian?"

"You know anything about how it began? About Jesus Christ and his disciples?"

"Not a lot," I admitted. "They were Jews, though, right?"

"They were, yes. But it was also Jews – the religious leaders, to be exact – who had Jesus arrested and put to death. They were waiting for the Christ – the Jewish Messiah, that is. But when he came, they killed him."

I sensed that this was a tangled affair, which I didn't particularly want to start getting into right then. Instead, I switched the conversation around completely, and started to talk about myself. It wasn't just that I was reluctant to start delving into the obscure details of the Christians' beliefs. I was also anxious to unburden myself of some of my own worries, and Matthias seemed like someone I could confide in.

"I'm running away from home." I blurted it out, just like that, and as soon as the words were out, the reality of it suddenly hit home to me far more painfully than it had up till that moment. Now it was Matthias' turn to stop and stare at me.

"Running away? What on earth for?"

"Like you say, I'm one of the poor devils your father has caught in his net. Except that by this stage I think I owe him more than I'll ever be able to pay back. I tell you, I've come to the conclusion that there's no other way out. I'm just trying to get together enough money to get out of Thuburbo and set up somewhere as far away as possible. Needless to say, your father wasn't being much help."

"You'd better be careful. He has friends that you wouldn't want a visit from. People who get on the wrong side of him tend to disappear – killed, perhaps – I don't know. But more often he has them caught and sold off at the port in Carthage as galley slaves. That way he gets a bit of money, and they just conveniently vanish. It all has to be kept quiet, of course."

Of course, I had known that there would be dire consequences if I failed to pay Simeon back, but I had not really thought about what the consequences might be. Now I shuddered at the thought of being hunted down by some hired thugs and murdered, or, a worse fate probably, spending the rest of my life at the oars of a galley. Matthias obviously noticed the worry on my face.

"But I doubt if he has much influence outside of Thuburbo Minus," he added. "Your plan of running away is probably your best option." There was a pause, and then he went on, "As a matter of fact, I think it's probably my best option too."

"But didn't you say you were going to stay with the Christians?"

"Well, I could for a few days. But my father told me he wanted me out of town, and I believe he meant it. If he discovered I was still here I wouldn't be surprised if I got a visit from one of his henchmen sooner or later."

"You mean – he'd actually try and have you killed?"

"As far as he's concerned I've committed the worst blasphemy possible. Most Jews regard anyone who becomes a Christian as deserving the death penalty. I'm afraid he might not shrink from avenging the family honour, and I certainly don't want to stay around to put it to the test."

I rolled my eyes. "You really are crazy, you Christians. What can possibly be worth all this trouble?"

He laughed. "The truth. When you've found the truth, what can you do but accept it?"

I considered this, and after some moments I discovered something about myself.

"You know," I said, "I think I have a different philosophy. If the truth is too hard, you just ignore it."

"Then you're blind, Marcus Saturus. A blind man walking towards a pit."

"Just leave me to it."

"I'll pray for you."

It was my turn to laugh, but without much humour. "Pray for me! A lot of good that'll do. The gods have got it in for me, that's what I think. What good have they ever brought me?"

"If you pray to a statue with stone ears, it's not surprising if it doesn't hear you."

"Pray for me to your god, then. We'll see if he hears you."

By this stage we were at the forum, and it was time to make some decisions.

"Listen," I said, "are you serious about running away?"

"Yes."

"Together?"

"It makes sense."

"What about money?"

"I may be able to get some from the bishop."

"I have twenty denarii that your father gave me last week, but that's not much." I desperately wanted to try gambling with it, to see if I could strike lucky just for once, but I didn't dare suggest this to Matthias.

"Listen, how about this. I'll go and stay with the bishop's family tonight, and see if he can spare me some money. Then tomorrow we can go to Carthage – that'll be a start at any rate."

"What then?"

He shrugged, and smiled. "We're in God's hands."

I looked at him, trying to assess whether he really was as reassured about this as he sounded. I was beginning to like his straightforward approach to life, although in another way it also scared the wits out of me.

"Tomorrow, here, at first light then."

We parted, Matthias heading off in the direction of the amphitheatre. As he went he turned and called back to me, grinning: "I'll pray for you!"

I turned for home, shaking my head at this crazy notion. But my heart was beating fast with excitement and apprehension as I thought about the adventure that lay ahead.

*

I was there the following morning at the spot where we had parted, with my money, some food I had managed to take without anyone noticing, and an extra cloak, but there was no sign of Matthias. I wondered if he had decided not to run away after all, and just lie low at the bishop's house for a while. I had been counting on him adding something to our meagre funds, quite apart from providing companionship and support, and I was very disheartened at his non-appearance. I had not waited long, however, before I heard my named being called, but not very loudly. The voice was coming from behind some crates of fruit.

"Saturus! Over here!" I looked and caught a glimpse of Matthias' head briefly appearing round the side of the crates. He beckoned me over with a furtive gesture. Glancing around nervously, I sauntered over to the crates, then crouched down beside him.

"What's the matter?" I asked him.

"I was followed from the bishop's house."

"Who by?"

"One of my father's friends. They must know about me already. Can you believe my father would do such a thing?"

I was about to say that I could, but decided against it. Instead I asked, "Where is he now?"

"I think I lost him. I dodged down a side street then doubled back by another route. But he probably realised I was heading in this direction." He peered cautiously over the crates again. "I don't see him anywhere right now. Let's go before he appears."

Already things seemed to have got more adventurous than I had counted on, and I wasn't sure I liked the idea. We walked in the direction of the Carthage road, as quickly as we dared without drawing unnecessary attention to ourselves. As we went I asked Matthias about the money.

"Optatus – that's the bishop – gave me thirty denarii. He was very nice about it, but said he couldn't spare any more. He also gave me a letter of introduction to any church I came across wherever I ended up, so that should help too." He pulled a small papyrus roll out of his tunic.

"Very nice," I said, without much enthusiasm.

Our next problem presented itself as we approached the Arch of Vespasian, an impressive triumphal structure straddling the road from Carthage where it enters the town of Thuburbo Minus. Matthias suddenly pulled me into the doorway of a villa.

"He's waiting there at the Arch!" he hissed.

"The one who was following you?"

He stuck his head out from the doorway briefly. "Yes – it's him all right!"

"What are we going to do? Go to the Matar Gate?"

"I don't know. Maybe he's got someone watching each of

the gates. Obviously the Carthage road is our most obvious route, but they don't know for sure I'm heading in that direction, do they?"

"They seem to know an awful lot, that's all I can say." I thought for a few moments. "Listen, if you want to avoid the gates I know a place in the south wall where you can climb down on the outside. There's a tree growing near the wall. You know where I mean?"

"I can't say I do," replied Matthias, "but I'm willing to give it a try. Listen, I'm sorry about this. You could go out by the gate yourself if you want to."

"No, it's all right. Let's stick together." Despite the added danger and the slight detour, I really did want to stay with Matthias. And although my heart was pounding, I was beginning to enjoy the adventure.

Ten minutes later we were scrambling down the old fig tree whose sprawling branches now offered a reasonably easy way of getting down from the top of the town wall. Once down we were into olive groves, and we began to make our way back to the main Carthage road. From there we gazed back towards the Arch of Vespasian, but there was no sign of anyone looking our way. We had escaped.

Our next task was to beg a ride to Carthage. It was the time of the wheat harvest, and it was not long before a loaded grain wagon came trundling down the road. We were in luck, for the driver was friendly and seemed glad of some company, charging us nothing for the ride. We sat atop the piled sacks of grain, relaxing in the sun and chatting with the driver from time to time. Soon we were out of the olive groves and vineyards that surrounded Thuburbo Minus, and into rolling wheat fields full of migrant workers who had come and set up their temporary shelters everywhere. I felt relieved to be out of the bustle of the town, to watch the harvesters busy at their labours, and to feel free of a burden which had been weighing me down for months.

It was late afternoon by the time we approached the outskirts of Carthage, and we asked to get off before we got into the city. We had already decided to save money by sleeping rough, hoping that we could find an unused harvesters' shelter to spend the night – an idea Matthias had suggested while we were passing through the fields that morning. We found one without difficulty, and after eating most of our remaining food, we spent an uncomfortable night in the straw hut. As I slept fitfully, I dreamed of dark figures lying in wait with daggers, and of the two of us wandering in strange towns I had never been in before.

5

In Carthage

We were both up before dawn, stretching aching muscles and picking the hay out of our hair. We set off as soon as it was light and had soon walked into the city. Matthias was all for getting on a ship as soon as possible and sailing to Italy. This would be simple, since there were plenty of gigantic grain ships sailing back and forth at this time of year, each of which had space for hundreds of passengers. The only question was how much the fare would be. I suggested trying to get on as stowaways, but Matthias would have none of this, saying it was dishonest. In the days ahead I was to run up against this obstacle repeatedly, and I became quite frustrated with his ridiculous moral standards, as I called them. He was apologetic, but explained simply that he was a Christian and would not break the law.

"You don't seem to have any qualms about failing to sacrifice for the welfare of the emperor – isn't that breaking the law?" I complained on one occasion.

"God's law first, and man's law afterwards." was his only answer.

Meanwhile we agreed that he would go down to the port and enquire about fares, while I went to the forum to buy food for the journey. The forum in Carthage must be one of the most magnificent in the whole of the Empire, being built on the top of a hill, with one end raised above the hillside on huge arches, and with an open view out over the sea and the lower parts of the city. I spent some minutes just gazing out at this sight, letting my eye wander down to the great baths complex that I knew so well, and then southwards to the port, where Matthias was now headed. There were a number of grain ships docked there, clearly identifiable by their size, and I imagined us on board one of them by nightfall.

It had been my suggestion that I did the shopping at the forum, and although I had not consciously planned to do what I did, I think that the idea must have been there, dormant at the back of my mind all along. For no sooner did I turn away from the view and head back towards the market stalls, alone, with a pouch full of money, than I found myself wandering over to the colonnade where I knew the betting agents sat. One of them recognised me.

"Well, young man – do you have some money to put on the races this afternoon?" he called.

"Yes, and I feel lucky today," I replied. "Tell me your longest odds."

That was how I parted with the twenty denarii that I had managed to keep intact up until that moment. Then of course, I had nothing to buy food with, which meant stealing it instead. This was not too much of a problem, since I had learned some tricks from Rufus in the past, and I had soon gathered enough to last us the three days it would probably take to sail to Italy. I then realised that I would have to confess what I had done to Matthias, since we would have to wait till the races were over before doing anything else. I cursed my own stupidity, realising that I did not really feel lucky at all, and that I would almost certainly never see the money again. When we met up again at the port, as agreed, I broke the news to him straight away, trying nevertheless to sound optimistic about my chances of winning.

"I was only trying to get us a bit more cash," I explained, in an attempt to make it sound like a sensible plan. Matthias was silent at first, saying nothing, but giving me a long stare that made me very uncomfortable. At last he spoke.

"Like I said before, Saturus, you're a blind man walking towards a pit." He paused. "Well, we'd better go to the races, then. I'll pray for a good result."

I thought of how many others at the races would also be praying for good results. The gods couldn't answer all those prayers at once, since only one result was possible. But something in Matthias' tone told me that he really believed that his prayers would be answered. I was curious, and even dared to believe it myself.

"You mean – you can really pray to your god and get things like that?" I asked.

He laughed. "I can pray to be delivered from the hands of a fool, that's all!"

We made our way through the streets to the far side of the city, and the circus.

"What did you find out about the fare, then?" I asked, trying to sound contrite.

"Twenty denarii apiece."

I stared at him in disbelief. "That's extortionate!"

"More than extortionate, my friend," he said with a smile. "Impossible, for us, unless we see a miracle at the circus today."

I felt another wave of remorse, as I considered this news. I felt like I had ruined everything, not just for me, but for Matthias too. We reached the circus and sat outside to eat some bread. Matthias, as I had noticed was his habit, looked upwards and muttered a brief prayer before eating. Then, as he was raising the bread to his mouth, he suddenly stopped and looked at me suspiciously.

"Did you pay for this food?" he asked.

I hesitated, thinking of simply lying to him, but I couldn't.

"Don't ask, and your conscience won't trouble you," I said, sulkily. He rolled his eyes and sighed. But he went on to eat the bread. Then, when the races were about to start, we went in and found a place near the finishing line. I had spent many exciting afternoons here with Rufus, but now I only felt a sick feeling in the pit of my stomach, dreading the worst. It was also strange to be there with Matthias, who told me that he had never been to the circus before. He took a detached interest in the proceedings, and, during the races while everyone around was cheering, he just stood in silence, watching intently and, I imagined, praying. I had put my money on the reds in the first race, a ten-to-one outsider, but the race was much closer than the odds would have suggested. It was not until the last lap, however, that the reds actually pulled into the lead, and I stopped cheering to gape stupidly at the scene in front of me. As the chariots thundered down the last stretch towards us, I turned to shake Matthias by the sleeve, to find that by this stage he actually had his eyes closed.

"We're winning! We're winning!" I shouted in his ear. He opened his eyes, looked at the chariots as they sped across the finish line, the reds just barely ahead, and then he started to laugh. I began to laugh as well, and we hugged each other there on the terraces, I with tears streaming down my face.

There were more races, but even I was not at all interested in staying to watch them, and we made our way to the exit, and started back to the forum. I was full of excitement after witnessing this incredible phenomenon.

"We could be rich!" I said, my mind racing over the possibilities. "We could put money on all the outsiders, then you could go and pray at the races – it wouldn't even have to work every time, even just half the time with long odds would still make us rich!"

Matthias had not said much and now he turned to me with an unreadable look on his face, still saying nothing. I began to feel foolish, though I didn't know why.

"What's wrong?" I asked, defensively. "Wouldn't it work?"

"I don't think so," was all he said.

"But worth a try, surely?" I pressed him. However, he only shook his head. I found the whole affair somewhat bewildering, and began to wonder if our good fortune had had anything to do with his prayers at all. Perhaps I had really just had a lucky day.

"Well, anyway," I went on, "we can be on board a grain ship and sailing to Ostia by tonight, and still have our pockets full of gold."

"Perhaps it should be my pockets that have the gold in them," suggested Matthias. "For safe-keeping, I mean."

My immediate reaction to this was to feel offended, and even to wonder if he was planning some way of abandoning me and making off with all the money, but I could not honestly imagine this happening, and I realised that what I had done that morning had proved that I could not be trusted with it myself. Reluctantly I agreed that he should look after the bulk of it.

We reached the port, and I gazed in wonder at the huge ships that were docked there, which I had seen from the forum that morning. The scale had not been apparent from that distance. I knew very little about ships and the sea, having grown up in an inland town surrounded by nothing but olive groves and vineyards, but I did know that these were some of the largest ships in the world, designed to transport the vast quantities of grain that Rome needed from Africa and Egypt.

The massive ships were all of a similar size and design. We assumed that they were all bound for Ostia, where the grain would be unloaded and carried overland to Rome, so we approached the nearest one, the *Poseidon*. After finding that it was indeed sailing to Italy, leaving early the following morning, we paid for places on board for the two of us and were allowed to board the ship right away to spend the night there. 'Places' meant nothing more than the word suggested. We would be on the vast deck along with crowds of other passengers for the two or three days it would take to reach Ostia. We had all the food we needed with us, so without further delay we made our way up the gangplank and settled ourselves in a corner which we hoped would not be too uncomfortable. There were quite a number of other passengers who had also boarded the ship already.

I was tired after a long day and after a bite of food I lay down, heedless of the wooden deck beneath me, and was soon lulled to sleep by the gentle, almost imperceptible movement of the ship beneath me, and the creaking of the timbers. Matthias lay beside me, staring up at the stars as they drifted on their course across the night sky. At dawn I awoke from a deep sleep to find him shaking me gently and whispering.

"Saturus, wake up."

With difficulty I blinked my eyes open and stared stupidly into his face, which was close to my own. He was not lying down, however, but had sat up and was leaning over me.

"Saturus, we have to get off the ship!" His voice was a whisper, but the tone was urgent.

"What is it?" I asked, trying to collect my thoughts. I had only just worked out where we were and why, and my whole body ached from sleeping on the hard wooden boards.

"I think it's going to sink!"

I sat up at this, and stared around in a panic. Some of the other passengers were already awake, but many were still sleeping. Everything seemed perfectly calm in the grey light of morning. The crew appeared to be already at work making the ship ready to sail.

"What's happening?" I said, "What are you talking about?"

"I had a dream. I've never had one like it – it was so real. We were on the ship, sailing to Ostia, and there was a terrible storm. There were huge waves coming over the sides, and water all over the decks. The ship went down and everyone was thrashing about in the sea, grabbing anything that they could to hold on to. I was clinging to a piece of wood, looking for you and shouting your name, but I couldn't see you anywhere."

I looked at him in a daze, not knowing what to think of this story.

"Listen, Matthias," I said at last, "don't you think it's just a bad dream?"

I could see doubt in his eyes, but also fear and desperation.

"I don't think so," he said. "I think it's from God."

"We'll never get them to give us our money back."

"It doesn't matter." He looked at me pleadingly. I felt terribly tired, and annoyed at this disruption to our plans. I was also extremely dubious about the dream, but his prayers at the races the previous afternoon had left an indelible impression on me, and I found that I could not dismiss it as lightly as I would have the previous night. Reluctantly I struggled to my feet.

"All right," I said. Then I looked around at the other passengers sitting or lying all around us. I suddenly had the impression that those who were still sleeping looked like so many lifeless corpses. "What about everyone else?"

Matthias gazed about him too.

"What can we do?" he said. "I don't mind trying to speak to the captain, to tell him about the dream and explain why we're disembarking. I don't see that we can do anything more."

We picked our way to the head of the gangplank, where a soldier on guard stopped us and asked where we were going. Matthias explained that we had decided not to sail on the ship and wished to speak with the captain before we disembarked. The soldier seemed doubtful about this request, so Matthias went on to describe his dream. Evidently the soldier had something of a superstitious outlook, for he immediately called to another soldier at the foot of the gangplank, to say that he had to report to the captain, and then led us aft to where a stairway led below deck to a low door. Another soldier stood guard outside, and when our companion explained that we wished to speak with the captain, we were ushered through the doorway into a small cabin where two men were bending over some papers.

"Yes?" said one, addressing the soldier who had brought us.

"Legionnaire Appius Pudens, guard duty, reporting sir. These two passengers would like to speak with you about an urgent matter, sir."

The captain, for so we assumed him to be, looked at us in annoyance.

"It had better be urgent," he said. He addressed the soldier: "You may return to your post."

The soldier saluted, and with a brisk "Hail Caesar!" he was gone. The two men were looking at us in expectation. I now felt acutely embarrassed about our errand and wished that I had sent Matthias here on his own. What, after all, had this business to do with me? As for Matthias, he too appeared to be nervous, but he launched into his story boldly enough. When he had finished and was standing under the somewhat hostile stares of the two men, I felt obliged to put in a word for him myself.

"It may sound rather incredible, sir," I said to the captain, "but I have good reason to believe that my companion does indeed have certain, er, powers of communication with the gods."

The captain drew himself up and addressed us coldly.

"I can assure you both that it is not yet the season for storms in these seas," he said. "If you insist on leaving the ship because of some superstitious omen, you are free to do so. You should note, however, that no refunds on fares can be paid. Do you have anything further to say? If not I would be grateful if you could leave us to the business of getting this ship to Ostia as soon as possible."

And so we were dismissed. We made our way back to the gangplank, where the soldier saluted us.

"Any luck?" he asked.

"None whatsoever," said Matthias. "Are you sailing with the ship?"

"Me? No, thank the gods." And he looked around with a troubled expression at the passengers on the deck, who were now being joined by many more. We had to push our way past those who were coming up the gangplank, and finally we were back on the quay. Within an hour, we had watched the *Poseidon* weigh anchor and sail out of the harbour. Meanwhile, we were poorer by forty denarii, and we had the task of finding another ship to board. In the full light of day, without a cloud in the sky and the lightest of breezes blowing, the reality of what we had done now seemed to me utterly ridiculous, and I said so. Matthias himself now looked a little embarrassed, as if he too was now having second thoughts about what he had been so convinced of in the night.

"Well, what's done is done," he said. "Anyway, I have an idea. Come with me."

I followed him as he led the way across to one of the porticoes arranged around the port which housed the offices of shipowners, merchants and other related businesses. There was an inscription above the doorway of this one announcing the occupant's name: 'Gaius Clodius Lucullus, Shipowner'. Matthias indicated a symbol drawn beside this inscription, composed of the two Greek letters, chi and rho.

"What's that?" I asked.

"The first two letters of the word 'Christ'," he said. "Wait here." And without another word of explanation, he went inside the office. I stood outside, contemplating the Greek symbol. It was some minutes before he emerged grinning, and brandishing two small clay tesserae.

"What's that?" I asked.

"Places on the ship *Alatus*, bound for Hadrumetum."

"Hadrumetum?" I was astonished. "I thought we were going to Italy!"

"What does it matter?" he said. "Hadrumetum is far enough away isn't it? Anyway, you don't need to take them if you don't want to – I paid nothing for them."

"How on earth did you manage that?" I asked, even more amazed.

"Like I told you, this shipowner is a Christian." He gestured to the Greek letters again. "I explained my, er – family circumstances, and asked if he could help me. He told me there's a large church in Hadrumetum and suggested we should go there."

"What did you say about me? I'm a Christian too now, am I?"

"I said you were my companion, and that you had already been a help to me. He didn't ask any questions."

I wondered what help Matthias was referring to, but I didn't tempt fate by pressing the point. Meanwhile I was adjusting to our sudden change of plans, and deciding that Matthias was right. It did not much matter to me where we ended up, as long as it was well away from Thuburbo Minus. Hadrumetum, I guessed, was a good four days' journey from Carthage, overland down the coast road, though the ship would be there in a day and a half.

The *Alatus* turned out to be a much smaller vessel than the *Poseidon*, carrying a cargo of spices and cloth to the ports of the African coast. In an hour we were on board, sailing out of port into the open sea, and looking back in wonder at the magnificent sight of the city of Carthage glittering like a jewel in the morning sun.

6

The End of the Road

During the voyage we spent some time discussing what we planned to do when we reached Hadrumetum. Matthias' main concern was to seek out the Christians, a desire which I did not share with him at all. Not that he was without apprehensions about this himself. It was a strange city for both of us, and much larger than Thuburbo Minus. All he had was the name of an olive oil merchant who had an office by the port, who was supposedly a Christian. The shipowner in Carthage had told Matthias to contact him when we arrived. He was hoping that this man would introduce him to the other Christians. Perhaps one of them could even find work for him somewhere. As for me, I had decided to try to find a potter who needed an apprentice. There was a certain amount of risk in this, in that if I became known in the pottery business in Hadrumetum, in time word could easily get back to my father about my whereabouts. I therefore thought up a false name, and a totally fictitious story to give to anyone I got to know in Hadrumetum, to avoid such an eventuality.

As our little ship neared the port of Hadrumetum, the wind was beginning to freshen, and ominous storm clouds were gathering in the northwest. It made us both think of the *Poseidon*, now somewhere off the coast of Sicily. During our voyage, with clear skies and a calm sea, Matthias' dream had begun to seem to both of us like nothing more than the product of his own fears at sailing for the first time in his life, but now it was much easier to imagine the worst.

"I thought you didn't get storms till later in the year," said

Matthias to one of the crew, indicating the clouds on the horizon.

"Aye, that's true as a rule," came the man's reply, "but when they do come this early they can be pretty fierce. Don't you worry, though, son – we'll be safe in port before anything hits us."

But that, of course, was little comfort to us.

We did indeed reach port safely and disembarked. It did not take long for Matthias to find the oil merchant's office, but it turned out that he was away on business, and was not expected back until the following day. Matthias felt it was unwise to speak to anyone else first, so we left without explaining our errand. I was quite relieved at this, as I had really wanted to avoid contact with any more Christians, and now it seemed possible that I would be able to manage this after all.

So we set off together to explore the city, enquiring about where the potteries were located and heading for the part of town where most of them seemed to be. Each time we found one, I went in alone, to avoid the complication of explaining who Matthias was. The first few that I visited had no need of me, but then we came across a small workshop belonging to a man named Laetantius, who gave me a friendly welcome and listened to my story. I gave my name as Gnaeus Speratus, which was actually Rufus' real name – Rufus was just his nickname.

"My father had a small pottery business in Simitthu," I told him, thinking of Rufus' colleague Calenus. "It's a small town and there wasn't much work. Eventually he had to close the business down – that was just a couple of months ago. He wanted me to carry on the family trade, however, so he sent me away to see if I could get taken on as an apprentice in Carthage. I found no-one there who would have me, so I decided to come down the coast to Hadrumetum. I know the pottery business as well as anyone."

"Well," said Laetantius, looking me up and down, "it so happens that I have no sons of my own and I've been thinking of taking on an apprentice. You seem like just the lad for the job. You'd have to be willing to do the menial work at first, though. Then, if you prove your worth, I'll see about giving you a bit more responsibility. Do you have anywhere to stay?"

"Er – no." I hadn't given this much thought, but now that I seemed to have struck lucky finding employment, my mind began to turn over the possibilities. Perhaps I could search for some cheap lodgings nearby. Laetantius put an end to this, however.

"That's no problem," he told me. "I have an attic above the workshop where you can sleep. I'll give you bed and board and a weekly allowance of two denarii at the start. We'll put it up if your work merits it. How does that sound?"

It sounded to me like little better than slave labour, but I knew that I'd been lucky to find anything given the circumstances. What's more, Laetantius seemed like a fair and honest man, and I was confident that I would soon 'prove my worth' as he put it, and start to earn a bit more.

"Very well," I said. "When do I start?"

"Right away. You can put your things up in the attic, then I need some fresh clay mixed. It's in that tub over there – the temper's all ready beside it, and you'll get water from the cistern in that corner. You know what to do, of course?"

"Er – yes, yes of course." I was somewhat taken aback by the speed at which things were developing. I was aware that Matthias, whom I hadn't mentioned, was waiting for me outside. I climbed a steep wooden ladder which led to an opening in the ceiling, pushed my small bundle through it, and hauled myself through. The attic was dimly lit from a small garret window, and had a few pieces of equipment and sacks of something piled at one side. Otherwise it seemed to be clean and dry. I peered out the garret window, which overlooked the street. Matthias was there, sitting against a wall.

"Psst! Matthias!" I tried to keep my voice low. He looked around, having heard his name.

"Up here!" He looked up and caught sight of me.

"What's happening?" he said. I put my finger to my lips, afraid that Laetantius would notice and start to question me about him.

"He's taken me on. I'll see you down by the port later on,

when I can get away." Matthias looked surprised, then grinned and waved.

"Well done! See you later."

I clambered down the ladder again, and was soon hard at work mixing the clay.

＊

That evening I ate a simple meal with Laetantius and his wife who rented a modest apartment nearby. After dinner I excused myself and made my way down to the port once more in search of Matthias. He had spent an uneventful afternoon wandering the streets of Hadrumetum, and was now preparing to spend an uncomfortable night on a pile of fishing nets. I told him about Laetantius and my apprenticeship.

"It's not much, but it's a start," I said. We agreed to meet at the same place the following evening to see how Matthias had fared with the oil merchant. The following day was one of hard work for me, of the sort that I wasn't used to, and it was with weary steps that I trudged down to the port once more when evening came. Matthias had good news. The oil merchant, whose name was Tertius, had proved to be very friendly and had agreed to take Matthias on as a clerk in his office, even though he didn't really need one. He had also helped him to find lodgings nearby at a reasonable rate, so he was all set up. The next day was Sunday, when the Christians apparently met early in the morning and he eagerly talked of how he would be able to go along and meet them. He seemed to have completely lost his former apprehension, and even suggested that I might like to go with him and find out about joining a catechismal class.

"Listen," I told him, "I'm very pleased that you've found these people, but I don't want to have anything to do with them. And if I were you I'd be very careful what you do. They know you're Jewish, right? And there could be some of those fanatical types who'd like to see you dead in a city this size as well, couldn't there? Not to mention the civil authorities who consider you to be their enemies as well. I don't want anything to happen to you."

I really meant this. I had grown fond of Matthias over the last few days, and it worried me that he might be arrested at any time, or even that he might simply get his throat cut in some dark alley. What happened, of course, was that over the following weeks we gradually saw less and less of each other. I spent my days hard at work in Laetantius' workshop, while he was down in Tertius' office by the port. We had little reason to meet. I began to explore the possibilities which Hadrumetum offered for a young man to enjoy himself, which were far greater in scope than in Thuburbo Minus. There was a large amphitheatre, and a circus, plenty of baths, and the night life was all I could have dreamed of. Then, of course, there was gambling. All of this, needless to say, Matthias spurned as 'worldly pleasures', and something inside me told me that he was right. I had escaped from the wreckage of my life in Thuburbo fully intent on making a clean start elsewhere. Matthias' simple, wholesome approach to life was really what I had envisaged for myself, but I found that I could not so easily break with my old ways. It was simply too enjoyable, too alluring, too easy, to wander down to the gaming houses and brothels of the city in the evenings. The only trouble was that my meagre income was soon eaten up by such distractions. As soon as we had both got settled in our separate positions, Matthias gave me half the remaining money, suggesting that I should try and keep it safe in case of future needs. I said I would, but of course, we both knew that this was a lie. A few days later it had all gone.

It was about a week after our arrival in Hadrumetum that we heard the news. Matthias heard first. Everyone in the port was talking about the huge grain ship that had been caught in a terrible storm off Sicily and had sunk with no survivors. Most of those who had drowned were, of course, the passengers who had been crammed onto the crowded deck for the voyage. It was a terrible tragedy, everyone said, but for Matthias and me, who did not need to be told that the name of the ship was the *Poseidon*, the story was chilling and horrifying.

I told Laetantius the next day, but he had apparently already heard the news.

"They shouldn't be allowed to carry so much cargo on one ship," he said. "Those grain ships are so heavy in the water – they're floating death traps."

I wanted to tell him that I had been on board that ship, that I should now have been drowned at the bottom of the sea if it hadn't been for Matthias' dream, but somehow I could not bring myself to say it. I had already told him so many lies about myself, it was too complicated now to try to tell him something of the truth.

True to his word, Laetantius soon began to entrust me with more responsible tasks when he saw that I knew what I was doing. This was a great relief to me, as the only sort of work I had been given at first was what the slaves had always done in my father's workshop. He also increased my allowance to four denarii per week, but this was still a pitiful sum compared with what I had been used to borrowing from Simeon. It occurred to me once to try to seek out a money-lender here in Hadrumetum, but I realised immediately the impossibility of persuading anyone to lend me so much as an as. I had no family here and was completely unknown. What means could I ever have of paying back a loan?

My need for cash began to turn into an obsession with me. Whenever I saw any money during the course of my daily routine I found myself eyeing it covetously, wishing that I could somehow make it my own. And then, of course, the solution became obvious to me. I had been entirely successful at stealing the food in Carthage during our flight from Thuburbo – what was so different about stealing money? The easiest place for me to do this was Laetantius' workshop. Clients who came to buy his wares always paid in cash, which was stored in a wooden box on the counter. Often the box was kept locked, but not always. I noticed that Laetantius trusted me, often leaving me alone in the workshop even when the box was not locked. And so I began to help myself, telling myself that the money was, in a sense, due to me anyway, since Laetantius had set my weekly allowance so low. I did not take much at a time – I was fearful at first that Laetantius might be keeping a careful note of how much was in it and would notice the discrepancy immediately, but this did not happen.

Laetantius was a devout worshipper of Mithras, the Persian god of truth and light, and each day at about the fifth hour he went out to make prayers and libations at the temple of Mithras, which was only a few minutes walk from his place of work. During this time I was normally left alone at the workshop, and it became my habit when this was the case to check whether the money-box was unlocked, and if so to help myself to a little cash from it. One day he had just gone out and I had slipped over to see if the box was open. It was, and I lifted the lid, greedily eyeing the coins inside. I had taken three denarii and was wondering if a fourth would be too noticeable, when I heard footsteps behind me, and a hand on my shoulder.

"So it is a thief I have for an apprentice." I turned in terror to see Laetantius glaring at me. Without stopping to think I pulled myself away and made for the door, still clutching the money I had already taken. He lunged at me and pulled me down, the coins flying across the floor as I fell against a bench with racks of newly fired plates stacked on it. The whole thing went over and most of the plates smashed as they toppled to the floor. In desperation I squirmed out of his grasp once again and got to the door. There was another crash as Laetantius tripped over the fallen bench and landed on the floor himself. This gave me the chance I needed to get a start on him. I fled down the street, knocking passers-by to right and left. Laetantius was not far behind me and was yelling to people to stop me, but luckily for me no-one seemed quick-witted enough to do anything before I was already past them and gone.

I had youth on my side, and though I was not too fit, neither was my employer, so I hoped that I would be able to get far enough ahead of him to be able to give him the slip. In fact, it was not long before his yells ceased and I stopped to look behind me. There was no sign of him. No doubt he had thought better of leaving his workshop deserted with the money box sitting open on the counter and had gone back. He could be after me again before long, however, and others in the street were looking at me suspiciously, having evidently witnessed something of the commotion caused by my flight, and now wondering whether to apprehend me. I therefore took to my heels once more, this time seeking out narrow quiet streets that took me as far away from Laetantius' workshop as possible. Soon I felt safer and slowed to a walk, still keeping a careful look out all around me for anyone who might be in pursuit.

At last I stopped and looked around at my surroundings. I was in a poor neighbourhood which reminded me of the street where Simeon lived in Thuburbo. The houses were mean and dirty and there was an unpleasant smell coming from somewhere. I wanted to sit down and rest, but I was still fearful of being seen and recognised, so I slipped behind a section of partly broken down wall where I would be out of sight of the street. There was a rubbish dump there, the source of the smell, but I was too exhausted to seek out some other resting place, so I slumped down amid the refuse to take stock of my situation.

I was alone. I had naturally been congratulating myself on getting away from Laetantius, but it now came home to me with an awful suddenness just how alone I was. There was no question of my going back to the workshop. My few belongings were lost therefore, and even the money I had been trying to steal had slipped from my hand in the struggle. I had nothing in the world now but the clothes I was wearing. And even more terrifying, I had no-one to turn to for help. Laetantius' business was not large, but he was a member of the potters' guild of Hadrumetum, and there was no possibility of my being able to find another employer in this town. I thought briefly of Matthias, my only friend here, but I had not seen him for over two weeks, and anyway, I knew that he would have nothing but condemnation for me when he heard my story. I wondered if I should try and lie to him, claim that I had somehow been unfairly treated and thrown out, but I knew that I could never do such a thing to Matthias.

The next possibility I considered was that I could move on to some other town and seek some sort of work there, where nobody knew me. It seemed like a reasonable option, indeed probably my only option, but for some reason, which I could not at first identify, the thought filled me with a great weariness and depression. After some moments' consideration it came to me why this was so. This was a solution that I had already tried once. I had run away from my home and family in Thuburbo Minus and started a new life in Hadrumetum. But now it seemed plain to me that it was not really a new life at all – it was simply my old life begun again in a different setting. My old life, with its folly and weakness, and the pitiful inevitability of disaster waiting to engulf me.

My thoughts wandered back over the years, trying to see what had gone wrong. I thought of my family – my father and mother and my younger brother Lucius. They had loved me as one who belonged with them, but I had turned my back on them and abandoned them. Tears rolled down my cheeks as I now thought for the first time about how much I had hurt them. Long before I had run away from home, I had already abandoned them in my heart, choosing rather to go after the pleasures that were so enticing to me. Matthias had shown me friendship and trust, but I had let him down too, and had turned my back on him. And then there was Laetantius, a good and honest man who had been far kinder to me than I ever deserved, and what had I done to him? As soon as his back was turned I had had my hand in his money box.

At this point it seemed like there was a voice inside my head shouting at me, telling me that I had let down everyone I had ever loved. Everyone who had ever shown me kindness I had betrayed. The most horrific thing about this was that I knew that it was absolutely true. The voice went on relentlessly, detailing every foolish decision I had ever made in my life and reminding me of every time I had shown contempt for the love and friendship that those around had shown me. As I sat there on that odious pile of rubbish I wept till my body shook at what I had done with my life. And gradually a black depression overwhelmed me and I staggered to my feet. The final image that swam before my mind's eye was of the imagined faces of the passengers on board the *Poseidon* as the great ship slowly sank beneath the waves, and one by one they fell screaming into the water. I knew now that I should have been one of them. Matthias' dream had been for him alone. I should have stayed on that deck and drowned in the depths of the sea, ending this life that I could now see was so futile and empty.

In something between rage and black despair I started to stumble down the roadway. I knew only that I was heading for the port, not to board a ship this time, but to give my body to the waves. To throw myself down into the depths of the sea and rid the world of my own worthless existence. I did not know these streets, but somehow my footsteps seemed to be guided in some fateful fashion. I was only dimly aware of people passing by staring at me. I no longer cared about anything, and in that at least I found some relief from the depression that tormented me. I barely noticed the temples and shops which I was now passing as my feet took me closer and closer to the port. The voice in my head was goading me on, urging me forward each step of the way, telling me that soon I could be free of all my burdens. At last I emerged in the open space of the quays. It was busy and crowded and I hurried out along the massive breakwater that formed the outer wall of the harbour. Soon I was alone and I looked down into the dark green waters of the sea, rising rhythmically towards me and falling away, seeming to invite me, drawing me down into their depths to embrace me. I knew that this was my destiny. Perhaps there was a glimmer of doubt that arose in my mind as I fell, but the cold of the sea as it hit me drove everything from my mind. I had never learned to swim, of course, and I sank down under the water. I looked up toward the greenish sunlight shining down through the surface. My last memory was of drinking in a huge mouthful of sickening salty water, and then all went black.

Part Two

THE NOBLEMAN'S DAUGHTER

7

The Refusal

The ladder was very high – or so it seemed to me. My brother, who was two years older than me, had already climbed it and was calling to me, shouting that you could see for miles from up there. He thought he could even see Carthage in the distance. I had never been up a ladder before and I was pretty sure I didn't want to go up this one, but he was insistent – I had to come up, I had to see the wonderful view, it was easy, there was nothing to worry about. After hesitating for several moments, I finally plucked up courage, set my foot on the lowest rung and, glancing up at his cheery face peering over the parapet at the top, started to climb. As I got higher I was vaguely aware of a rising panic somewhere deep inside me, but I continued climbing, mechanically, hand over hand, one foot up, the other foot up.

I was perhaps two-thirds of the way up when I looked down at the ground. That was my mistake. For the twelve years of my carefree life up until then I had not known any such fear. At that very moment it took hold of me, body and soul, and would not let me move a single muscle. I stared at the wall in front of me, through the rungs of the ladder, around which my whitened knuckles were immovably clamped. The shapes swam in front of my eyes. I tried to open my mouth, to cry out and tell Gaius what had happened to me, but my throat was dry, and my lips wouldn't move. I was aware that he was speaking to me, but there was a ringing in my ears, and I couldn't hear the words. They seemed to be coming from a long way off, though he must have been only a couple of metres above me. I don't know how long I remained like that – it seemed like hours to me – a nightmare stretching on endlessly, without hope of ever waking. In reality, it was probably only a few minutes – then the worst of my panic subsided and I could hear Gaius more clearly:

"Vibia! Answer me! What's wrong?"

"I... I can't move. I'm stuck." I managed to get the words out, breathlessly.

"How are you stuck? You're fine. Look, you're nearly there. Just a few more steps."

"I don't know what's wrong – but... but I can't move."

"You'll have to – you can't stay there! Anyway, you're blocking the ladder – I can't get down till you move out of the way." Perhaps he only meant this as a light-hearted jibe, but almost immediately he must have realised the consequences, if I really was unable to move.

"Are you serious, Vibia?" A note of panic was rising in his voice. "You really can't move? But if we're found here we'll really catch it, you know that! And it'll be all your fault!"

The building site was, of course, strictly out of bounds. The thought of what my father would say if he found me halfway up the ladder, and in the state I was in, filled me with an altogether different sensation of fear.

"Listen, Vibia," said Gaius, taking control of the situation, "here's what we'll do. If you can... oh, no!"

I looked up quickly to see what the trouble was. He was staring down at the ground behind me. I knew immediately that he had seen someone coming. Someone who would obviously have seen us too, by that stage. I was filled with dread at the thought of looking down myself once more, but I needed to know who it was that had discovered us. If it was one of the slaves we would probably be all right, but –

"Gaius! Vibia! By all the gods, what do you think you're doing!" My worst fears were realised – it was the voice of my father. Why, oh why did it have to be him? And how on earth could he have known where we were? I learned later that we had been noticed by one of the slaves heading in the direction of the building site. My father wanted Gaius for something and had been told where he might find us both.

How I got down I don't really remember. I know my father came up below me and helped me down, rung by hideous rung. Gaius kept up a barrage of encouragement and reassurance from above. Then finally I was down, sitting in the dust at the foot of the ladder with my head between my knees, shivering like someone possessed. My father was berating Gaius, laying most of the blame on him as the older, and therefore supposedly the more responsible of us. The result was that neither of us was allowed out of the house for a week. My father clearly felt terribly concerned about what had happened to me and this saved me from the worst of his wrath, but I knew he was very disappointed with me, his only daughter and his best-loved child, and this hurt me deeply.

Didn't our family have enough to worry about, he demanded, with Dinocrates lying sick for week after week and the doctors unable to do anything for him? This reproach from my father was the hardest to take. Dinocrates, my youngest brother, was only six years old and until six weeks ago a happy, healthy little boy. Now he was struck down by a wasting disease that was slowly disfiguring his face. The possibility of losing him hung over us all like the black shadow of some gigantic evil bird. We had tried every doctor in the town of Thuburbo Minus, and my father had brought one from Carthage too, but none of them had been able to do anything for him. Diversions such as our adventure on the building site had helped Gaius and I to forget for a while the horror of what was happening at home, but now, confined for a week, and spending long hours sitting in my room, I could not escape the awful thought – Dinocrates was going to die.

*

A few days later my father arrived at the house speaking in Greek with a stranger, with whom he disappeared into the room where Dinocrates lay. They remained with him for some time, with slaves coming in and out on various errands. One was sent off with careful instructions to buy certain herbs, another to fetch boiling water and dressings. The stranger was clearly a doctor, but not one whom I had seen before. Eventually he emerged with my father, and, after he had given him some last instructions in a low voice, there was the chink of gold passing between them and he left as quickly as he had come. It turned out that this was a famous physician from Rome who was lecturing in Carthage. My father, at considerable expense, had persuaded him to come and look at his son. After bleeding his young patient, the doctor had prepared a dressing which was to remain over the wound for a week without being removed. By that time the doctor would be back in Rome, but we had high hopes that when the dressing was removed we would at last see some improvement.

The wound had first appeared as a harmless looking red spot which Dinocrates had said was terribly itchy, and he had scratched at it incessantly. After a while it had grown hard and wart-like, and then it had disappeared. However, some weeks later other sores had suddenly appeared around the same spot on his cheek, and the whole left side of his face was now horribly swollen and disfigured. His mouth and nose seemed particularly badly affected so that he often had difficulty eating and even breathing at times. He was in constant pain and often cried out. Sleep gave him some relief, but never for very long, and the nights were often disturbed by the sound of his moaning and crying out. It broke my heart to see him like this, and I waited impatiently with the rest of the household, to see whether the doctor from Rome had been able to help him.

Finally, the day came when the dressing was to be removed. The whole family gathered around as my mother gently peeled away the bandage. Dinocrates seemed to be in great pain, and as the last layer came off there was a hiss of indrawn breath from several of the onlookers. Far from there being any improvement, Dinocrates' face now looked far worse than it had before. The sores appeared to be actually eating away at his face and the wound looked horrific. It was at that point that I lost hope in any kind of medical cure. If Dinocrates was going to live, it was going to be through a miracle from the gods.

We had, of course, made prayers to Aesculapius, the god of healing. More than once since Dinocrates had first been taken ill

I had accompanied my mother to the temple. It was one of the smaller ones in the cluster of public buildings around the forum, but one of the stricter ones. Before going there we had had to observe a three day ritual of abstinence – no pork or beans, no bathing or hairdressing. When we arrived at the entrance to the temple we had to take off our shoes and leave them outside. I found it an oppressive place, dim and smelling of incense. The priest asked us about the nature of the illness, and then went through a long and complex liturgy, the object of which was to enquire of the god Aesculapius what action should be taken to cure Dinocrates.

I stood watching the proceedings with a kind of hopeless resignation, hardly aware of what was happening. Why should the god Aesculapius care in the slightest whether my brother lived or died? I knew there were stories of those who had been miraculously cured by following the directives of the god – people who had been blind, lame and such like – but I knew of no-one personally who had experienced this, and somehow I could not really believe these fantastic-sounding tales. I was brought out of my reverie by the priest who seemed to be drawing things to a conclusion.

"The most wise and beneficent Aesculapius requires the sacrifice of a young goat, not yet one year old. The animal shall be burned on his altar here, then the ashes shall be mixed with wine and applied to the wound. The god has been pleased to give his assurance that this will result in a complete healing of the ailment."

We followed these instructions, but I felt that I was simply going through the motions without any real hope of success, and it was with something of a shock that I realised that my mother seemed to be doing the same. Looking back I can now say with certainty that most of the members of my family, upright and respectable though we were, thought no differently than me about such things. We did our duty out of habit and custom, and for appearance's sake, but our hearts were never in it. I believe this is one of the reasons for what later happened to our family. It was to become a family torn in two, but the cause of the tearing was a deep and unfathomable love and devotion which we never knew in our dealings with the gods of Rome. My mother and I returned to the temple to make special prayers for his healing after the prescribed treatment, but, needless to say, it all had no effect whatsoever. The horrible wound continued to spread over Dinocrates' face.

*

It was a few days after we had removed the dressing made by the doctor from Rome that my mother came to speak to me in private.

"Vibia, dearest," she said to me, "a word with you in my room."

I followed her there, wondering what this was all about.

"I want you to help me," she confided, after she had dismissed the slaves and we had sat down on her bed. "It's rather a delicate matter, and... I don't want anyone to know about it – not at the moment, anyway."

This was not at all the sort of conversation I was accustomed to having with my mother, and my curiosity was aroused, although I also felt a certain apprehension, so unexpected was her manner.

"What is it, mother?" I asked, trying not to betray my emotions.

"Vibia, you know how ill Dinocrates is, and we are all at our wits' end trying to do something for him." I could now sense a certain agitation in her voice, and could see it also, in the way she was not looking at me directly, but letting her gaze flit around the room, as if she were searching for something. "There is one thing we haven't tried, and I have come to the conclusion that we must – for Dinocrates' sake if for no other reason."

At this point she did look at me directly, as if to see how I was reacting to her speech so far. I tried to look encouraging, but I felt completely bewildered.

"I wouldn't even have considered it," she went on, "but there is nothing else left to us – you can see that as well as I can, I think."

"But what is it you're talking about, mother?" I asked at last, in some exasperation.

"To speak plainly, my dearest, I was discussing the whole matter with your aunt, Pescennia, this morning and she told me that she knows of a sorceress who – who might be able to help us."

" A sorceress, mother!" I exclaimed, in a shocked voice.

"Shhh! The servants will hear. Vibia, I want you to try to understand – I don't want people to talk, but I really think she may have some power in these matters. Pescennia says that, by the arts of this woman, a friend of hers was cured of a terrible stomach complaint which she had had for years."

I felt like the foundations of my life were being shaken and pulled from under me. We had always been told that sorcery was all just so much superstition and quackery. And as far as I knew, the only people who resorted to such things were poor people who couldn't afford a proper doctor. But then, just a few days ago we had been praying to Aesculapius. We had listened to his priest rattling off a lot of mumbo jumbo about some mysterious rituals which would cure Dinocrates. Was it really any different to go to some magic-worker with an array of potions and spells? To be sure, our visits to the temple of Aesculapius had proved a fruitless exercise, but what if that was not where the real powers were to be found these days? And if other people had really been convinced by the results she could achieve – was it not worth a try? If only for Dinocrates' sake, as my mother had said? These thoughts flashed through my mind, and I tried hard to reconstruct my opinion of sorcery with a new, more open-minded outlook. At the very least perhaps we should put it to the test and see for ourselves. My mother, meanwhile, was looking at me intently, trying to read my thoughts. A question suddenly occurred to me.

"Mother," I asked, "what has all this to do with me particularly? If you don't want to tell anyone else, why are you telling me?"

"First tell me that you are willing to go along with me in this matter – otherwise I shall not say any more about it."

I considered for a moment, then I gave my reply:

"Mother, if you think it might do some good, I am willing to go along with you."

"Very well. Now listen carefully and see what you think. I asked Pescennia to go to this woman and find out if she could offer us any hope, and if so, how the... matter... should be undertaken. She has just called on us to say that the woman would like me to come to her home next Wednesday evening, but that I must bring a young unmarried girl with me, to take part in the proceedings. I am assured that no harm will come to you, but I beg you to help me out in this, Vibia. Will you do it, for Dinocrates' sake?"

For some reason, even at that moment, I felt a sick feeling in the pit of my stomach at the prospect of this encounter. I could think of nothing I would wish for less than to have to accompany my mother and perform who knew what strange rites in the house of some vile crone – I had already pictured her in my mind's eye – but I knew that my mother's last words left me no choice. After a moment's struggle within myself, I agreed, in a choking voice. My mother swore me to secrecy, and I left to go and be alone in my room – alone for a while with my thoughts, and fears.

*

I was standing, completely naked, with the witch in front of me. My mother was nowhere to be seen, but I had a vague sensation that she was present somewhere in the room, hidden in the shadows. The room was dimly lit by a single smoky oil lamp, and from a clay pot on the floor there rose the smoke and sweet overpowering smell of some strange incense. Around the walls, on shelves, were arranged countless phials and bottles, books and scrolls, and many disgusting-looking objects, some of which were identifiable as parts of dead animals. On the floor were painted shapes and symbols, most of which seemed to relate to what I knew of astrology. The witch's face was terrible to look at. Her long black hair was completely loose, and her green eyes shone like a cat's in the night. I was transfixed – I could not move a muscle of my body – I could only stare in terror at her awful face. Her lips were moving, but at first I could hear no words. Gradually, however, I began to hear the whisper of her voice. She was chanting something in a language which I could not recognise – certainly it was neither Latin nor Greek. Then her eyes closed, and her voice rose to be perfectly audible. Some of the words were Latin now. She seemed to be invoking some god or other being, and these invocations were interspersed by strings of words which I did not understand, the very sound of which made my flesh creep. Her voice rose and fell as she chanted the rhythmic syllables, her eyes remained closed, and her arms began to trace eerie shapes in the air in front of her. All of a sudden I became aware of a presence behind her – a dark and indistinct shape which seemed to form and dissolve before my eyes. Gradually, as the witch's chanting continued, the shape took on a more distinct and solid form, and I could make out the features of its face. It was certainly not human, and the very sight of it filled me with a deathly chill. I wanted to run away, but I still could not move. Just then, the witch drew a strange-looking dagger from somewhere in the folds of her tunic and took a step towards me. As her voice rose, she raised the dagger also, and it was clear that she was going to strike me. The shape behind her seemed to be bending over her in a grotesque way. I could stand it no longer – I wrenched myself to one side, screaming:

"No, mother! I cannot do it! I cannot do it!"

I felt my mother's hands on my shoulders – they seemed to be pushing me back, towards the awful apparition from which I was trying to escape. Then I realised that I was in my own bed, struggling to sit up, sweat pouring from my brow. My mother was sitting beside me, holding me by the shoulders.

"Vibia, it's all right – it's just a bad dream. Hush, my dear."

I stared back into her eyes, and it was as if I could still see that horrible black shape behind her.

"I cannot do it, mother!" I repeated, "I swear, I cannot do it!"

Just then, my father came into the room as well.

"What are you talking about, my daughter?" he asked, "You cannot do what?"

"It's nothing," said my mother quickly, "It's only a bad dream she's had. Go back to sleep, Vibia – everything is all right."

She hurriedly ushered my father out of the room before I could say a word more, and I heard her as they went away, saying:

"You know what she's been like since that day she was on the ladder. Poor girl, it still comes back to her."

Not another word was spoken between my mother and me after that, concerning the sorceress. I believe she passed word to her by my aunt that we would not be coming on the specified day.

8

The Passing of Winter

Winter drew on, and Dinocrates' condition gradually but relentlessly worsened. On New Year's Day, the Festival of Aesculapius, we had made our last visit to the temple, but even on that auspicious occasion the god seemed to turn a deaf ear once more to our supplications. By now we had lost all hope, and we now prayed only that Orcus would come quickly to claim his victim, relieving Dinocrates, and all of us, of the torment of his suffering which continued day after day, week after week. His face was now hideous to look at and he was too weak to do anything. He simply lay on his bed, uttering occasional moans. Our family was like a household in mourning, the only thing missing being death itself. For me, I believe this sickness of the soul went deeper than for most. I had gnawing questions in my mind which I threw out into the void, receiving back stony silence as my only answer. I felt that the hopes offered to me had let me down so many times that I could no longer believe in anything. Did the gods really exist at all? If they did, what sort of strange game were they playing with our lives? The alternative, that all around was meaningless, blind chance pursuing us all tirelessly and relentlessly to the grave, seemed like a dark abyss into which I peered and from which I recoiled in horror.

The new year, however, brought news from abroad which took even our sorrowful and preoccupied minds away from our immediate circumstances. Affairs of state, and the doings of the Emperor Commodus in particular, were the subject on everyone's lips these days. It was common knowledge that the emperor was now completely insane – at least that was how most people explained his behaviour. He had publicly announced that he was the god Hercules, and his fanatical obsession with the amphitheatre had driven him to appear in the arena himself, the emperor of Rome facing wild beasts before a howling mob. Fortunately, the affairs of government were being attended to by competent ministers and advisers, but during recent years many of these had lost their lives, accused, some rightly, some wrongly, of plotting against his imperial majesty. In addition, it was rumoured that Commodus' excesses were milking the system dry, and that the imperial coffers were almost empty. Things were reaching a crisis point, when, on New Year's Eve, the emperor proclaimed, as expected, that he would assume the consulship for the coming year. What was unexpected was that he had decided to appear at the ceremony the following day dressed as a gladiator. That night he was quietly strangled in his bed, and before the New Year dawned the Senate had met to proclaim the prefect of the city of Rome, one Helvius Pertinax, emperor in his place.

*

Some weeks later, I believe it was in early March, when the worst of the winter storms were over, and Dinocrates still lay dying in our house, my father took me with him to visit Carthage. I had never visited the city, indeed I had rarely travelled further than a few miles from the town of Thuburbo Minus. Carthage was about a day's journey away, and I eagerly accepted this offer to go there for the first time with my father now, to see the exciting sights and hear the unfamiliar sounds, to gaze at the wonders and soak in the beating pulse of the Empire's second city. My father was going there on business, as he often did. I think he wanted to give me the opportunity of escaping for a couple of days from the melancholy atmosphere of our home. Also, being very fond of me as his only daughter, he welcomed the chance to spend some time in conversation with me on the road there and back. It had not escaped his notice how withdrawn I had become, and he clearly wished to try to help me by encouraging me to talk about my troubles.

"Why do the gods not come to our aid when we appeal to them father?" I asked as we rode along in our covered wagon between young cornfields and olive groves. One of the slave-women of our household had come with us to look after me. The sun was shining and the birds were singing, and the injustice of life seemed all the more hard to accept in such a pleasant setting. My father's face looked sad. He sighed, and stared away into the distance for some moments.

"Dearest daughter," he replied, "I know that you are going through a time of bitter schooling just now, being taught lessons that are not meant for one so young as you. But you must understand that the gods are not our slaves, to answer to our beck and call. We can only ask for their favour and accept whatever answer comes."

"Do you really believe in the gods, father?"

"Vibia! What talk is this? My dearest, what have we taught you all these years? Listen to me, now. Consider this great and mighty Empire of ours. Is it not the most wondrous thing that has ever existed on this earth? Do you think we can maintain the peace and prosperity that have spread over the whole world merely by our own human efforts? No, my daughter! It is the gods who give us all these blessings. It is they who send rain in winter and harvest in autumn. Who make wars cease and bring new life into the world. Yes, sickness comes, and death too. But life goes on. We are all part of something much greater than the ups and downs of our own small lives. It is this greater thing that the gods will always preserve, if only we do not give them cause to abandon us."

Here he looked at me with a slight frown, but whether it was in warning, or simply to try to see into my troubled mind, I could not tell.

"And Commodus?" I asked. I had a habit of exasperating him like this. I know he was proud that I had a good head on my shoulders, but sometimes he probably wished I would accept things more easily, without having to question everything I was told.

"Commodus." He sighed again. "That dark episode is over,

and we can thank the gods for that, at least. I know that Pertinax is not popular with everyone, but he is trying his best to right the wrongs of a decade. I believe that we can look forward to happy and prosperous times once more, out of the shadow of tyranny and madness. It is beyond me to say why the gods allowed the Empire to go through such a time, but I have not lost faith. Rome is still there. And look! We are free, and we are blessed here in this peaceful land."

He gestured around him at the hills and fields that we were riding through, and the sight did indeed lift my spirits for a while. It was good to live here in Africa, with its abundant harvests, where war and strife were things of history, and the intrigues of Rome seemed far away.

As we approached the city, the road ran alongside the massive piers of the great aqueduct that had been built to bring water from the mountains far away. A huge building could be seen on the edge of the city, and I asked my father what it was.

"That, my dear, is the amphitheatre. In all the world there is not another like it, except for the great Flavian Amphitheatre in Rome itself. Some day, no doubt, you will go there and see it from the inside, but for now, is the sight of it not magnificent enough even from here?"

I could indeed see by this time that the building was circular in form, having four storeys of massive arches rising one above the other. Many other buildings could now be seen on the city skyline, most notably the temples of the Capitol on the top of the Byrsa hill, but none rose higher and gave a more massive appearance than the great amphitheatre. I was curious to know what such an enormous structure looked like from the inside, but I was not sure that I would be so eager to witness some of the more gruesome spectacles that I knew were put on there to entertain the citizens of the city.

When we arrived at the gates of Carthage we had to leave the wagon and continue on foot, since no wheeled vehicles were allowed in the city during the daytime. My father offered to get me a covered litter to ride in, but I persuaded him not to, preferring to be able to look around and see as much as possible, and not miss anything of the life of the great city as we walked through its streets. It really was nothing like what I was used to in Thuburbo. The first thing that struck me was the number of people. At times we could hardly move for the crowds, and whereas in Thuburbo our family were well known and highly respected, and generally treated with deference whenever we walked through the streets, here we were just faces in the crowd, being pushed and jostled like everyone else.

The buildings were higher than what I was used to seeing in Thuburbo, too. Here the apartment blocks rose up as high as six storeys, which meant that the narrow streets between seemed very dark and closed in. The lack of space was made worse by the shops and stalls which spilled their displays of goods out into these narrow passages, and by those such as barbers and hawkers who carried on their business right in the middle of the public thoroughfares. I was glad that I had refused the litter, as I could see that our progress would have been almost completely halted for much of the time. I gazed up at the towering buildings, wondering how they managed to stay up without collapsing. However I sound found the answer to this riddle. As we passed along one street we witnessed the rubble of a building which actually had collapsed being shovelled into carts to be taken away.

In time we reached the forum. The sudden open space, crowded though it was, was a tremendous contrast, not to say a relief, from the claustrophobic streets that we had been fighting our way through. All around us rose huge temples and other civic buildings, the most magnificent structures I had ever seen. This was where my father's business took him. He had to see to some matters at the Curia, the town hall which was situated on one side of the forum.

Meanwhile, the slave-woman, whose name was Appia, accompanied me as we strolled over to the south-east side of the forum. This side had no buildings on it, but was more like a huge balcony, from where one could see that one was on the top of a hill, the Byrsa hill, overlooking the sea. This, of course, was the first time I had seen the sea with my own eyes, and the sight of it took my breath away. It was a beautiful turquoise colour, and stretched across a wide bay to where the forested slopes of a mountain with two peaks rose up on the other side. To the east, on the far side of the bay, more hills stretched away into the distance, and then there was nothing but open sea all the way to the horizon. Closer in, immediately below us, the streets of the city were laid out as they ran down to the seashore. On our left the view was dominated by another massive structure, which I guessed to be the baths, but baths the like of which I had never seen before in my life. I later learned that these were the Antonine Baths, the largest in the world. Even Rome had nothing to compare with them. To our right the eye was drawn to two stretches of water which were actually within the city, and which were obviously the ports, as they were filled with sea-going vessels of every shape and size. The nearer port, which was circular in shape, was evidently in the throes of a massive building project, with the scaffolding clearly visible even from where we stood.

We had an hour or so before we had to meet my father back at the Curia, from where we would go to the house of some friends of his where we were going to stay the night. I suggested that we go down to the seashore, and Appia agreed to this. As we made our way down into the bustling narrow streets again there were more strange sights and sounds awaiting me. At one small square a man with four performing dogs had drawn a crowd to watch the creatures jump through burning hoops and walk on their hind legs.

Along another street we glimpsed a strange and noisy procession which was heading down towards the seafront. Some of the people in it were waving palm branches, and others were playing flutes and pipes or shaking metal rattles. Appia explained that these rattles identified the people in the procession as devotees of the goddess Isis. Others in the procession were dancing and a choir was singing as they walked along. It was a joyful procession, and the people were obviously enjoying themselves. I was struck by the stark contrast between these people as they worshipped this strange goddess from the east, and the empty rituals with which we served the traditional gods of Rome, and which I now felt meant so little to me. I wondered to myself what it was that these people had found that made them so happy. They sang that Isis the great mother goddess would protect her children in this life as she would also keep them safe beyond the grave. I thought of Dinocrates once more.

We reached the seafront ourselves and I gazed in wonder at the gently lapping waves. I watched as the ships sailed back and forth, their great sails billowing in the breeze, or their oarsmen straining to the rhythmic beat of a drum. After some time, we made our way back up to the forum, where my father was waiting for us.

"And how do you like Carthage, my daughter?" he asked me.

"It is like nothing I have ever seen before," I replied.

"It is good for you to see it, Vibia. This is our great Empire. This is what the gods have given us. Look around at these magnificent buildings, at the wealth and freedom we have, and do not take these things lightly. Above all, do not wonder that the most magnificent buildings are the temples themselves, where we pay homage to the gods to whom we owe so much. Let us worship them, and enjoy their bounty for many years to come."

My father's friends, whom we were going to stay with, lived in a beautiful town house about ten minutes walk from the forum. They had two young children, a girl and a boy, who seemed to take to me immediately and clambered all over me. They took me into the little garden which was in the centre of their house, and we played there until dinner time. Over dinner, the talk about politics was, to me, rather dull, but some of the details stuck in my mind and I recalled them a few weeks later, when one of the names I had heard mentioned came to be on everyone's lips.

"I received a letter from Clodius Albinus last week," our host was telling my father. "You remember him?"

"Oh, yes – 'the Glutton of Hadrumetum' we used to call him. Isn't he governor of some distant province these days?"

"Britannia, in fact."

"Ye gods! The poor devil."

"Not at all. He seemed in good spirits. He is an ambitious man, you know. These frontier provinces are just the place for such a man to prove his worth."

"In that case, good luck to him. I wish him well."

"In any case, he is one to watch. I got the distinct impression that he was looking for support among his old schoolmates and acquaintances."

"Support for what?"

"Whatever he has his beady eyes on, I suppose. He was very diplomatic, needless to say."

*

My father's optimism concerning the days of prosperity and freedom that were returning to the Empire proved sadly misplaced. Within a month we heard how the Emperor Pertinax had been murdered in his palace by a group of soldiers, and no less than four rival claimants had risen up to battle one another to take his place. What happened immediately after his death was perhaps the most shocking of all. The Praetorian Guard calmly stepped forward and announced that they would grant the purple to whoever offered them the biggest prize. Thus did a wealthy senator named Didius Julianus earn the right to become Emperor of Rome for the price of 25,000 sestertii a man. It was after this scandalous episode that the other three claimants, acting, as they said, in the public interests, each came forward to claim the imperial throne. One of them, of course, was none other than Clodius Albinus.

"He eats too much," was my father's comment, "but he may make a good Emperor. It is the bloodshed that we are going to witness before this affair is over that is the saddest part."

It was just a few weeks later, as the weather began to get warm once more, that my brother finally died. A beautiful marble sarcophagus was ordered, and his body was laid to rest in a small tomb not far from our family home.

"If anyone should dare to disturb this resting place," read the inscription on the tomb, "may he be cursed by all the gods, and may he go down soon to his own grave in sorrow."

In my grief, I cried out, though I did not know to whom I

cried, asking that my little brother would be safe and happy, now that his suffering was over. But the empty words that were being uttered over the grave by the priest gave me no comfort, and a dark emptiness seemed to fill my heart. That night I dreamed I was standing at the tomb, and a flock of huge black birds came down breaking into it easily with their great yellow beaks. They pecked at the little sarcophagus, splintering the marble until they could get in and carry off Dinocrates' body. They flew away into a dark and thunderous sky, and I did not know where they were taking him. I stood there weeping, as the rain began to fall, drenching me with the tears of heaven.

9

A Secret Discovered

The rain poured down on the marble flagstones, and dripped from the red tiles of the roof as I stood with my mother just inside the doorway, waiting for the litters to arrive. Inwardly, I was fuming. We were going out to the dressmaker's to order a new tunic for me. I didn't want a new tunic. I already had more tunics and shawls than I knew what to do with, but my mother's opinion was that many of them were old and shabby, and hardly any were of really high quality. So we were going that day to get me a tunic made of silk, so that I could be dressed appropriately when we went out to the theatre or to dinner at the homes of other notable families in Thuburbo Minus. And in order to impress the dressmaker concerning the sort of clients we were, I had of course, to look my best for this outing too. For what seemed like interminable hours the hairdresser had worked on my hair, the maidservants had fussed around me, applying my make-up and offering suggestions and advice about which jewellery to wear, and finally it had taken a considerable time just to select what clothes I would wear for the trip. When I was finally ready, I still had to wait for my mother, who, incredible as it seemed, had taken even longer in her own preparations. The sun had been shining when I had got up that morning, but now dark clouds had rolled over and a steady rain had begun that looked like it would not let up for the rest of the day. This, of course, added considerably to my frustrations. It was not very far to the dressmaker's, but now, instead of walking, we had to wait while covered litters were fetched for my mother and me.

The litters finally arrived and we splashed across the rain-soaked flagstones and climbed in, already somewhat damp and dishevelled. I propped myself on one elbow, pulled aside the curtain to see out, and tried to look on the bright side. I told myself that my parents wanted the best for me. Hardly a week went by when I was not presented with some small gift or other – a gold hair band, some expensive perfume from a far-off province, or a beautiful glass phial to keep it in. I was their only daughter, and it seemed that nothing was too good for me. And I did appreciate the things I had. I knew that I would enjoy wearing a new silk tunic, knowing that all eyes were on me, admiring me and envying such tokens of wealth and luxury. And yet, I was not content. I felt guilty about this, of course, but no matter how I tried to ignore it, I had a profound sense that there had to be more for me in life than expensive clothes, elaborate hairstyles and the chance to show them off on outings and at dinner parties.

After a few minutes we arrived at the dressmaker's, splashed through some muddy puddles once more, and went into the shop.

"You're very quiet, Vibia," my mother said, interrupting my train of thought, "is something the matter?"

"No mother, nothing." I tried a rather forced smile. "Just this awful weather."

"Well, at least we have litters," she said, peering out the door of the shop at the less fortunate pedestrians passing in the street. "Now, tell me my dear, have you thought any more about the colour? I really think we should work on finding some shade of yellow, don't you?"

"Yellow?" I tried to picture myself in a bright yellow silk robe. It seemed faintly ridiculous. "Yes, mother. I think yellow would be fine. What do you think, Felicitas?"

This last was addressed to the young slave-woman whom we had brought along with us. My mother looked at me and raised her eyebrows at this breach of decorum, but then turned her attention to Felicitas. She was quite young, only a few years older than me, and I had taken a liking to her since we had bought her and her brother the previous summer. Since then one of the other slaves, by the name of Sextus, had taken her as his common law wife. Of course, a slave would not normally be expected to offer advice about fashion to the ladies of the household, but I genuinely wanted to know what she thought, and on a rebellious impulse had decided simply to ask her. She blushed, and I realised that I had embarrassed her. She managed to stammer a reply.

"Indeed, I think Madam would look gorgeous in yellow."

I flashed her the merest flicker of a smile, and she immediately looked down at her feet. The dressmaker's was a large establishment, one of the most prestigious in the town, and there were shelves all around the walls, stretching up to the ceiling, filled with rolls of linen and silk of every conceivable colour. My mother explained our business, and we were soon deep in deliberations about the style, the colour and what sort of edging the tunic should have. I tried hard to take an interest, but my heart was not in it. At one point, as the dressmaker's assistant had just been dispatched to bring back a roll of silk that had already been examined and rejected twice, I glanced over at Felicitas, who was looking rather bored, and rolled my eyes. I believe it was all she could do to stop herself from giggling out loud.

In the end, we ordered a bright yellow long-sleeved silk tunic, with rich and colourful embroidery around the hem, and I believe I did indeed look gorgeous in it. And I had the perfect opportunity to do so a few days after it was delivered, when we were invited to dinner at the home of a friend of my father's, Gargilianus, who lived in a sumptuous villa a short distance from the town.

Although I had occasionally been with my parents at such parties before, sitting at their feet as one of the children, this was the first time I had been assigned a place at the table, which made me rather nervous. To make matters worse, I realised as soon as we were ushered into the dining-room that I had been given the place of honour, reclining on the top couch, to the right of Gargilianus himself. My parents were over on the left-hand couch, also in honoured positions, but rather far from me. On my right was Gargilianus' son, Lupercus, a young man of about twenty, tall and rather thin, who seemed mainly interested in talking about matters to do with money. The other thing he seemed interested in was me, and I began to suspect, as the dinner wore on, that this was perhaps the reason for the seating arrangement. Lupercus was not eating much himself, but he continually plied me with titbits, which seemed to amuse and delight his father, whose eating capacity more than made up for his son's.

There was certainly plenty to eat, and an enormous variety of dishes, and I have to admit that I tried quite a few out of sheer curiosity after my natural hunger had long since been satisfied. To help us prepare ourselves for the onslaught of each successive course, we were treated, while we waited, to some very tasteful entertainments which Gargilianus had laid on. The first of these was musical, a woman who sang folk songs to the accompaniment of a flute, and later there were dancers, acrobats and, last of all, a recitation of poetry. Lupercus seemed rather bored by these distractions, and in between making whispered comments to the young man on his right, he continued to offer me bowls of olives, capers and pistachios, as if I might actually still be hungry.

The poetry was from Virgil's 'Georgics', which conjured up delightful images of farming life and the countryside. I had not been much exposed to the classics up till then, as my father had not been inclined to continue my education past the age of twelve, and I myself had not felt any need for further studies. I was aware that my elder brother, Gaius, was advancing in his studies and even my younger brother, Cornelius, had recently left the primary school to begin his lessons with the grammarian, but what they were actually studying remained something of a mystery to me. Now, however, I felt as if I was coming under the spell of some magic that I had never encountered before. The verses overflowed with exotic names of places from far away and long ago, and praises to the gods of the woods, fields and countryside. As I listened my eye wandered about the room, looking at the rich tapestries which covered the walls, whose designs depicted lush woodland landscapes, peopled with gods and goddesses, fauns, hunters and shepherds.

I felt as if my mind had been set free to wander in these ancient landscapes, where mortals could meet the gods face to face, and revel in the bounty of all that they gave. These idyllic thoughts were, needless to say, frequently punctuated by the attentions of Lupercus, which I tried to meet civilly, if not with any warmth.

"And tell me, Perpetuus," Gargilianus was addressing my father as we sipped wine after the main meal was finally over, and the conversation had come around, inevitably, to politics, "what do you think of our esteemed Emperor Severus' glorious victory over the eastern upstart?"

News had recently come from the province of Syria of the defeat and subsequent capture and execution of Pescennius Niger, one of the rival claimants to the emperorship, who for the last two years had been regarded as sole legitimate emperor by the eastern provinces. It had been a bizarre period. No-one had seriously wanted to see the empire split in two, and yet Roman armies had been fighting one another to decide who would emerge as master of the whole.

"Severus is a gifted general, of that there is no doubt," replied my father, "and for me the final outcome was never really in question. I am glad that the episode is over, and that we have an empire reunited under one head once more."

"You speak the truth," said Gargilianus, "but don't you think..."

Here he cast a conspiratorial glance around the assembled company, and gestured with his wine bowl, as if drawing us into some murky plot with him. He lowered his voice slightly as he went on.

"Don't you think that the purple might sit a good deal better on the shoulders of our old friend Clodius Albinus? It is all very well to be able to fight battles, and I dare say Severus is popular with his troops, since he pays them so well, but there is something about him that I find a little... distasteful." Here he took a mouthful of wine, but immediately spat it out so that it spattered on the ornate mosaic floor.

"A little strong for my liking," he explained, and held the bowl out for a slave to add more water.

"Albinus is a glutton and a drunkard," said another of the

guests, "and even if I could envisage him being able to take on Severus in battle and win, I would not support the venture."

"Come, come," Gargilianus went on, shifting his ample girth on the couch, "there is nothing wrong with a robust appetite. I only wish my son had more of one." He glanced over at Lupercus, and perhaps noticing that I looked rather tired, he added, "But I fear that we are boring the ladies with this talk of politics. Tell me, my dear, how did you find the entertainments?"

"Sir, you are an excellent host," I replied. "The meal has been most enjoyable. I particularly appreciated the poetry."

"Ah yes, the Georgics! You are familiar with our great poets, then?"

"Not really, my lord. I have not had the opportunity to study."

"Ah, Perpetuus," he turned to my father, "you are not of that enlightened company who hold that our daughters have as much need as our sons to be cultivated by the study of the old classics?"

"You who have no daughters of your own," said my father dryly, "do not realise that young women have other things to occupy themselves than burying their noses in books all day. Beauty, modesty and the makings of a good wife do not come by learning grammar and history."

"Now there you have me. What would I know about the upbringing of young women?" He looked at me with a somewhat repulsive grin. "But it is true that your daughter will certainly make a most excellent wife for some fortunate young man, of that I have no doubts whatsoever. Let us hope that that happy day will not be too far in the future."

At this I kept my eyes firmly averted from Lupercus, whose gaze I could feel upon me without looking.

"You are too kind, my lord." I said, nervously fingering the gold bracelets I was wearing. After that the talk turned to other things, and finally the party broke up and the guests departed. On the way home I tried hard not to let my thoughts dwell on the subject of Lupercus, but rather to try to recall the verses of Virgil's poetry I had listened to, that had held such unexpected charm for me.

The next afternoon, when I had returned home from my daily visit to the baths, a time of day when I often found I had nothing particular to occupy me, I decided to go and investigate the library. My father, like most men of his rank, had, over the years, acquired an impressive collection of books, which were kept in a room in an out-of-the way corner of the house. My father took great pride in this collection, and would take people there if he was showing them round the house, to make sure they noticed what a cultivated family we were. Nowadays Gaius made use of it too. There was a couch at one side of the room, and he could sometimes be found reading there, outside the times of his normal lessons with the grammarian. He had been there today, but was just leaving as I got there, on his way to the baths himself, I supposed.

"Hello, Vibia." he greeted me cheerfully, "Are you looking for someone?"

"I'm looking for Virgil." I replied, giving him a mysterious frown. He laughed.

"I believe his bones are buried in Neapolis, my darling, but you'll find his poetry on that shelf over there. And what, may I ask, brings my sister on such a quest?"

"I'm going to study the classics," I announced. I had not consciously decided this up till that moment, but I realised that, ever since the suggestion had fallen from Gargilianus' overfed lips the previous evening, I had been turning the idea over in my mind, and becoming more and more enchanted with it.

"Indeed!" he said, raising his eyebrows, "Well, good luck to you – I look forward to hearing how you get on." With that he disappeared off down the passage.

"*Bene lava!*" I called after him. "Enjoy your bath."

I went over to the shelf he had indicated, and found that it contained a large number of rolls of the books of the Aeneid. I pulled one down, carried it over to the couch, lay down and carefully unrolled it. I began to read, and was soon completely engrossed. I do not know how long I lay there reading – I was not very quick at it, to be sure, and I found the Latin rather difficult compared to the simple texts we had worked with at primary school – but the light was fading and I was unconsciously bending to peer at the letters as they became ever harder to read, when I heard my name called from some distant quarter of the house. I started up from the couch, feeling a sudden wave of guilt at my clandestine activity. I hastily rolled up the book and put it back in its place on the shelf. Then, turning to leave, I found myself face to face with my father, who was standing in the doorway, frowning at me.

"Vibia! What is this nonsense about you studying the classics? I thought Gaius was trying to have some sort of joke, but I find that he was speaking the truth."

"Father!" I ran to him and clasped his arms in my hands, looking up into his frowning face. "You must let me study – please! Can you not get me a tutor so that I can read these books properly? I have been here all afternoon, and I don't remember when my heart was last so full of excitement. I have been reading…"

"Enough!" he said, holding up his hand and shaking off my grip, "I will hear no more of this. I can see I have Gargilianus to thank for this idle notion. I shall have to speak to him when I see him next. Meanwhile, I insist that you put this ridiculous idea out of your head. You are not going to study, daughter. That is all I have to say about it. Now – come, it is time for dinner." And he strode ahead of me down the passage.

I did not follow him, but instead ran to my room in tears, and lay there on my bed, with the verses I had been reading going round and round in my head. Like Queen Dido of Carthage, abandoned by her lover Aeneas, I felt as if I had nothing left to live for, and angry tears ran down my cheeks, slowly forming a damp patch on my pillow.

I was still like this when my mother came in some time later and sat down beside me. She stroked my hair gently for a while, saying nothing. Finally I rolled over and looked up into her face. She looked sad and troubled.

"Mother," I said, wiping my cheeks with my sleeve, "I just want to study. Surely there is no harm in that?"

She turned away, unable to look me in the face, as she

replied, "Dearest, your father doesn't want it. I am afraid that that is the end of it. Please try not to get him upset about this. Come – you must have something to eat."

I suddenly realised that I was very hungry, and I went with her in silence to see what was left of the evening meal. My mind was racing now, however, and I was planning how I could defy my father and study on my own, in secret. If Gaius could be persuaded to help me – though he had certainly not been much help so far, I told myself ruefully – I thought that it might not be at all difficult to get books smuggled to my room in the after- noons, where I could read them without anyone knowing what I was doing. Gaius could help me choose what to read, and explain things to me that I didn't understand. By the time I went to bed that night, I felt much happier. Indeed, I was positively elated at the prospect of my secret project.

As it turned out, however, Gaius was much less enthusi- astic. My 'ridiculous' dream of studying the classics had been the main topic of conversation at dinner the previous evening, and my father had made it known to the whole family, in no uncertain terms, what his will was in the matter. My older brother was therefore not inclined to go against him, despite the fact that he undoubtedly had some sympathy for me. He tried to comfort me.

"Really, Vibia, I can tell you that it all gets rather tedious at times. All that grammar that you have to learn. And some of the books we read are downright boring, though I'd never tell Flavius to his face. You'd probably get fed up with the whole idea after a few weeks and wish you'd never started."

So I resorted to my younger brother Cornelius, and to my surprise, he immediately agreed.

"I think it's very unfair of father," he told me. "I don't see what can be wrong with you reading some books from the library. Just let me know and I'll get you whatever you want. What do you want to begin with?"

"What did you begin with?"

"Oh, the first thing we read was Terence's 'Adelphi'. You'll enjoy that – it's very funny."

And so began my somewhat unorthodox career of study.

Each afternoon, Cornelius came to my room with a roll from the library, which meant that I was never seen there myself. I also enlisted the help of Felicitas, the slave-woman, in the following way. During these afternoon hours I was supposedly occupied spinning yarn with a distaff and spindle. Since it was not possible to do this while simultaneously reading from a papyrus roll (I did try), I requested that Felicitas be there for anything that I needed. This was granted, and thereafter it was she who did the spinning, whilst also keeping a lookout for anyone who might be coming, so that I could hide the book before it was spotted. The whole affair was very amusing to her, and I started to talk with her occasionally when I had tired of reading, and to get to know her better.

Our system worked admirably for several weeks, during which time I worked my way through 'Adelphi', followed by several other plays and poems. I discovered that I loved reading, and soon became much quicker at it. After a while I moved on to my first attempt at reading in Greek, which I had spoken a little since being looked after as a young child by our Greek pedagogue, and which we had learned to read along with Latin at primary school. Thus it was that I had just embarked on Book One of Homer's 'Iliad', when disaster struck.

One afternoon, Felicitas came in from where she had been working just outside my door, telling me urgently that someone was coming. We had been through the procedure several times on previous occasions. I hurriedly rolled up the book and placed it carefully under my pillow. I was just taking the distaff and spindle from Felicitas when my father appeared in the doorway of the room.

"Greetings, my daughter," he said, and I detected a hint of anger in his voice. "Gaius tells me that there is a roll of Homer missing from the library. He was asking if I knew where it was – which I don't." At this point, and quite unexpectedly, he suddenly turned on Felicitas to address her rather than me. "Do you know anything about where it might be, child?" he asked her, in a threatening tone of voice. The poor woman did not know where to look. She looked first in my direction, and then, no doubt realising that this was inadvisable, looked back at my father with guilt all over her face, then finally looked down at the floor in confusion.

"Well, answer me!" my father pressed her. "Have you seen this book anywhere in the house?"

At this point I realised that my father had already guessed the truth, and I knew I could not leave Felicitas in this predicament. Indeed, my father had probably been counting on this. Slowly I drew the papyrus roll out from under the pillow and held it out to him.

"Is this the one that you are missing?" I asked him. He stared down at it and nodded grimly.

"Just as I thought. Vibia, you will come to my study in an hour's time and we will settle this matter once and for all." And with these words he left.

There was silence in the room for several moments, then Felicitas began to stammer an apology.

"My lady, I – I'm so sorry... It was all my fault, I -"

"No, Felicitas," I interrupted her, "I will hear none of that. You have done all you could possibly do for me, and I only hope you do not suffer as a result. Here – give me the spinning things."

She handed them over, and I began to work furiously, my mind in a turmoil.

10

The Dream

My father loved me dearly, of that I was not in any doubt. I believe he loved me more than he loved my brothers, even to the point that they sometimes became jealous of the way he treated me. That is the only explanation I can offer for what happened when I went and presented myself to him at the time he had told me to come. He was reclining on a couch, writing, and he looked up when I entered the room. He looked weary, not angry, as if he had gone through a great struggle in his own mind since our last encounter. He put down his pen.

"My daughter," he said, slowly and deliberately, "I do not know why, but I see that you have made up your mind to study, with or without my permission. It is not something I wanted for you, but seeing that you so ardently want it for yourself, and have proved that it is not merely a passing whim, since you have apparently been defying me for a period of months now, I have decided to grant you your wish."

He took a deep breath, and said, with an almost tangible effort of will, "You shall have a tutor."

I did not know whether to laugh or cry. After weeks of living in guilt and the fear of discovery, and after the previous hour of waiting to see what terrible judgement was going to be passed on me, my world was suddenly turned upside down, all my fears vanished in an instant, and my greatest wish came true. After a moment's hesitation, I rushed forward to embrace him where he sat.

"Father!" I cried, "That is wonderful! It will make me happier than anything else in the world."

He looked into my face, and I saw that he was holding back tears, something I had never seen before in my life.

"That is all I want," he said, embracing me in return, and his voice was softer than I had heard him speak in a long time. "I just want you to be happy."

Gaius and Cornelius were as astounded as I was by my father's change of heart. Cornelius, who had always been my ally, and partner in crime, so to speak, was overjoyed. My father never knew, as far as I was aware, who, if anyone, had been helping me, and neither Cornelius nor Felicitas suffered any repercussions from the affair. It was Gaius's teacher, Flavius, who recommended an old friend of his, a Greek freedman named Sosigenes, who was currently looking for employment and agreed to be my tutor. He was about the same age as my father, in his mid-fifties, and he was a Stoic. He was horrified to find that I had simply been ploughing my way through the classics without any 'explication' as he called it.

"But what virtue is there in simply reading?" he remonstrated, "They must be explicated! Do you think that the pursuit of learning is a worthwhile end in itself? Not at all, madam, we must apply these great writings of antiquity to the here and now, to our own lives. We must search for divine reason and the good of mankind!"

And so he went on. I liked him immediately. Although he was very particular about things like methods of study and the reasons for studying in the first place, I found him quite harmless and easily distracted from his own course when I wanted to go off on some tangent.

So we studied history, reading the works of Sallust and Livy, and I built up in my mind a clearer idea of what the Empire was, and how it had come into being. This was particularly fascinating for me in view of what was happening in the world at large. Having been named as Caesar, heir to the imperial purple by Septimius Severus, Clodius Albinus had promptly been proclaimed sole emperor by his troops. At this point my father, as well as Gargilianus and many others of the nobility of Africa, had come out openly in support of Albinus. It was not just that he was from Africa – Septimius Severus himself was from Leptis Magna far down the Libyan coast – but he stood for the interests of the aristocracy which Severus clearly did not. My father and his cronies were in the habit of portraying the latter as something of a thug. Such talk was quickly silenced, however, when Albinus was defeated in battle somewhere in Gaul, and promptly took his own life. Septimius Severus thus emerged as uncontested master of the Empire, and, whether we liked it or not, we were obliged to give him our allegiance. I took far more interest in these affairs as I was studying the history of Rome, and I sometimes discussed the current situation with Sosigenes.

We studied the Aeneid, too, of course, and it was a delight to me to see how my tutor brought to life these words of Virgil written so long ago, and applied them to the here and now, and to our everyday life. Together we delved even further back in time and read the Greek classics, which I had never really got started on before – the Iliad and the Odyssey, and the tragedies. These were especially close to my tutor's heart, being written in his own native language. He spoke to me in both Latin and Greek, but he clearly preferred the latter, and as time went by and I became more accustomed to it, he used his own language more and more.

Of course, as well as studying the classics, being under Sosigenes' direction I was also put to work reading Seneca and other more modern works by the Roman Stoics, including the 'Meditations' of the late emperor Marcus Aurelius. One day I was reading aloud to my tutor from Seneca's 'Natural Questions'.

"What is the principal thing?" I read. "To be able to endure adversity with a joyful heart; to bear whatever betide just as if it were the very thing you desired to have happen to you. For you would have felt it your duty to desire it, had you known that all things happen by divine decree. Tears, complaints and lamentations are rebellion." I stopped, and read these words over again to myself. Sosigenes was watching me, with his characteristic half-smile.

"You have a complaint?" he said. I was silent for some moments, my eyes still on the words in front of me, but no longer focused. My mind had gone back to those dark days of Dinocrates' illness and death. Here was an answer to my questions, which, though I had managed to put them to sleep, still woke from time to time to torment my mind and threaten to engulf me once more in dark depression.

"He would have been eleven years old last month," I said, looking up from the book in my hands.

"You are speaking about your younger brother." It was a statement, but Sosigenes raised an eyebrow, asking the deeper question.

"Must we just accept such things?" I said. "How can we desire that which gives us only pain and grief?"

"Pain and grief, my lady? What are they? What is pleasure? As long as you are in bondage to such as these, you will never be truly happy. What does this world have to offer us in the way of joy, happiness and pleasure? Nay, my lady, the world is a dark place, filled with misery and suffering. Children die, men kill one another, the innocent are tortured and beaten, all over the world people wallow in the direst pits of vice and depravity. Do not look to this world to make you happy, my child. The way of virtue lies in rising above the circumstances that surround you. Divine reason has ordained all things – what good is there in opposing that which is real, that which we go through, that which is, which always has been, which always will be?"

I sighed, trying to imagine such a viewpoint. But no, in the words of Seneca, I was a rebel. As I contemplated all the evil and suffering in the world it seemed wrong to me. Fundamentally and incontrovertibly wrong. I could not see how, by reason, Sosigenes had come to accept it as anything other, but here he was, telling me that all the pain and misery in the world was simply the divine will.

"I envy you your peace and contentment," I told him, "but I cannot envy you the price you have paid to find it. There is something inside me which tells me that there must be more to good and evil than simply the dictates of a divine will that does not care for one above the other."

"You must continue to search, my lady," he replied. "You are still young. One day you will find contentment. One day you will find the truth, and you will know that it is true."

Slowly and carefully, I rolled up the scroll I was still holding in my hands.

"Can we read some Homer?", I said. "I don't think I want to read any more philosophy today."

Sosigenes smiled, bowed, took the roll from me, and went to fetch another.

*

During this time Felicitas continued to act as my personal maidservant, so that this became her main duty in the household. I enjoyed her company, and often shared things with her as with a friend. I was aware that this was not really a fitting way to treat a slave, but I had no sisters to talk with and my brothers seemed to grow more distant from me the older and more like adults we became. For her part, Felicitas was devoted to me, and although she felt honoured by the way I treated her, and the way I chatted with her about personal affairs, she was always very respectful and obedient, and never tried to take any advantage of the favoured position in which she found herself.

One day she came to me to ask if she could accompany her brother Revocatus to the market. Her brother was one of the slaves who regularly went to buy food for the cook, and I knew that he sometimes took someone else along to help carry the baskets. On this particular occasion, Felicitas was unusually excitable, and it was not the usual time for Revocatus to go to the market, but since I was at that moment somewhat distracted with a passage of Euripides, whose Greek was giving me some difficulty, I did not really notice these details, and simply dismissed her with a wave. That night, however, I had a remarkable and disturbing dream which gave me cause to think back and recall what I had failed to pay any attention to at the time.

I was wandering in a desolate landscape, with dark clouds overhead. I did not know where I was but I had the impression that I was searching for something which I could not find. Suddenly a man stood before me, a few paces away, whose appearance was as I imagined one of the gods might look like.

His face shone like a white fire, so bright that I could not look at it, and his brilliant white clothes also seemed to shine with light. In his right hand he held a sword. I was terrified at the sight of him, and immediately fell face down in the road.

"What do you want with me, my lord?", I asked.

"Stand up, Vibia Perpetua," he said, and I was astonished that he addressed me by name.

"I do not know who you are, my lord," I replied, still trembling with fear. "How is it that you know my name?"

"I have chosen you, Perpetua. You will fight a great battle, and if you overcome by the power of my word, and by the strengthening of my spirit, you will be given the crown of life. I must leave you now, but when you seek for me, you will find me."

"Sir, how shall I find you?" I asked.

"Go with your servant Felicitas. She has already found the way to everlasting happiness, and she will show you too."

I looked up into the dazzling radiance of his face, and just then I felt my feet lifted off the ground. I was being drawn towards him, through the air, slowly at first, then faster and faster. I shut my eyes, bracing myself for the impact as I collided with him, but instead I felt a sudden searing heat engulf me, my arms thrown out in the air at either side, and a sudden sharp and terrible pain in my wrists and ankles. I was gasping, hardly able to breathe, hanging there stretched in the air, with the unbearable pain wrenching at my wrists. It began to dawn on me that this was what it felt like to be executed by crucifixion, when suddenly the pain was gone, indeed all feeling went from my whole body.

Now I sensed that I was lying on a cold flat stone, unable to move a muscle of my body. I opened my eyes, but the place where I was lying was utterly dark. I thought, "I'm dead. This is my tomb, and this is what death feels like. Lying forever, conscious, but numb and lifeless in utter darkness." The horror of this thought flooded through me, and I tried to scream, but I could not even open my mouth. Just then, there was a rasping, grating sound, and a chink of light appeared over to my left, not far away. The sound came again, louder and longer, and the chink grew gradually to become what was obviously a rough doorway.

Suddenly a warm blast of air came rushing through the place, and I felt a strange, tingling sensation seeping through my whole body, as the feeling came back gradually into every part of me. The warmth of the air was now increasing to the point where it was becoming unbearable, and seemed now to be coming from the very walls, which were very close all around me. Indeed, they seemed to be drawing closer, to be walls not of stone as I had imagined, but of living tissue, pulsating and collapsing in on me. I was now entirely enclosed and was being suffocated as they still kept drawing in, squeezing the breath from me. I thought I was going to be crushed, when I realised that the patch of light was still there, and that I was being squeezed towards it. "If only I can reach it and get out," I thought, "I will be able to breathe again." I could do nothing, however, to help my own progress as the hot, living walls held me in their vice-like grip and propelled me slowly forward. I felt like I was about to faint, when finally, with one tremendous heave, I was thrown out of the opening, and drenched in a bright, almost blinding light.

Looking up, I saw that this light was coming from the man's face. He was still there, but I was now right next to him, his face only inches from my own. The look in his eyes was something indescribable, but it was beautiful, and so pure as to be painful to behold.

His eyes held me in that unbearable gaze for some moments, and then he disappeared as suddenly as he had appeared at the beginning, and I woke up, amazed and bewildered. For a long time I lay there motionless, going over in my mind what I had just gone through. The whole dream was still very clear in my mind, not at all like the fragile tatters of memory with which one so often awakens. I pondered its meaning, for it seemed to me that this dream was unmistakably a message from the gods. Above all else, I wanted to know who the man was who had appeared to me, and had said such startling things to me, but nothing in his appearance or his words gave me the slightest hint as to his identity.

In the morning, I lost no time in telling Felicitas about the strange dream, and as I described the vision, and the appalling ordeal I had experienced in the dream, her eyes grew wide and shone with a joy and excitement that I had never seen in her before.

"My lady," she said, when I had finished by describing how I had been told to ask her about how to find the man again, "you are truly blessed! You have seen him and spoken with him face to face!"

"But who is he? That is what I want to know!"

"Jesus Christ, of course!"

I stared at her in astonishment, wondering if she had gone completely mad, or perhaps if I had myself.

"You mean that one who is worshipped by the Christians?" I had certainly heard of this sect, and knew a few things about them, and the way that they lived, but of their founder, Jesus Christ, I knew next to nothing. The idea that he could have appeared to me in a dream, saying the things that he had said to me, seemed altogether incredible. "I think you must be mistaken, Felicitas. What on earth would make you think it could be him? But wait…" A vague memory had come back to me. "Didn't he die by crucifixion?"

"Yes," said Felicitas, "the Christians have a cross as their symbol. But he came to life again after they had buried him."

The vivid images of the dream came back to me. Some sort of meaning seemed to be piecing itself together in my mind, but I was still utterly bewildered as to why this man should have chosen to come and reveal himself to me in such a way. I was staring down at a gold ring I was wearing, turning it round and round on my finger.

"What does it mean, Felicitas?" I said, turning to look at her.

"That I do not know, my lady," she replied, "but I think you must come and meet the evangelist."

"The evangelist?" I asked. "Who is that?"

"There is a man who speaks in the marketplace. It was my brother, Revocatus, who first heard him. My lady, he says the most wonderful things. It was him that we went to see yesterday, when I came to ask you for permission. He talks about Jesus, about the miracles he did, and the things that he said. He healed people who were sick and blind and lame, and when people were brought to him who were possessed by evil spirits, he drove the spirits out. Revocatus says that he has decided to become his follower."

Here, she hesitated, as if unsure of what she was about to say next. There was a pause.

"And what about you?" I prompted her. "What do you think?"

"I was not sure. You know, my lady, that the Christians are called enemies of the state, and there are many people who hate them?" This I was aware of. I had even heard of cases of Christians who had been tried and executed as criminals because they refused to participate in public religious rituals. I nodded.

"I was afraid," she went on. "But now – I mean, now that I have heard of your dream – now I think that I must follow him too."

"Felicitas," I said, "I think I want to meet this evangelist. Can we go today?"

"But of course, my lady." She paused, looking at me shyly. "And you, my lady… Are you going to follow Jesus Christ?"

I thought of my father and mother, and my brothers. The idea of my becoming a Christian and an enemy of the state seemed altogether preposterous. Our whole family would be the object of scandal and ridicule. How could I ever do such a thing to them, I asked myself. And yet, the memory of his radiant face was still there in my mind's eye. That sublime look that I had seen in his eyes. I knew now what it was. It was a deep and immeasurable love, and I did not know if there was anything I could do to resist it.

"Let me speak with this man in the marketplace," I said. "We will go this afternoon, after I have been to the baths. Tell me, Felicitas – what is his name?"

"His name, my lady?" She paused, trying to remember. "Oh, yes. His name is Saturus."

11

The Evangelist

"I am deeply honoured to meet you, my lady." The man bowed. He was perhaps in his mid thirties, handsome, with a pleasant face. He smiled, but something in his eyes told me that he was very sincere.

"The honour is mine," I replied. We were in a colonnade of the forum, in a corner which was, if not exactly quiet, at least not quite as noisy as the rest of the forum. I suddenly felt very strange, confused and unsure of what to say. I was here because a man in a dream had told me to follow my slave. Now that I was here, the whole affair seemed ridiculous, and I couldn't think of any words of explanation that would make it appear otherwise. The man, Saturus, was looking at me, his head slightly on one side, but he did not speak. He waited, apparently untroubled by my speechless state, as if it were the most natural thing in the world that I might take some time to decide exactly what to say. Finally I realised that I was not going to be able to explain myself in any way that would seem normal and sensible, so I plunged into my story regardless.

"I have come because of a dream I had last night," I said. He nodded, but did not speak. "A man appeared to me in this dream, telling me that my slave, Felicitas," I gestured in her direction, "had found the way to eternal happiness. She tells me that she believes the man was Jesus Christ, and that you can tell me more about him, and what the dream means."

I looked in Felicitas' direction and she nodded at me, encouragingly. I knew that she wanted to hear the dream again. So I told it once more, trying to recall every detail and the exact words which the man had spoken to me. Saturus listened intently. He seemed very moved by what I had to relate. When I had finished he looked at me and addressed me in an earnest tone.

"My lady, you do not know it, but you are very blessed."

"My slave told me the same thing," I said, "but I do not feel blessed – only bewildered. Tell me, sir, why was this dream given to me?"

"I believe the Lord Jesus has come to you and is offering you the gift of new life in him, my lady. But you have the choice. You can accept it, or reject it."

"But you would presumably counsel me to accept it – as you have done?" I gave him a brief smile.

"I would not counsel you to accept anything without counting the cost. As the Lord himself said, 'Anyone who does not carry his cross and follow me cannot be my disciple.' And of crosses you know a little already, I believe."

Once again I recalled the pain I had felt in my dream, which I had been trying to describe to him a few minutes before. A very real, horrible pain. Pain that I had seen real criminals going through, hung on crosses by the road outside the town gates. And I thought again of my father and mother, and the prospect of their only daughter turning into a criminal like those poor wretches, their bodies nailed up in public for all to witness their agony.

"My family could never accept that I should do such a thing." I told him. "Has your Jesus Christ thought about that?"

"'If anyone comes to me and does not hate his father and mother, his wife and children, his brothers and sisters – yes, even his own life – he cannot be my disciple.' Those are his own words."

"Hate my father and mother? And you? Do you hate your father and mother?"

Here he looked away, into the distance, then turned back to me with a troubled expression on his face, as if he was recalling some painful memory.

"My lady, I had already shown hatred and scorn for my parents when I met the Lord Jesus. What he asked of me was to return to them and beg forgiveness."

"You say you met the Lord Jesus, as you call him. Do you mean in a dream, like mine?"

Saturus smiled his solemn smile once again. "How I met the Lord Jesus – that is a long story, my lady."

"And I have long ears," I replied. "Since I have been ass enough to follow my slave to meet you, I might as well hear your tale."

He laughed at this, and then gestured to a stone bench set against the rear wall of the colonnade.

"Let us make ourselves comfortable in that case."

We sat down together and Felicitas stood at the end of the bench beside me. I was feeling rather hungry, so I sent her to go and buy some nuts. Then I turned back to Saturus, and he began. He told me how he had grown up here in Thuburbo Minus, the son of a potter with a respectable family business – I knew the workshop as our family had bought some articles there on several occasions. He told me of his father, his mother and his brother, and also of the reckless company he kept as he was growing up. He told me something of his debauched and profligate lifestyle, and of how he had fallen hopelessly into debt in order to finance it. All of this seemed hard to believe of the mild-mannered man in front of me, but he told his story with great humility, and often with evident pain at the memory, and I knew that he was speaking the truth.

After some time he had found himself so deeply in debt that he had no hope of ever repaying the Jewish money-lender whom he was borrowing from, even when he would come into his inheritance on his father's death. It was at that point that he had met the moneylender's son, a young man of about his own age who had recently become a Christian. His father had just discovered this and had thrown him out of his home. I learned then how, although the Christians had started out as a sect of the Jews, they were often hated by them even more than by the pagans. The two of them had decided to run away together, and, after a series of incredible adventures, they had ended up down the coast of Africa in Hadrumetum, where they had each managed to find employment.

Felicitas meanwhile returned with a dish of roasted

almonds, and I began to eat them idly as I listened.

"All would have been well, but for my own foolishness once again," Saturus continued. "I had fully intended to leave my old habits behind me in Thuburbo Minus, but I soon found that it wasn't that easy. Hadrumetum is a large town, and there was even more to tempt me there than there had been here. It was not long before I began to frequent the brothels and gaming houses of the city, where I soon squandered what little was left of the money I had with me. It then occurred to me to seek out a money-lender like Simeon, but I soon realised that, as a stranger without a family in the town, I would never be able to borrow anything from anyone. In any case, I knew that I did not want to go down that path again.

"My folly then reached new depths, as I began to look for ways of stealing money from my master, a potter by the name of Laetantius. He himself was an honest man, and not in the least suspicious. I soon began to find ways of helping myself to money when his attention was elsewhere. I think he became suspicious then, and one day he actually caught me at it. Once again I took what seemed the easiest way out of my predicament, and ran away, this time quite literally, with an irate master at my heels. But I was too quick for him, and gave him the slip, and I was soon alone, wondering what on earth to do next.

"At that point I felt myself sliding into a deep mire of despair. I finally saw what a mess I had made of my whole life. In running away from home, I now realised, I had been trying to run away from myself, but my own folly had stayed with me. In blackest despair I decided to take my own life by throwing myself into the harbour. I really had no reason to go on with my life, and it seemed to me that there was no-one else who would care one way or the other whether I lived or died. In a sort of waking nightmare I made my way down to the port, walked out onto the harbour wall and threw myself off. As I plunged into the dark waters of the sea I was certain that death was about to take me. Then I lost consciousness.

"The next thing I remember is lying on the cold stone of the harbour wall, retching up what seemed like several amphorae of salt water. I could hear voices around me, chattering excitedly, telling each other that I was alive after all. Then I heard a familiar voice: 'Saturus', it said. Only one person in Hadrumetum knew my real name, and I managed to open my eyes and gaze round to where the voice came from. Matthias, kneeling by my head, was staring down at me, and in his eyes I saw a strange mixture of terror and joy. It seems that he had caught sight of me as I stumbled past the merchant's office where he worked, and, seeing that there was clearly something wrong, had quickly finished up what he was doing and left to go after me.

"At first he couldn't find me, but then, as I began to make my way out along the breakwater, his sharp eyes spotted me and, suspecting the worst, he began to run after me. He was no more of a swimmer than I was, but when he saw me jump he shouted for help and several people came running. I owe my life to a young fisherman who was the first to spot my body and dived in to bring me out. It was only a matter of minutes before I came round, coughing and spluttering and emptying my lungs of the salt water.

"They took me back to Tertius' office – that was the merchant who had given Matthias a job, and who was a Christian. From there I was taken to his home, where I was cared for by his family. It wasn't until the following day that I managed to muster the strength to tell Matthias my story. But tell him I did, and I hid nothing from him. I think I was still in that state of utter indifference about my own life, and I no longer cared what he thought or did in response to my tale.

"Well, as I had anticipated, Matthias had only words of condemnation for the things I had done since we arrived in Hadrumetum together. But he said little about this, seeing that I had already condemned myself, and was truly filled with remorse for my past life. What he did talk to me about was his God, the Christians' God, who loved me, he said, even in spite of my life up to that point. This I found difficult to accept, of course, but he tried hard to convince me, telling me stories about Jesus Christ, who was sent from God into the world to show us how much God loved us. This Jesus, he said, showed love for poor and rich alike, for holy men, for prostitutes and for those such as myself who had come to ruin by their own folly.

"'We came to Hadrumetum to begin a new life', he told me, 'but it was not really a new life, as you yourself have pointed out. It was only the old life, begun again in a different setting. Listen to me, Saturus, and try to accept the truth – only Jesus Christ can give us a truly new life.' It is a strange thing to tell, but something inside me convinced me at that moment that the words I was hearing were the truth. There and then, lying on a couch in Tertius' house, I begged Matthias to tell me how I could have such a new life. He explained to me that all I needed to do was to stop trusting in myself to try to sort out my own life, and to trust Jesus Christ with it instead.

"The following day my strength had fully returned, and he took me to meet the bishop of the church there, a godly man whom I soon came to love and respect as a true father. The first step, however, which the bishop was very insistent upon, was that I went back immediately to face my master Laetantius, and accept whatever consequences came to me. For me, this was the true moment of decision in my life, and I thank God that the bishop did not allow me to shrink from it. I nearly didn't do it – it was certainly in my mind to run off once again and try to sort out my life by myself, on my own terms. But as Matthias had pointed out to me so plainly, I was utterly incapable of doing this. I simply had to trust the command of Jesus, to return to Laetantius and beg his forgiveness.

"What happened next was a sore trial for my new-found faith. On returning to Laetantius, I fondly imagined that he would show me mercy, but instead he immediately seized me and had me arrested and thrown into prison. Matthias, who had come with me, pleaded with the potter to give me a second chance, but he proved to be a hard man, and would hear none of it. This, then, was the first consequence of my decision to hand my life over to Jesus Christ – that I languished in a filthy prison for several days, and was then found guilty of theft and subjected to a public beating.

"It is a strange thing, and difficult to explain, but in spite of this ordeal, while I was going through it I felt an inexplicable joy within me. For the first time in my life I felt truly clean and forgiven – no, not by Laetantius, it is true, but by God who had created me and who loved me, and to whom I prayed daily in that dark, overcrowded prison cell. Matthias came to visit me while I was awaiting trial, bringing one of the deacons from the church with him. They supplied me with food and blankets and stayed to pray with me on several occasions.

"After my punishment and release, I joined a group of others who wanted to join the church, and each week we attended a catechismal class together, to prepare us for baptism and full membership of the church. We were also allowed to attend some of the church's meetings, and these for me were blessed times indeed. I felt truly happy for perhaps the first time in my whole life. My biggest worry was that I could not find work. All the potters in the town had heard about me from Laetantius, so the one trade that I knew was closed to me. The Christians helped me out materially, but they were unable to find me any employment.

"Finally, Matthias suggested that I come back here to Thuburbo Minus and tell my family everything. The bishop also encouraged me in this, offering to write a letter of introduction to the small church here explaining my circumstances. Once again I was being challenged to face the consequences of my past folly, and once again I struggled with the decision. But I knew that my Lord Jesus had been faithful to me before and would be again.

"Well, I will finish my tale briefly, since I have already taken too long over it, and even your long ears must be growing tired of listening. I returned to my home and family, and at first they did not quite know what to make of my tale. My father's initial fury at my daring to return at all soon subsided, giving way to perplexity and amazement at the change that had come over me. In the end he and my mother also gave their lives to Jesus Christ, so impressed were they by what had happened to me. It was not long after that that my brother Lucius also joined us.

"Of course, I was petrified too of being discovered by Simeon the money-lender, and for some time I went about the town furtively, always on the lookout for the old crook. It was a great relief to me to discover one day that he had been apprehended by the authorities and was no longer in business. So in the end I was even freed from that burden as well.

"As I mentioned, my father died some years ago, and Lucius and I now run the business together. It is going well – my brother is a shrewd businessman – and I am not always needed there, so I spend as much time as I can spreading the good news of Jesus here in the marketplace, and in neighbouring towns as well. That is how I first came in contact with your slaves Revocatus and Felicitas.

He paused, looking at me as if trying to guess my thoughts.

"And that is my story. I am sorry if I have bored you with it my lady, but I enjoy telling it, and you did ask to hear it."

"Not at all," I replied. "It is a fascinating story."

I paused, my mind wandering over the things he had been speaking about, and over my own recent experience. I had a hundred questions that I wanted to ask him, but for the moment, I contented myself with one of the most puzzling ones.

"Coming back to the present," I began, "in my dream, this Jesus spoke of a battle to fight. Can you tell me what that could mean?"

He thought for some moments before making his reply.

"To be honest, my lady, I cannot offer you any definite answer. I can only say that the Christian life is indeed a battle. Every day we battle against evil desires within us and against the ignorance and darkness around us. In this battle the devil, whom Jesus Christ called the prince of this world, is our enemy, prowling around us unceasingly, seeking some way to make us fall."

"You are not making it any easier for me to choose to follow Jesus Christ," I remarked. "I must hate my father and mother, must battle daily against some devilish being, and, if your own experience is anything to go by, I might end up being thrown into a dark dungeon, or even being killed for that matter. It hardly seems like an attractive choice, you have to admit."

"You have met him, my lady," he replied, "and only you can judge whether it is an attractive option to follow him."

Here he struck a raw nerve. It was easy to dismiss the whole thing as foolishness and utterly impractical for anyone such as myself – Felicitas and Revocatus as slaves were, ironically, much freer than I was to take such a step – but the haunting image of his face in my dream would not go out of my mind. I knew Jesus was calling me, but the cost seemed too great. I felt a sudden urge to get away from this man who was making me feel so uncomfortable.

"Well," I said, in an altogether different tone of voice, "I have taken enough of your time, sir, and I thank you for it, but I think I will be getting on my way." And with this I rose to go.

"One more thing, my lady," he said, getting up himself. I turned to him.

"Bishop Optatus would like to speak with your father."

I could not conceal my surprise at this announcement. "What on earth for?" I said.

"Your slave Revocatus has asked to be a candidate for membership of the church. I have spoken for him, and Optatus himself has spent some time with him, examining him as to his suitability. But it is our practice with slaves to interview their master also, to ascertain whether there is any cause for complaint about their way of life or their service."

I stared at him in amazement. "You do not make it easy for a person to get into your church, do you?" I said.

"On the contrary," he replied, "the church will welcome anyone who truly wishes to follow Jesus. If you learned nothing else from my own tale, you must at least have gleaned that. But a person who wishes to come forward for the washing and rebirth which baptism symbolises must do so naked, as it were, not hiding anything."

At this point Felicitas touched my sleeve, and I turned to her.

"My lady, I would like to say something."

"Go ahead," I said. She turned to Saturus.

"Sir, I too would like to be considered along with my brother."

"I will certainly speak on your behalf to Optatus," he replied, "and he will wish to meet with you as well, of course. After that he will no doubt wish to pay a visit to my lady's household, to speak with her father about both of you."

By this time I was starting to get somewhat irritated, though I hardly knew at what. I quickly explained where the house was, and at what hour he could expect to find my father at home. I then left him, with a formal greeting, and not a word to Felicitas, who followed meekly behind. I could tell that she felt hurt, and probably guilty at offending me in some way, but I was not in a mood to speak to her, and we returned home in silence.

12

Further Encounters

It was a few days later when Sosigenes and I entered the courtyard of our house, where we commonly sat for the day's
lessons, to find Saturus standing there, studying the ornate
fountain at the centre. He turned to look at us, and smiled.

"Sir, my lady, greetings." he said, "I have been admiring the
beautiful architecture of your home."

I was in some confusion as to how to explain to Sosigenes
who Saturus was, and how I knew him, but clearly it had to be
done.

"Ah – Sosigenes, I don't think you know this gentleman.
His name is Saturus. He has become acquainted with some of
our slaves, with whom he has been discussing his religion."
Then, to Saturus, "Sosigenes is my tutor."

"I am honoured to meet you, sir." said Sosigenes, in Latin,
though he preferred to speak in Greek whenever he was
amongst our family. Saturus surprised me by replying in
passable Greek.

"The honour is mine, most esteemed teacher."

"I see you are an educated man." replied Sosigenes, "May I
enquire what your religion is, that you have been discussing
with members of the household?"

"I am a Christian, sir. I studied your language at school, of
course, but more recently I have become better acquainted with
it through the writings of our holy apostles, which were first
written in Greek."

"Indeed." said Sosigenes, and I detected a slight note of
condescension in his voice. "I myself have seen and studied

some of these writings. I found them a little – shall we say, fantastic? They speak, do they not, of the founder of the Christian religion being God in human form, performing countless miracles, being executed and then rising from the dead – you will correct me if I am wrong in some detail?"

"You are entirely accurate in what you report, sir," replied Saturus, "and for that I must say that I am thankful, for there are many who malign us and falsely accuse us of all kinds of monstrous beliefs and practices. In the past I myself was guilty of the vilest slander against the Christians. It is therefore refreshing to find a man who is more concerned about truth than about gossip and rumour."

"And by Truth I take it that you mean Divine Reason, that Logos from which precedes the order and pattern of all things that exist around us and within us?"

Ah, I thought to myself, here we go – now the swords are drawn. Sosigenes was obviously intending to try to convince our visitor of the self-evident truth of his own stoic philosophy. But Saturus seemed entirely at home with such debate.

"There is ultimately only one Truth," he replied, "and that is found not in any system of philosophy, but in the person of our Lord and Saviour, Jesus Christ, who himself declared 'I am the way, and the truth, and the life.' He it is whom the apostle John described as the Logos, or Word of God, through whom all things were made. It is true that he appeared in human form, though he has existed from eternity, and is still alive today. Perhaps your pupil mentioned to you that she has had the blessed privilege of meeting him?"

At this a look of consternation came over Sosigenes' face, a rare enough event, needless to say. He turned to look at me. As for me, I was at a loss as to how to explain this statement, and inwardly I was furious with Saturus for bringing up the subject of my dream. As I was saying nothing, Sosigenes spoke.

"She had not mentioned anything of this, er – encounter. Perpetua, perhaps you could enlighten me…?"

"I had a dream." I said. "I saw a man in the dream whom the worthy Saturus –" I shot him an evil glare, "thinks was this Jesus Christ."

"Ah, dreams and visions!" said Sosigenes, in a lively tone. "My lady, I find it surprising that you should have had some sort of revelation from the gods without even mentioning it to me." He then addressed Saturus: "I have always taught my pupil the value of such things. She is progressing well in her understanding of the Truth, and I have great hopes for her."

It was true that Sosigenes had lectured me at length concerning his own beliefs, but I felt indignant that he thought that I had been convinced by his arguments. I was certainly not a Stoic, and I was annoyed that he was portraying me as his disciple, a faithful follower of the Stoa. In fact the whole conversation was beginning to irk me, and it was with some relief that I heard footsteps at that moment. I turned to see my father coming from the reception room accompanied by an older man of about Sosigenes' age, whom I took to be the bishop Optatus.

However, judging by the look on my father's face, he had been just as irked by this visit of the Christians to our house as I was. He was being polite, but I could tell that he could scarcely wait to see the back of them.

"I trust then," he was saying, "that I have satisfied your desire for information regarding these members of my household, and that you will not find yourself inconvenienced by having to make any further visits."

Optatus, whom I did not recognise, but whom I guessed by his speech and bearing to be a man of some rank, seemed to be coping remarkably well in the face of my father's less than hospitable treatment of him.

"Once again, sir," he said, "I apologise for impinging on your valuable time, and I must thank you for your long-suffering co-operation in this matter. I realise that you have little sympathy for the whole affair, but I ask merely that, if you notice any change in the general demeanour of these two, whom I henceforth rejoice to name as members of my flock, you will ascribe it to the transforming work of the Holy Spirit in their hearts, and will give glory to the God who has rescued them from sin and darkness."

"Please be assured," replied my father in an icy tone, "that I and my family have never ceased to do homage to all the gods as is fitting for every citizen of Rome, and I will do my utmost to ensure that no member of my household is found to be wanting in this respect."

Optatus bowed stiffly, then glanced in our direction, where Saturus stood waiting.

"Since that is the way things stand," he said, "I think my brother and I should be on our way."

Once they had gone, my father turned to Sosigenes and me.

"I trust that other good-for-nothing troublemaker was not taking the opportunity of poisoning your minds too with these treacherous superstitions?"

"He was indeed attempting to explain his religion, sir," said Sosigenes loftily, "but since it is such a tissue of fanciful nonsense, I am afraid he met with little success."

I was praying silently that he would not mention anything to my father about the dream, thus revealing both that I had had previous contact with Saturus, and that I myself might be harbouring sympathy for the Christians. But Sosigenes was far too discreet to do such a thing, and he left it at that. My father, giving no reply but a contemptuous snort, marched off, to look, as I guessed, for the two slaves whose waywardness was the root of all his trouble.

*

Later that evening I drew Felicitas aside to have a private talk with her. I could see immediately that she had been beaten, and I was shocked at this. My father prided himself in being a humane master and I could never remember him ever beating the slaves for anything. But now Felicitas had marks on her arms and face, and one eye was swollen. Nevertheless she seemed in good spirits, which was almost as surprising as the thought of my father beating her.

"My father did this to you?" I asked, unable to hide my shock and anger.

"No, it was not your father," she said. "It was Sextus."

This gave me something of a sense of relief, and, as I considered it, it made more sense. Clearly her husband Sextus was also opposed to her new faith, and no doubt whatever measures my father had taken against Felicitas and Revocatus had affected him also in some way. I knew from Felicitas that he had a short temper, though he kept this well hidden from the family, and generally carried out his duties satisfactorily, though without much attention to detail. I knew too that Felicitas was not very happy with their relationship, but had stuck with him up till now, there being no obvious alternative. Despite my relief that it was not my father who had perpetrated this violence, I was still angry and upset, and was determined to see that Sextus was punished for it.

"We must tell my father!" I said.

"No, please, my lady," Felicitas replied, "don't do that!"

"But why not? Such things should not be happening under our roof."

"My lady, I know he has done wrong, but I don't want him to be punished for it." She paused, apparently in some perplexity, as she tried to explain her feelings. "I have given my life to Jesus now," she said eventually, "and I am trying to live by his teaching."

I sighed and raised my eyes to the ceiling. Clearly it was my fate to be plagued by this man and his incomprehensible teachings.

"And what exactly does he teach about such things?" I asked in exasperation. "That men who beat their wives should be allowed to do so, thus encouraging them to do it again?"

"He taught that if anyone hits you on one cheek you should let them hit you on the other. And if anyone maltreats you for being a Christian, you shouldn't try to get your own back or curse him, but rather you should bless him and pray for him." She smiled at me. "So I'm praying for him."

I wrestled with this idea in my mind for some moments, while looking at the marks on her body that I could see, and imagining those I couldn't. It was the simplicity of her faith that both impressed and scared me. Eventually my thoughts gave way to the practicalities of the situation.

"Let me see to you then," I said. "Did he hurt you badly? And what are you going to tell people about the state you're in?"

"Really, my lady, it isn't as bad as it looks, I'm sure. I'll wear long sleeves and just say it was an accident – I walked into something, maybe."

"Felicitas, I am afraid of what you *are* walking into. I suppose it's too late to ask you to reconsider?"

"My lady – you have seen him. Don't you understand my joy in being his follower?"

And once again that shining face was before me in my mind. The face that, I realised now, I was trying my best to forget about. And the more I learned about this obscure Jewish prophet and his teaching, the more I became convinced that it was a matter of all or nothing to follow him. And I was still desperately scared of giving all.

"Come on," I said, ignoring her question, "let me bathe those wounds."

*

The Parentalia began some days after this, the festival of the dead, when we remembered those who were no longer with us, and honoured their memory with offerings and gifts. It seemed natural and right to be doing this for grandparents, uncles and aunts who had passed away, but for me it was a painful time because of the memory of my little brother. We had buried him, as was the custom for children, within the town walls, in a small plot of ground not far from our house. One day during the festival I had been to visit his grave, taking Felicitas with me as usual. We were on our way home again, and I was trying to turn my thoughts to other matters.

"I hear that you and Revocatus have both asked to have your afternoon off moved to Sunday," I said to Felicitas. "Why is that?"

"It's the catechismal class, my lady," she replied. "We're going to go to the bishop's house to meet with other new converts, and he will teach us the beliefs and practices of the Christians. Then we can be baptised."

"And what does Sextus have to say about that?"

Felicitas paused before answering, and I gave her a worried

look, but she seemed cheerful enough.

"He doesn't want me to go, my lady. But I told him that I was going to go anyway, no matter what he did. I expected another beating, but he didn't lay a finger on me. Plenty of angry words, of course, and threats too, but I think he realised he couldn't stop me." She giggled at her own stubbornness, and I smiled too.

"You are a courageous woman, Felicitas."

"Mule-headed, others would say, my lady."

"In any case, I want my father told if he ever does lay hands on you again, do you understand?"

At this point Felicitas stopped and touched my arm.

"My lady."

I looked at her and saw that she was looking down the street. Following her gaze I was startled to see a familiar face approaching us. It was Saturus. Involuntarily, my heart leapt at the sight of him, but then, as I gathered my thoughts, I decided that I didn't want to talk with him at that moment. Unfortunately, by that stage he had seen us and was coming up to greet us.

"My ladies, I wish you good day!" he said, smiling at us. Then he evidently noticed the wine flask and libation bowl that Felicitas was carrying.

"Oh," he said, somewhat embarrassed at his light-hearted mood. "Excuse me. I see you've been to the cemetery."

"Not to the cemetery, exactly," I said. "My younger brother is buried not far from here."

"Your younger brother?" he said, raising his eyebrows. "I'm sorry, my lady. I didn't know you had had such a tragedy in your family."

"It was seven years ago now," I told him, and I could feel tears coming to my eyes. "He was just seven at the time."

"My heart is sad to hear such a thing," he said. "But I'm sorry if I have upset you by talking about it."

"No, please," I replied, brushing my tears away. "It is good to have someone to talk to about it."

"Would you like to tell me about him?" he asked.

I looked around. We were still standing in the middle of the street where we had met.

"Oh, but I mustn't keep you," I said. "I'm sure you have more important things to do this morning."

"To tell you the truth, my lady, I had nothing in particular to do. I was walking the streets somewhat aimlessly, I have to confess, but perhaps the Lord led me to you for a reason of his own."

At this suggestion I felt slightly uncomfortable, but for some reason I still wanted to stay with him and talk about Dinocrates, about my feelings and my doubts. However I also felt rather self-conscious about standing talking with him in the middle of the street.

"Perhaps we could go to the forum," I suggested.

"Whatever you wish, my lady." And with that we set off.

"We called him Dinocrates," I began, smiling at this despite myself, "but that was just a nickname."

"I've certainly never heard of a Roman with that name," he said. "Why Dinocrates?"

"He was always happy playing with others or by himself, but he was never happier than when he was building with a set of wooden blocks he had. He built houses and towers and temples, then he would come and fetch whoever was near at hand to come and admire his masterpieces. Our pedagogue was often the adult who was there with him, a Greek from Alexandria, who thought these creations were wonderful. He used to say that my brother would be a great architect when he grew up, and it was he who gave him the nickname Dinocrates, after the architect of his native city. His real name was Vibius, after my father, so the nickname stuck because it avoided confusion in the family."

"I'm sure you must all miss him."

"Yes, of course. My father has shown me great kindness and love since he died. I think he was trying to lessen the pain and loss, but somehow I still feel an emptiness inside."

"It can take many years to recover from such a tragedy," said Saturus.

"No," I said, and I could feel some deeply buried emotion welling up within me. "It is not just a question of getting over a family tragedy. I feel I have suffered a wound that time can never heal."

He looked at me questioningly, but said nothing.

"Tell me," I said. "You believe in a God who is good, do you not?"

"I certainly do."

"And does he care about us, his creatures?"

"He loves us with an unfathomable love, my lady."

The image of that face flashed before my mind's eye once again. An unfathomable love. And yet my question remained.

"If that is the case, then why is there so much pain and sorrow in this world?"

"My lady, I have told you already, and not only I but the Lord himself according to your own account, that this world in which we live out our lives is a battlefield. There is a battle being fought all around us between good and evil. The God of light and truth is at war against the forces of darkness and evil, and the legions of Satan his enemy. It is Satan's will to kill and mar and destroy all that God has created good."

"Then what hope is there for us? If that is how you explain things, evil seems to be winning the battle. The world is full of death and destruction."

"No, my lady. It is not as black as you paint it. I admit that it can be hard to see, and many things are now hidden that one day will be made clear, but God is all-powerful. In the end, his victory is certain."

"How can you know that?"

"Because the greatest enemy he faces is death itself, and that enemy he has already defeated. Death was defeated that Sunday morning two hundred years ago in Jerusalem when Jesus Christ came out from his tomb alive. Because Jesus lives, we also will live. Death cannot touch us."

"You mean you will never grow old and die? I don't believe it. And what about all those Christians condemned to death, who have died before the eyes of a crowd of jeering spectators? What do you mean, death cannot touch you?"

"Our bodies will grow old and die, or be torn by wild beasts if that is our lot. But our spirits will never die. Here in this life our Lord Jesus is with us, living in us by his Spirit, but we do not see him as he really is. Death means being with him and knowing him more fully than we ever can in this world. Do you understand, my lady?"

I considered these things for some moments.

"So you're saying that is why those poor wretches are not afraid to die for what they believe?"

"What is death, but the very Gate of Heaven? That is God's victory – that he has turned the greatest weapon of the enemy into something that cannot touch those who put their lives into his hands. He is at work in this dark world, my lady, you can be sure of that, rescuing daily those who are otherwise doomed to destruction. Just as he rescued me from the murky waters of the sea."

"And Dinocrates?" I said, after a pause. "Can he be rescued?"

"That I cannot tell you, my lady. All I know is that he is in the hands of God, and that God loves him as he loves you and me. But one thing I do know."

"What is that?"

"You, my lady – you can be rescued."

"My lady." It was Felicitas, who was looking across the forum. "Look – my husband, Sextus."

Sure enough, he was there, watching us, and when he saw that we had seen him, he turned quickly away and headed back in the direction of our house. My mind was in confusion, and I knew that I needed time to think things through on my own. Also, I was worried about Sextus. It seemed certain that he would report the fact that I had been seen with Saturus in the forum. How was I going to explain this to my parents? I turned back to Saturus.

"I must thank you once again for your time," I said, "but I am afraid I must go now."

"Think about what I have told you, my lady. And may the Lord himself convince you of the truth."

"Good day to you."

"Good day, my lady. And the Lord be with you, my sister." This last was to Felicitas.

We left, and hurried back home, arriving there to find my mother and father standing waiting in the vestibule. There was no sign of Sextus, but I knew instinctively that he had already spoken to them. My mother looked worried, and my father looked grim. He gestured to Felicitas to leave us, and when she had gone he turned to me.

"It is the one who was here with that fool of a bishop, isn't it?" he asked me.

"Father," I said, "it is nothing, really. We met by chance in the street. We got talking about this and that."

"This and that? You were talking about this vile religion he is spreading, weren't you? Yes, you need not even try to deny it – I can see the guilt written all over your face."

I looked pleadingly at my mother for some support, but she was saying nothing. And then my father uttered the awful words, which I had been unconsciously dreading for years.

"My daughter, your mother and I have decided that it is time you were married."

13

The Agreement

"No!" The one word I spoke was uttered with a vehemence which surprised even myself. "I cannot do it, father. I cannot."

"But why not, Vibia? Lupercus is a fine young man. He's handsome, is he not? And Gargilianus is a wealthy man these days. What more do you want, my dearest?"

"Father, I know what this means to you, and I can see that Lupercus would be a good husband, in his own way." I sighed. "But I don't love him, father."

Ever since that evening at their villa, when I had been so entranced by Virgil's poetry, gentle hints had occasionally been dropped to remind me that this match was still what my parents had in mind for me. We had been to their home again on several occasions and they had been to ours. I could see that, from my father's point of view, it was the perfect match. He and Gargilianus had grown up together, and now they wished to unite their two families together in marriage – the happy union of two of the most highly respected families in the town.

"Listen, my daughter. I don't know what is going on between you and that meddling Christian, but if you have the slightest notion of marrying *him* you can put it out of your head right now!"

"Father!" I was shocked at this idea. "I tell you that there is absolutely nothing between us. He must be in his mid-thirties, father. By all the gods, I swear it never crossed my mind to marry him!"

But even as I uttered these words, the thought took root in my heart like a tiny seed. And, small as it was, I knew that it was there, and that it was going to grow. I realised that perhaps I did indeed love Saturus, and the thought served only to redouble my despair, for I knew that my father was right – I could never marry him. At this point my mother mercifully intervened.

"I don't think we should rush things, Perpetuus," she said. "Vibia obviously needs some time to think about it. After all, it is her future we are talking about. Dearest," she said, addressing me, "why don't we let the matter rest for the moment. We can all give it some thought and see if, in time, we might find some solution."

I could not imagine any 'solution', as my mother put it, but at least the pressure was off me for a while. About a week later I was called to the vestibule of our house, and when I got there my heart sank at the sight of Lupercus standing there with my father. They had evidently been in conversation, but they stopped and looked round as I approached. Lupercus bowed and smiled.

"Greetings, my lady."

I said nothing, but gave a slight bow of acknowledgement. My father seemed rather uncomfortable.

"Vibia," he said to me, "Lupercus has asked if he might speak with you alone for a few minutes. I told him that you would of course be happy to grant him this request." He gave me a meaningful look. "Why don't you show him into the reception room?"

With a heavy heart I led the way over to the door and gestured to Lupercus to enter. To my irritation, he made a great show of insisting that I go in first.

"Please, my lady." he said, gesturing in turn. I sighed and went ahead.

When we were alone, and had settled ourselves on two couches facing each other, I opened my mouth for the first time.

"I cannot imagine that this will take very long."

"My good lady," he said, "I'm sure you are right. And to this end I want to suggest that we be entirely open and frank with one another. It will save us both a great deal of time and heartache."

"Please feel free to be as frank as you wish," I replied

coldly. "For my part, you can be sure that I will do likewise."

"Good," he said, apparently unruffled by my icy tone. "Your father has informed me that he recently proposed our betrothal to you – something which, I cannot hide it my lady, I have been looking forward to for some years now. He tells me, however, that you had some – er, objection to his proposal."

"That is quite correct."

"I can see that this objection is based on, shall we say, a certain lack of reciprocity in our feelings toward each other."

"Let's be frank, Lupercus, as you yourself requested. I don't love you. Call me a revolutionary upstart if you wish, but I had in mind to marry someone whom I loved."

Lupercus flinched momentarily, but quickly recovered.

"May I ask if you had someone particular in mind, my lady?"

For a moment the wild notion came into my head of announcing to Lupercus that I intended to marry Saturus. I tried to guess whether my father had made any hint to him of his own suspicions, but I decided that this was entirely unlikely. It would have had the possible consequence of putting Lupercus off marrying me altogether, thus spoiling his own plan outright.

"There is no-one at present," I told him, though it pained me to utter the words. "I do wish, however, to have the freedom to choose my own marriage partner. And I must say that I find it somewhat barbaric the way our parents have been plotting and scheming with our future. Anyone would think we were living two hundred years ago to judge by their expectations."

"My lady, please be assured that I would not dream of marrying you if you were not willing."

The wave of relief must have been visible as it passed over my features.

"Well," I said, with a conclusive air, "that is settled then."

"There is just one thing more," he said, and paused. I gave him an enquiring look. To my surprise, Lupercus glanced toward the door, then lowered his voice before going on.

"Your father also indicated to me the reason he had for proposing our betrothal at this particular moment."

It flashed across my mind that my father had, after all, told him about Saturus, but it would be difficult to reconcile this with Lupercus' apparently conspiratorial air.

"You have begun to take an interest in the sect known as the Christians."

He paused, evidently awaiting some kind of confirmation from me.

"I will not hide from you that I find certain aspects of their life and faith attractive. Their founder, the one they call Jesus Christ, in particular holds a certain... fascination for me." And once again the face was there in my mind. Somehow that image seemed to have burned itself into my consciousness, and I could not rid myself of it.

"Very well," went on Lupercus. "Your father is very concerned about your dabbling in such things, and, from an old-fashioned perspective, I can see his point. I myself, however, have no particular objections to this sect. I know that there are some shocking rumours about them, but I do not think there is a shred of truth in them. I am acquainted with one or two of these Christians myself, and I have found them to be good and upright people who deserve none of the slander that is so often aimed against them."

He paused, waiting to see my reaction to his speech so far. I tried to reveal nothing, but inwardly I was curious as to where all this was leading.

"That is why," he continued, "I am willing to make a deal with you. As I already mentioned, I have been looking forward to our betrothal for several years. I cannot hide the fact that I find you a very attractive woman, and nothing would make me happier than to have you as my wife. Moreover, I am convinced that we could both be very happy together. If you will agree to marry me, to give me the chance to prove this, reluctant though you may be at first, here is what I promise you in return. I am willing to allow you complete freedom to explore the Christian religion, or any other such avenue that you may wish to, without any restriction or disapproval on my part."

That, then, was why he had been so anxious that no-one outside the room should overhear his words. Such a deal would be entirely unacceptable to my father, and for the first time I began to have a glimmer of respect for Lupercus as someone who might after all have some measure of independence of thought and action. I was naturally flattered, too, by his ardent desire to have me as his wife, and the lengths to which he was going to try to win me over. As for how I should respond to his proposal however, I found myself completely unable to make a decision right then and there. After some moments' consideration, while he watched me patiently, I spoke up.

"I see that the matter is indeed perhaps not quite so settled as I had previously thought. I would urge you not to hope too fervently for a favourable response, but I am willing to consider what you propose, and give my answer when I am settled in my mind."

"That is all I ask, my lady," he said. "I shall await your response as patiently as I can."

"I will endeavour not to keep you longer than is necessary," I replied, and with this I rose to my feet and indicated the door. This time he went first, and I followed. The vestibule was deserted, apart from two slaves who were stoking the brazier. I sent one of them to fetch my father, and, once he had come to say his goodbye to Lupercus, he turned to me with a hopeful air.

"Well, my dear," he said, "have you changed your position at all?"

"Perhaps," was all I offered him. "Let us say that he gave me some things to think about."

*

I spent many hours over the next few days considering what Lupercus had proposed. Often I was by myself, going over the various issues endlessly in my mind. One of the first things I did, however, was to tell Felicitas about it, to ask her what she thought. It was a tremendous relief to have someone else to talk to, even though she was extremely hesitant to offer any advice.

"Please, Felicitas, don't be shy," I told her. "I really do want to hear your opinion."

"It's not that I'm shy, my lady," she said, "but I'm sorry to say I think I'm as torn as you are. I really don't know what advice to give you. Of course I want you to share that same joy that I have in knowing the Lord Jesus, but I can see that there's a bitter price to pay. I also know about being stuck with a husband that you don't really love, and all the pain and sorrow that can lead to, as well."

"Perhaps I would grow to love him in time. I certainly found, when we had our little conversation together, that there was more to him than I had previously imagined."

"You say he's sympathetic to the Christians, my lady. But not interested himself?"

"To be honest, Felicitas, I think there are only two things he is interested in. One is his family business, and the other is me."

Felicitas giggled, then checked herself, embarrassed. "Beg pardon, my lady. But you should be flattered, really."

"I am, Felicitas, but I am also wary that being flattered is a form of blindness. I want to keep my eyes open, and I do not wish to be influenced too much by the fact that he obviously wants me so badly."

"What if you just said no, you won't marry him, my lady?"

"I am sure my father would make life intolerable for me if I did that. Not deliberately, to be sure. But he would make it his business to know everything I was doing and everywhere I was going, and everyone I spoke to. I really don't know which he is more concerned about. The possibility that I might want to marry Saturus, or the possibility that I might want to become a Christian."

"You marry Saturus, my lady?" and she giggled again. "But he's ancient!"

"Thirty-five perhaps."

Felicitas suddenly stopped giggling and looked at me. "You don't want to marry him, do you, my lady?"

"Oh don't be ridiculous, Felicitas," I snapped. "He's a potter's son. He's thirty-five years old or more. My family detest him. What on earth would I want to marry him for?"

"I'm sorry, my lady," said Felicitas meekly, "I shouldn't have said such a thing."

"No, no, please," I said, realising I had hurt her just because she was so painfully close to seeing the truth. "It's just that I'm on edge trying to make up my mind about all this. I wasn't angry with you."

All this did not seem to get me any nearer making a decision, however. Each of the choices before me seemed to lead to a prison of some sort, and I had to choose which one I was going to be locked in. On another occasion Felicitas plucked up the courage to raise a matter which had evidently been troubling her.

"If you did marry Lupercus," she asked rather hesitantly, "what would become of me, my lady?"

So caught up with my own dilemma had I been that this question had not occurred to me up till that point. But after a few moments' consideration the answer seemed quite plain to me.

"Why, Felicitas I would ask my father to let you come with me, as part of my dowry. You and Revocatus."

"And Sextus, my lady."

I remembered the role he had played in my father's discovery about my interest in the Christians. Would he continue to spy on what I was doing and report it to my father? Even so, what could my father do about it then?

"And Sextus, too, I suppose," I said, resignedly.

"Would your father agree to that, my lady? For you to have two Christians with you, under your roof?"

"Perhaps," I said grimly, "the thought that Sextus could keep him informed of my doings might persuade him to agree to it."

Then an idea occurred to me. "I could make it a condition of my agreeing to marry him. If I told my father I was still reluctant, but would go if you went with me, I'm sure he would agree. After all, it's not as if he's been trying to keep me away from you so far."

Felicitas paused before asking her next question. "Do you still want my advice, my lady?"

"Yes, of course, Felicitas."

"I think you should marry him, my lady. That's my advice, for what it's worth."

"It is worth a great deal to me, Felicitas."

And soon after that, I came to my decision. Felicitas was, right, I told myself. Of the two prisons I was being offered, my marriage to Lupercus seemed the less dark. I therefore went to my father the next day and put my proposal to him. Of course, he was suspicious about my request concerning Felicitas and Revocatus, but he knew that I had been fond of Felicitas long before she joined the Christians. Who knows, he may even have been intending to give her to me of his own volition. In any case, he agreed, so pleased was he that I was willing to marry Lupercus. Immediately, the preparations began.

*

The formal betrothal was held soon after this, and everyone involved seemed happy enough. Needless to say Lupercus lavished a large number of expensive gifts on me, and presented me with a solid gold ring. But as I admired the gifts one by one – clothes, perfumes, beautiful and rare ornaments – I knew that the greatest gift he was giving me remained a secret from those around us who had come to witness our betrothal. The freedom that he had promised me seemed to me far more precious than any of the costly treasures that I was holding up for the assembled company to admire. During the banquet held afterwards it seemed to me that Lupercus drank too much wine and I became rather uneasy at one point, thinking that he was going to disclose how he had managed to persuade me to agree to our betrothal.

"My future wife is a strong-willed woman, it is true," he was saying, "but I do not expect there to be any problems between us on that account."

"Show her who's boss!" called one of his friends, an obnoxious individual who was completely drunk.

"Diplomacy, that is all that is needed, my friend Gelius," said Lupercus. "A little give and take and everyone will be happy."

"And how is it that you persuaded my dear sister to marry you at all, Lupercus?" This was my older brother Gaius. "You have been very evasive about that little detail."

At that point I managed to catch his eye, and whether he had been about to say anything compromising or not, all he said was: "Natural charm, my friend, natural charm." He gave me a sweet smile, as if to demonstrate how talented he was in this area, and I spoke up in order to stave off any further speculations.

"It is true that I was somewhat hesitant about our proposed union, for a time," I said, "but that was merely because I had not had the opportunity to get to know the most esteemed Lupercus properly."

"I could tell you a thing or two about him," volunteered the drunken Gelius, but then, after downing a bowlful of wine in a single gulp, he appeared to forget what these things were and lapsed into a bemused reverie of his own.

Gargilianus, who appeared to be enjoying the banquet immensely, especially the copious amounts of food on offer, then spoke up.

"It is, purely and simply, a blessing from the gods which has united our two families by this happy agreement. I count myself fortunate indeed to be able to have the lovely Perpetua as my daughter-in-law. Those beneficent gods Pilumnus and Picumnus have indeed smiled upon us, and in their honour I propose a toast to the young couple: long life and happiness to them!"

It was at that moment, I think, that I first dared to believe that I could be truly happy with Lupercus, despite all my fears and misgivings.

The weeks and months that followed were busy and full, and I found little time for reflecting on my choice or speculating about what the future might hold. My father was obviously still suspicious about my movements and I felt very restricted in terms of where I could go and what I could do in the times when I was not occupied with the various preparations for the marriage. I did not see Saturus again during that time, for example, and although it was painful, I was relieved about this. After the first pangs of longing had subsided I found that I could put the thought of him to the back of my mind and almost forget that he existed. Felicitas of course saw him every Sunday afternoon when she went with Revocatus to their catechismal class at the bishop's house. It was actually Saturus, not Optatus, who seemed to be doing most of the teaching, and I often asked Felicitas how the class had been, hoping for some snippet of news about Saturus, though not daring to ask about him by name. Needless to say, she tended to concentrate on the content of the course, rather than on the teacher, but I found this fascinating in itself. I almost felt as if I were following the course myself, listening at second hand to Saturus as he led his disciples through the foundations of the Christian faith.

*

We were to be married in June, and the months passed quickly by. When the day finally came I was a bundle of nerves while the slaves, supervised by my mother, strove to get me ready exactly as custom dictated. This was the kind of thing which I disliked at the best of times, but on this occasion it seemed ten times worse. By the time my hair and head dress had been completed, my whole head felt like it had been caught in a thorn bush. Then the traditional wedding garments were brought in – the plain tunic, tied at the waist by a simple woollen girdle, the bright yellow cloak and sandals, the bronze collar, and the bright orange veil, secured on top of my head by a wreath of myrtle and orange blossom. I have no doubt the effect was stunning, but all I felt like was a statuette in a festival parade.

At last I was ready, and I stood, with my family around me, outside our house, to wait for the arrival of Lupercus. The weather was hot, and I was beginning to sweat profusely in all my finery, so it was a great relief when the party finally arrived and we were able to retire to the reception room for the wedding sacrifice. The ewe which had been selected for this ceremony was brought in and duly slaughtered, and the auspex, a crotchety old priest, stepped forward for his ritual examination of the innards.

As we waited impatiently for him to pronounce a favourable outcome, I caught the eye of Felicitas, who was standing slightly to one side. I put on an exaggerated yawn, to show my feelings about the rigmarole that had to be observed and she let out the tiniest giggle, which was, nevertheless, audible in the silence. My father frowned at her and she cowered in embarrassment. I took care not to look in her direction again.

There seemed to be some complication with regard to the sheep's entrails, and my father went over to mutter a few impatient words to the auspex. There was a brief, though evidently heated exchange between them, and I suddenly had an awful premonition that he was actually going to announce that the marriage was ill-omened. However, after some moments the man seemed to find something in the gory mess that satisfied him, and he duly gave his guarantee that the auspices were indeed favourable. There was an almost audible sigh of relief from the assembled company, and the witnesses then came forward and Lupercus and I exchanged our solemn vows. Then everyone burst out cheering, and I turned to Lupercus. We were husband and wife.

I realised during the days that followed that I had deliberately been concentrating on all the details of preparation in order to put my deeper fears to the back of my mind. I had come to appreciate a number of things about Lupercus, but I was still not in love with him. Nevertheless, his love for me was unmistakable, and he made it clear over the next few days that his greatest desire was for me to be happy as his wife. We settled into our new home, with our small complement of slaves, including, of course, Revocatus, Felicitas and Sextus. Gargilianus appeared to have spared no expense in equipping our home with all that we could wish for, and my parents had also provided some articles and ornaments. In short, we were the classic newly-wedded couple living in comfort and contentment.

But of course, I had not forgotten the deal I had made with Lupercus, and nor had Felicitas. The first Sunday after the wedding, she came to find me.

"My lady," she said, "it is Sunday today. Would it still be possible for Revocatus and I to spend the afternoon at the bishop's house?"

"Why, of course, Felicitas, that goes without saying," I replied.

She hesitated before going on to ask her next question.

"We wondered, my lady," she began, clearly in some embarrassment, "that is, now that you are free, so to speak – perhaps you might like to come with us?"

This suggestion should not have come as a surprise to me, and indeed I had considered the possibility on several occasions, especially while listening to Felicitas as she told me about all that passed during the classes. Somehow, however, I had always pushed the idea out of my mind. One thing that I dreaded was the prospect of meeting Saturus once again, this time as a newly-married woman. I had no idea how I would feel when I saw him again for the first time after so many months, nor how he would react to me. But the other encounter which I was dreading was with someone else, someone whom I had met only in a dream, but whose face still haunted me, and whose eyes I could still picture gazing into mine, calling me to give up everything in order to follow him. I knew that this was a moment of decision, and I sensed that my whole life hung in the balance. I looked at Felicitas, and I saw the joy and eagerness written all over her face. There was something else, too. I could not explain why, but I was sure that I detected a likeness as I looked in her eyes. The likeness of those eyes that were calling me. In a moment, I made my decision.

"I will come," I said.

Part Three

THE NEW FAMILY

14

First Impressions

"I understand your desire to join us, my good lady," Optatus was saying, "but you must realise that we do have certain formalities which must be observed before one can be accepted as a candidate for the catechumenate."

"I don't think you quite understand, sir," I replied. "I did not come here because I wanted to. I am here because I was told to come."

"You were told to come? And who was it that told you, might I ask madam?"

"Jesus Christ."

At this the look of mild irritation on the bishop's face was replaced with one of complete astonishment. He could find nothing to say before Saturus intervened.

"Perhaps I might speak on my lady's behalf," he said. "I first met Perpetua several months ago when she came to speak with me about a dream she had had."

"A dream?" said Optatus, looking surprised. There were two other catechumens present in addition to Felicitas and Revocatus. They were seated on the wooden benches arranged around the walls of the reception room which served as our meeting place. They had been looking rather bored up till now, but at the mention of a dream they immediately turned to me with curious looks.

"It seems that our blessed Lord Jesus appeared to her and spoke with her," continued Saturus. He turned to me, evidently for confirmation and I nodded, but said nothing.

"And he instructed you to come to this house?" asked the

bishop, his voice betraying a certain incredulity.

"Well, not in so many words," I said. "He told me that my slave Felicitas would show me the way to true happiness. It was she who suggested I should come here."

"And this all happened some months ago," said Optatus. "You were not, then, in any hurry, my lady?"

I felt all the eyes in the room upon me, waiting for me to explain my delay.

"I came as soon as I could, sir. I have just recently been married. My husband is a little more – tolerant, shall we say – than my father."

"Hmm. I see," remarked Optatus, and I sensed a certain softening in his tone. "So you are here against your father's wishes?"

"I am."

"Does he know you are here?"

"Not yet."

Optatus appeared to consider this for a few moments. In the silence I could hear a wheezing sound. It was one of the other catechumens, who had been introduced to me as Secundulus, and who appeared to have some difficulty with his breathing.

"A hard man, your father, as I recall," said the bishop. "Our prayers go with you as you break the news to him that you have decided to join us. Perhaps you would like one of us to come with you?"

I thought about this, but I could not imagine that my father would be helped to accept what I was doing by the presence of either Optatus or Saturus.

"That is kind of you, sir, but I think I would prefer to speak to him alone."

"As you wish, my lady."

At this point Saturus intervened once more.

"Might I suggest that Perpetua be admitted to the class, to study along with the others. She has had a good education, and I am sure she will be able to catch up what she has missed so far by reading on her own."

"Might I say something, if you please sir?" This was

Felicitas. Optatus turned to her and nodded. Felicitas went on: "My lady knows quite a lot about what we've been studying. I've been telling her about it each week. I'm sure she'll not have any problems if she joins us now."

"So," said Optatus, and he gave me the hint of a smile, "you have been studying along with us anyway?"

"Not exactly. But I have taken a certain interest in the class." Here I allowed myself a glance at Saturus. He smiled back, but it seemed to me that he knew nothing of my feelings for him.

"And I take it," went on the bishop, to Saturus, "that you are willing to vouch for the good lady's suitability as a catechumen in all other respects?"

"Entirely," said Saturus. "She is an upright woman of good family and upbringing. I believe her to be here out of the purest motives. And in any case, if the Lord Jesus himself has called her, who are we to turn her away?"

"Yes, yes, quite," said Optatus. "I did not mean to imply that I was thinking of turning her away. But there are formalities to be observed, as I have already said. Well, if that is agreed, can I ask the other members of the group if there are any objections to Perpetua joining you at this stage in the course?"

Felicitas and Revocatus shook their heads, but one of the others, Saturninus by name, spoke up.

"Not quite from the same class as the rest of us, is she?"

He had not said anything up till that point, apart from a brief greeting when we first arrived. I felt angry at this rather blunt and rude comment, but I said nothing. Saturus once again spoke up in my defence.

"You will recall, Saturninus, the account of the Lord Jesus' encounter with the rich young man?" Saturninus looked blank, so, after a moment's pause, Saturus went on: "We are told that the Lord looked at him and loved him – even though he came from a higher class. I think perhaps he would be pleased if you did likewise."

I was glad to see that Saturninus looked suitably chastened by this, and I was grateful to Saturus. At this point the wheezing Secundulus spoke up.

"She is my sister," he announced. "If she is here at the invitation of the Lord himself, I welcome her."

And so I was accepted into the class, and the lesson for the day began. The bishop actually left at this point, handing over to Saturus to do the teaching. This did not surprise me as Felicitas had told me that he often did this. We were seated on benches in the *exedra*, the reception room of the house. In the wall opposite the entrance there was a small alcove, just as there was in my father's house. There it was where the altar to the household gods was set up. Three times a month the family would gather there while my father performed the necessary rituals. Here, however, there were no household gods, no portraits of the family's ancestors, and no family records. Instead there was a large cross painted on the wall, beneath which there stood a wooden table, and on the table a pile of papyrus sheets which seemed to be tied together at one side. Saturus now took these sheets and opened them out, announcing that the reading for the day was from the Proverbs of Solomon. I relished the thought that I could now sit and gaze at him while we listened. He began to read:

"'A wife of noble character who can find? She is worth far more than rubies. Her husband has full confidence in her and lacks nothing of value. She brings him good, not harm, all the days of her life.'"

As he read on, describing more and more about this 'wife of noble character', I felt smitten. Here I was, newly married to a husband who had put absolute trust in me, gazing at the man standing before me reading these very words, and wishing in my heart that I was married to him instead. I felt sure now that Saturus had no inkling of my feelings toward him, or else why would he have chosen to torture me by selecting such a passage to read. And yet, was it just by chance that these words were being read to me now? All at once I knew the answer. The passage had been selected, but not by Saturus. It was the other one who had chosen it, and he had chosen it especially for me. The face was there once more in my mind's eye, still gazing at me, still loving me with an incredible love, but pointing deep into my heart, and laying bare the secret that I had not dared to tell anyone, even Felicitas.

My eyes strayed away from Saturus and rested on the cross painted on the alcove wall. It was a stylised symbol rather than a picture of an actual cross intended for executions, but nevertheless it recalled to my mind the brief moment of agony I had experienced in my dream. Outstretched arms, burning pain, breathless, hanging. And the thought came clear into my mind once more: to follow him means giving up everything. Saturus had finished reading and was expanding on some of the themes in the passage, referring now and then to the writings of the Apostles to support some point he was making. Was I willing to give up my love for Saturus, even kept as a secret? Could I give it up, even if I wanted to? No – that was not the important question right now. What I had to decide first was whether I was willing. Did I want to be that wife of noble character which Saturus had read about, to deserve the full confidence of my husband who had freely allowed me to come here? Yes, I did. But I also wanted to be allowed to feed my secret longing for Saturus. Could I not have both? As Saturus continued speaking, the secret battle raged on in my heart.

I missed quite a bit of what was being said as I wrestled inwardly with these questions. I became aware after a while that Saturus had finished speaking and the others were asking him questions of their own. Felicitas I noticed was asking about how she could be strong in the face of her husband's opposition to her faith. Saturus quoted something about loving your enemies and praying for your persecutors. I could see that Felicitas was having her own struggles that afternoon. She had always appeared strong and courageous to me in her dealings with Sextus, but I detected a different side to her here, as she shared her doubts and struggles with the group, and asked them to pray for her.

Saturninus, the only one of the men present who was married, asked what to do if you had a wife, but she wasn't of noble character. I laughed along with the others at this question, but inside I felt ashamed. Perhaps Saturninus' wife, like me, was in love with someone else. In reply Saturus reminded him, and all of us, that Jesus had loved us even when we were people of the most despicable character. He didn't mention it now, but I was sure that all those present had heard his own story and were remembering it as he spoke. The Lord Jesus, he said, expected husbands who were following him to love their wives whatever their character, noble or not.

When no-one had any more questions everyone stood up, raised their hands outward from their sides, and one by one each said a short prayer. Some of the group prayed for Felicitas and Saturninus, asking God to give them the strength to love their partners in marriage despite the difficulties they faced. I stood too, and put my hands up like everyone else, but I did not say anything.

After this the lesson seemed to be over and I felt thoroughly discouraged. It all seemed too idealistic, too radical, too hard. Before we left each member of the group went forward and Saturus placed his hands on their head and said a brief blessing. I hung back and went up to him last. I bowed slightly, as the others had done, and felt the warmth of his hands pressing on my head as he uttered the blessing:

"The peace of Christ be upon you, Perpetua. Be filled with his Spirit."

At that moment I felt a sudden wave of intense energy flood through my whole body. The sensation reminded me of my dream when the warm wind had suddenly come rushing into the cold tomb where I was lying. The experience left me tingling all over, even after Saturus had taken his hands off my head. I looked up, and there was probably a look of shock on my face.

"Are you all right?" asked Saturus.

"Yes," I stammered. "That is… yes, yes – I'm all right."

He gave me a curious look, and then went on:

"Perhaps you could stay here for a while longer. I think the bishop will want to speak with you."

I knew that the others would be going through to the dining room now, where the other members of the church would soon be arriving to take part in the evening's fellowship meal.

"Of course," I said, but I felt very nervous about this. "Felicitas will stay with me."

"Naturally, my lady."

The bishop had a long list of requirements which catechumens were expected to observe. Many of these I was already familiar with, having been with Felicitas over the last few months. There were, for example, instructions concerning a daily routine of prayer. There were set times for praying, morning and evening, and at the third, sixth and ninth hours. Prayers were usually said too before meals and before going to the baths. Wednesdays and Fridays were to be observed as fast days, that is, no food or drink was to be taken before the ninth hour, though the evening meal was taken as normal. The bishop also took me to another part of the house and showed me the church's library. Copies of all the scriptures were there, the Jewish scriptures translated into Greek, and the writings of the Apostles, as well as some other writings that were considered useful for the edification of the church. He showed me how they were all arranged and labelled. These writings were not written on scrolls, but on collections of papyrus sheets, bound together at one edge, as I had noticed with the book of Proverbs that Saturus had been reading earlier on. I soon learned that this was the way that the Christians preferred to make copies of their books.

"You may come here and use the library for personal study any time you wish, my lady," he said. "In particular, it would be good if you read by yourself the various portions which the others have been studying over the past few months. I have no doubt that our sister Felicitas has been faithful in passing on the instruction she has received," here he glanced at her with a slight smile, "but nothing can be a substitute for reading or hearing the scriptures for oneself."

"Yes, of course," I said, wondering how long it would take me to catch up with all that the group had already studied.

The bishop then invited me to stay on for the fellowship meal and meet the other members of the church. I felt overwhelmed by the prospect of this, so I excused myself, saying I was rather tired.

"You will join us next Sunday, then," he said, and I sensed that it was more of a command than an invitation. "During the meeting you will be introduced to the church and formally admitted to the catechumenate."

After that Felicitas and I left, and I was glad to have some time alone with her as we headed home together. It was a warm evening, and we walked slowly and in silence for some minutes.

"You were very quiet, my lady," said Felicitas, eventually. It had not occurred to me, but she was quite right. I was a married woman of only a few days standing, we had just sat through a lesson about the characteristics of a wife of noble character, and I had said absolutely nothing. I wondered if the others had thought this odd, too. I wondered what Saturus had thought.

"Are you all right, my lady?" The same question that Saturus had asked.

"Does he always put his hands on your head like that at the end?" I asked her.

"Yes – it's the blessing. It's part of the lesson."

"Have you ever… felt anything when he did it?"

"Felt anything, my lady? I don't understand. You feel his hands on your head."

"Something happened when he did it to me. I felt something going through my whole body. Like a wave or a rushing wind, then a tingling all over."

Felicitas stopped and stared at me in astonishment.

"Oh, my lady – the Holy Spirit! Didn't he say that to you? 'Be filled with his Spirit'?"

"He did, yes. But what does that mean?"

"Well, it's sort of like Jesus living inside us, helping us to live for him. I can't explain it very well, my lady. Perhaps you should ask Saturus."

"Helping us to live for him." I repeated her words, and thought about how discouraged I had been during the lesson. "It certainly seems very difficult to follow him. I'm sure I would need a great deal of help."

"He does help us, my lady. But you must pray for his help – pray every day, like the bishop said. You remember when Sextus beat me for going to the class, back when I started?"

"I do, Felicitas – I wanted to have him punished, but you didn't want that."

"I did, my lady. After he did it, I was angry, and I cried. I was going to come straight to you and see that he was punished for what he had done. I prayed then, and I knew that Jesus didn't want me to do that. Saturus had just been speaking to us before that about forgiving and praying for those who mistreat us because we're Christians. I prayed then, 'Jesus, I can't do that. You'll have to help me.' And he did. I really did forgive him, and I've never given up praying for him since then. And he's never beaten me again, anyway."

"But how can you forgive a thing like that so easily?"

"Well, I tell myself that in a way it's not really him. It's Satan trying to get at me through him. Satan's his master as much as your father was, and he has to do what he's told. We were all like that before. But I'm praying that he'll be rescued. Bought back from Satan so he can be free."

I looked at her, and marvelled at the simplicity of her faith.

"You're amazing, Felicitas," I said.

"Not me, my lady, please," and she looked genuinely shocked. "It's Jesus living in me, like I tried to explain. He's the one that's amazing."

I thought about what I had felt when Saturus had put his hands on my head.

"So he's living in me now, too, is that what you're trying to say?"

"Of course, my lady. Aren't you his follower, too, now?"

Up until that moment, I had not put it to myself as bluntly as this. My experience at the bishop's house that afternoon had not been altogether encouraging in terms of helping me to make a final decision. But I realised now that, in my heart, the decision had been made. There was no going back.

"Yes, Felicitas," I said, "I am his follower."

When we got back home I went straight away to find Lupercus. He was in his study, poring over some accounts.

"You were away a long time," he said, but in surprise rather than annoyance. "How was it, my dear? Is your curiosity satisfied?"

"There is something I have to tell you, Lupercus," I said.

"What is it, dearest?" He looked worried at my tone.

"I have become a follower of Jesus Christ."

He looked completely astonished at this blunt announcement, and I felt sorry for him, in a way.

"You mean… you mean you've joined the Christians?" He was trying to sound calm and relaxed, but he could not hide the hint of dismay in his voice. "I thought you were just going along to see what it was like?"

"I have not been as honest with you as I perhaps should have been, my dear," I replied, taking his hand in mine. "I think I was intending to join them all along."

He looked into my eyes, and I could see that he still loved me. It pained me to see him so troubled because of what I was doing. I now appreciated all the more what he had done for me in letting me go in the first place.

"Listen, Perpetua," he said, evidently struggling to choose his words, "I still stand by what I promised you. If this is what you want, I accept it completely. You are a Christian. I am married to a Christian." He smiled awkwardly. "Only let the gods preserve us from whatever that might mean for us!"

He took me in his arms, and I held him close, feeling a love for him that I had not felt before. I thought of Saturus, and felt a wave of guilt once more at how I had been sitting gazing at him that afternoon. Silently I prayed: "Jesus, I want to be a good wife. Please, please help me!" The tears trickled down my cheeks, leaving wet marks on the shoulder of Lupercus' tunic.

15

Brothers in Christ

I had no doubt that word of my decision to join the Christians would quickly spread through the household and inevitably reach the ears of Sextus. I therefore resolved to get to my father before he did, so that he could hear of it from my own lips. I was terrified of his reaction, nevertheless, and as Felicitas and I made our way to my father's house, I searched in my mind for words to use that might soften the blow for him, and save me in turn from the worst of his fury. I wondered if the bishop had really prayed for me, as he had said, and how such a prayer might be answered. I had tried to pray myself that morning, and this had been the main focus of my prayers – asking for strength to face my father.

When the moment came, and I made the terrible announcement to him, I believe my prayer was answered, to some extent at least. Having been quaking with fear all the way there and as I waited for him in the familiar surroundings of the courtyard, when he actually appeared my fear seemed to melt away. Instead I felt a tremendous compassion for him. If only I could help him to understand my decision, and what it meant to me, perhaps he would accept it more easily. His immediate reaction, however, showed little understanding.

"By all the gods in heaven, daughter!" he roared. "What do you think you are doing? I cannot imagine how you could act so selfishly after all that your mother and I have done for you. Does it not occur to you that if this news gets about the town – that the daughter of Vibius Perpetuus is a Christian – our family will not be able to hold our heads up in public again. It is all very well for your wretched slaves," and here he glared at Felicitas who was cowering in the shadow of a column, "to tag along with whatever superstitious charlatans they want to follow, but you, daughter – don't you realise that you have responsibilities? Or have you just decided to turn your back on us all, to satisfy your own whims and fancies?"

"Father," I said, trying to convey the compassion I still felt, amid the terror that also gripped me in the face of this onslaught, "I have not made this decision without thinking of you and the rest of the family. In fact, it was the very first thing I thought of. I love you, father, and it pains my heart if you have to suffer for my actions. But I want you to understand that I really have no choice. I cannot be true to myself and not follow Jesus Christ. Would you have me live a lie, father? Surely that is as ignoble as anything you are accusing me of?"

I do not know whether my words appeased him at all, but they certainly did not seem to. He raged on, blaming himself for allowing me to study and thus get the notion that I could think and do whatever I chose. He asked if Lupercus knew, and when I said he had accepted it, he launched into a tirade against my husband as well. I tried to put in a word when I could, but I soon ran out of things to say anyway, and by the time we left I was utterly miserable. When I got home, I went straight to my room, lay down on my bed and wept.

A few days later I went back to the bishop's house, more out of a sense of duty than anything else, to investigate the church library and do some of the reading he had spoken of. He showed me where to find the first few of the set lessons that made up the course.

"You might like to have a look at this too," he said, pulling down one of a series of new-looking books from another shelf. "We have just received this from the church at Carthage – our own copy of the latest treatise by Quintus Tertullian."

I took it from him and studied the first page. It was in Latin, and was entitled 'The Apology'.

"Quintus Tertullian?" I asked. "Who is he?"

"He is a rhetorician who joined the Christians in Carthage a few years ago. Since then he has made a name for himself as a brilliant speaker and writer, defending the Christian faith and putting the pagans into confusion. I am encouraging every member of the church who can to read this work. It is a masterful defence of all that we believe in."

I stayed there reading for an hour or so. It took me back to the days when I had been studying under Sosigenes, although the texts I was reading now were quite different from the classics. Some were Greek translations from the Hebrew writings of the Jewish prophets, and others were more recent writings by the first Christians, most of which had been translated into Latin – memoirs about the life of Jesus, and letters written to churches about the Christian life. I still found much of the teaching very hard, and often found myself asking "How could anyone really live like that?" but I remembered what Felicitas had said on the previous Sunday night. Pray for strength. I tried to do this there and then, each time I came to some exhortation or example that seemed particularly formidable.

What I really loved, however, were the accounts about Jesus' life, and the stories he had told. The Latin was very plain compared with what I was used to studying, but this made the accounts all the more exciting, because it was clear that these were events which had really happened, not myths and legends from the mists of antiquity. The writers of these accounts were not poets or historians. They were ordinary men who had lived alongside the man I had met in my dream. They had, like me, seen him face to face, and they too had had their lives transformed by the encounter.

*

On Sunday we all went back to the catechismal class again. This time I tried my best not to spend too much time looking at Saturus. I found gazing at the cross on the wall was an effective strategy for this, though it was an effort, and I felt a little foolish at times. The lesson was based on the saying of Jesus: "Do not judge and you will not be judged." Saturus gave some examples of how we might subtly be judging other people critically without even realising it, and I searched my mind to see if I had been guilty of this. I was just congratulating myself that this was at least one area in which I didn't feel too convicted when our teacher paused for questions. After a few moments' silence Saturninus rose to his feet.

"I don't have a question," he said, "but I wanted to say something."

"Please go ahead," said Saturus.

To my surprise he turned to me, looking rather awkward.

"I wanted to say to Perpetua – well, about last week. I wasn't very welcoming, as you no doubt all noticed. Well, I just wanted to say sorry. I've been sitting here listening to the lesson, and I've been thinking – that's me. That's me all the time. And last week I was in a foul mood, and ready to take it out on any member of the aristocracy I could lay my hands on. It's no excuse, I know, but we'd just heard from our landlord that he wants to throw us out of our house. He'd given us a month to find somewhere else. I was thinking – these rich folk just think they can do whatever they like, and I didn't want one of them coming to join our class. Anyway – I'm sorry."

I sat there, feeling bewildered at this speech. I realised I had better say something. Everyone had now turned to me to see my reaction.

"That's – er – all right, really," I said, rather lamely. "I have to say you angered me at the time. But now that I hear your circumstances, I can quite understand. May I ask who your landlord is?"

"Some overfed toad by the name of Gargilianus. What he..." Saturninus stopped abruptly, looking at me in dismay. No doubt he could see the look of shock on my face. He clutched his hair in his fists and screwed up his eyes. "Oh, no! There I go again! Of course – you probably know him, too."

"He's my father-in-law," I said, hardly daring to move a muscle of my face. The truth was, I wanted to burst out laughing at the predicament that Saturninus was in. Still clutching his hair, he sat down heavily, brought his forearms round to cover his face and uttered a groan.

"You're right, though," I said, grinning at the others, "he is overfed. I think 'toad' is a little harsh though."

Saturninus looked up in surprise, and I smiled at him. Now it was his turn to look bewildered.

"What – you think I hadn't noticed?" I asked, laughing.

"No, no. It's just – I thought you'd be offended. I'm sorry. Again."

"That's all right. So you live in that apartment block on the Decumanus 4 North?"

"That's right – not for much longer, mind."

"Well, we'll see about that. I may have some influence over him in the matter – he's very fond of me."

"You mean…" Saturninus looked stunned. "You mean, you'll speak to him on my behalf?"

"Of course," I said. His face broke into a grin, then he stepped across to me and, to my astonishment, planted a kiss on each of my cheeks.

"My lady," he said, and it was the first time he had called me that, "you're an angel of God."

After our class the other members of the church began to arrive for the fellowship meal, and I began to get nervous. Optatus had explained the procedure for accepting me into the church, which included an exorcism. All catechumens underwent this apparently, in order to make sure they did not enter the church under the influence of any evil spirits, of which they may not even be aware. Felicitas assured me that this ritual usually passed without incident, but she also described having seen demons coming out of a few people, especially those who had previously practised sorcery, or had come from the pagan priesthood. Secundulus, I learned from her, had been a priest of Saturn, and his exorcism had been quite spectacular, with at least five demons being cast out of him while he writhed and shrieked on the ground.

Before the meal began the bishop opened by saying a prayer, then he asked me to come to the front. When I had done so he asked Saturus to introduce me and to formally propose me for the catechumenate. Saturus described to the whole gathering how Jesus had appeared and spoken to me in my dream. I found this rather embarrassing since the experience seemed to mark me out as something of a celebrity in the church, and I was not at all sure I enjoyed the attention it earned me. Then came the exorcism, but, to my relief, nothing in particular seemed to happen during this, and I felt no different afterwards. The bishop completed the ceremony by gesturing with his hand to make the sign of a cross on my body, and pronouncing that I was henceforth a child of God and a catechumen preparing for baptism.

The food for the meal consisted of contributions brought by each of those attending. Between courses, instead of the entertainments I was used to, there were prayers and sometimes we sang a hymn of praise to God. We sat around the tables, rather than reclining, which had the advantage that there was more space to fit everyone in. At one point one of the elders, those who helped the bishop with the leadership and running of the church, went to the front and announced that he had a prophecy from the Lord. With the bishop's permission, he went on to describe what he believed Jesus was saying to the church. This I found fascinating. I knew, of course, of pagan oracles, but I had not realised that Christians too had prophets among them through whom God spoke to his people.

"The Lord wants us to know that a time of testing will soon come to us," he said. "I do not know what form this will take, but he wants us to be ready. Our enemy the devil has many ways to attack us, but if we stand firm by the power of Jesus' word, and by the strengthening of his spirit, we will see his victory."

These words seemed strangely familiar to me, and then I realised that they were the same words Jesus himself had spoken to me in the dream. I shuddered at this thought. Perhaps the time of testing that this elder was now speaking about would be the great battle which I would have to fight. I did not want to fight a battle. Not yet. I simply wanted to learn more about Jesus, to be baptised, and become a full member of the church.

After the meal we all rose and washed our hands. Then lamps were brought in and we continued by singing more hymns and psalms. Finally the formal part of the meeting drew to a close though most people stayed on for a while to talk with one another. The elder who had spoken in the meeting came over to me at this point and introduced himself to me as Aspasius.

"I was particularly interested to hear about your dream," he said. "Perhaps you would like to describe it in more detail."

I did not really want to, but I did anyway.

"And please don't tell me that I'm very blessed," I said in conclusion. "That's what everyone says to me. What worries me is the part about fighting a great battle. All I want is peace and happiness!"

"Then let me say rather that we are blessed to have you in the church," he said. "It is always a joy to see the Lord bestowing spiritual gifts on his people. You haven't had any other, er – experiences, have you?"

I thought of what had happened when Saturus had laid his hands on my head the previous Sunday, but I hesitated. However, I thought, this elder was as good a person as any to ask about what it meant. I briefly described what had happened and what I had felt.

"My slave Felicitas told me she thought it was the Holy Spirit," I added.

"She was absolutely right," he said, his eyes shining. "You say it was Saturus who placed his hands on you?"

"Yes," I replied. "Apparently he does it every week to each of us."

"It is as well he is your teacher," remarked Aspasius. I was not sure about what he meant by this, but when he saw the puzzled look on my face he went on: "There are some in the church who, I regret to say, have fallen from their first love, and have lost the zeal for Christ that they once knew. Saturus, however is not one of them."

"I have been very impressed with his zeal, and that of the others I have met so far," I said, still wondering exactly what he was talking about. "I should have thought the bishop would soon deal with anyone in the church whose zeal was lacking." I thought of the long list of instructions he had pressed me with the previous week.

"I don't think you've quite understood the situation, my

lady," he said. He glanced around before going on: "I'm afraid I would count the bishop among those who were on slippery ground with regard to their zeal."

I was shocked at these words, and was still completely baffled by what he was trying to say, but I was becoming increasingly suspicious of him. Suddenly the text we had been studying that afternoon flashed into my mind. I hesitated for a moment not knowing whether to say what I wanted to, but in the end it came out anyway, almost involuntarily.

"We were reading a fascinating passage this afternoon," I remarked nonchalantly, "taken from the memoirs of the apostle Luke."

"Indeed?" said Aspasius with a polite smile. "Perhaps you could tell me about it?"

"The focus of our lesson was the part where Jesus taught: 'Do not judge and you will not be judged.'" I gave Aspasius a meaningful look. "I was wondering if you were familiar with that saying?"

"I – well, yes…" Aspasius seemed to be at a loss for words, and his face reddened slightly. "I am certainly familiar with those words of our Lord," he managed to say in the end. "I hope you didn't misunderstand what I was saying about the bishop. I realise that you are new to the church and have many things yet to learn. Perhaps I should not have troubled you with these matters at such an early stage."

"On the contrary," I replied, "I am keen to learn all I can about the church. Particularly if it concerns the Lord Jesus and how we might follow him better."

Aspasius was spared any further discomfort by the inter-ruption of the bishop himself, who at this point called the gathering together to make an announcement. I quickly excused myself and hurried off to rejoin Felicitas and Revocatus. The bishop's announcement concerned a visiting speaker who was going to be coming to Thuburbo Minus in a few weeks time. It was none other than the rhetorician from Carthage, Quintus Tertullian, whose latest work the bishop had been showing me in the library a few days before.

"I do not need to impress upon you," Optatus was saying,

"how privileged we are to be able to welcome this gifted brother to the church here. I have no doubt that everyone will make it a priority not to be absent from this meeting. Can I ask you, if in the course of the next few days you see any who are not present this evening or who have already left, to pass on this piece of news, so that none might be prevented from being there out of ignorance."

The bishop then closed the meeting in prayer and the assembled company left in small groups, with many farewells being passed between them and good wishes for the coming week.

Felicitas, Revocatus and I left together. As we walked home, enjoying the cool of the evening air, there were many things I wanted to talk about. The first thing I asked was whether they had got to know the elder Aspasius at all.

"I noticed you were talking with him, my lady," said Revocatus. "He's a fine speaker, I know that, and this evening wasn't the first time he's brought a prophecy to the church, but I've never had a conversation with him. What did you think of him?"

I was not sure how much I should repeat of his words to me. I did not want to fall into the trap of being judgmental myself, at least not out loud to others, but I wanted to understand more of what he had been talking about.

"He seemed to think there was some problem in the church," I said, carefully. "He mentioned that there are some in the church who are lacking in zeal."

"I've heard that he's been influenced by the Phrygians," said Revocatus. "There's a group of Christians who are devoted to the teachings of a prophet named Montanus, who came from Phrygia. I'm not sure what it's all about my lady, but I heard that they fast a lot, which put me off!"

"Two days a week seems quite enough to me," I laughed.

"They do extra fasts, and they don't break their fast at the ninth hour – they continue until nightfall. There's quite a few of them in the church at Carthage, I think, and there are a handful in the church here who talk a lot about their teachings."

"I think it's wrong that there should be groups like that in the church," put in Felicitas. "Everyone should agree on what is right, and then we can all do it together."

"But who decides what is right?" I asked, beginning to understand the depth of the problem.

"The bishop, I suppose," she said.

"And if the bishop of one church disagrees with the bishop of another church – what then?"

"Well, there's the bishop of Carthage. I think he's sort of in charge of everyone. In Africa, I mean. Then there's the bishop of Rome, too."

"What would happen if the bishop said something which I thought was wrong?"

"He hasn't, has he?" asked Felicitas, looking horrified. I laughed again.

"No, no, my dear – it's just a hypothetical question. I forget that you've never studied philosophy! Well," I said, changing the subject to something less troubling, "I must say I was impressed with Saturninus, anyway. Wasn't he funny when I told him who Gargilianus was?"

"Do you really think you'll be able to help him, my lady?" asked Revocatus.

"Oh, I think so," I replied.

When we got home I found Lupercus relaxing in the courtyard, taking in the cool night air. I decided that there was no time like the present.

"Come on," I said to him. "We're going to visit your father."

Needless to say, he was completely taken aback by this announcement. I had never before shown the slightest inclination to spend time with his family out of choice, though I had often visited out of duty.

"What on earth has come over you, my dear?" he asked. "I'm delighted that you want to visit him, but – well, it's not at all like you."

"Oh, I just had a notion to see him this evening," I said, grinning. "I thought perhaps we could take him some small gift as a token of our affection for him. Can you suggest what might be suitable?"

"Take him something to eat," said Lupercus. "You can't go wrong there."

16

The Visitor

"Well, my dear," said Gargilianus, biting into one of the peaches we had brought, "I hear you've become a Christian."

"I have," I replied, wondering what line he was going to take.

"Very curious," he said, examining the flesh of the peach where he had bitten into it. "What on earth made you decide to do that?"

I wondered what I should say in response to this. I decided to keep it simple.

"Jesus Christ himself called me to follow him. He spoke to me in a dream."

"Ah!" said Gargilianus, looking surprised and bemused. "Now that sounds very interesting. A little dangerous though, don't you think, my dear?"

"I'm afraid it is, yes," I said. "But when you have found the truth, can you be content with a lie?"

"Hmm. Very noble, very noble. Just be careful of yourself, that's all. If anyone tries to make you do something you don't want to -" here he rubbed a plump finger and thumb together, "a little money usually does the trick. I find Severus' lackeys are particularly accommodating in this respect."

"Thank you for the advice," I said.

"And you." He turned to Lupercus and pointed at him with a frown. "I hope you're not about to go and join this crowd too, are you?"

"Absolutely not, father. I confess that I admire my wife's courage and idealism, but I can assure you that no eastern mystics have been haunting my dreams of late."

At this Gargilianus laughed out loud. The whole thing was going far better than I could have hoped. I now dared to broach the subject of the eviction of Saturninus and his family from their home. Gargilianus seemed surprised that I should be concerned about them, but he was ready to discuss the matter. Apparently the whole building, which Gargilianus had owned for many years, was in an advanced state of disrepair and he had decided to pull it down and build another on the site.

"But what are they going to do?" I asked. "He cannot find another apartment at a rent that he can afford. They will be out on the streets – his wife and two little children begging for a living, or sold into slavery."

"Really, my dear – you make it sound so melodramatic!"

"And what if it were your grandchildren who were being put out of their home?" I said. This, as I had calculated, struck a chord with him.

"Dear, dear, really, Perpetua! Now you're going too far. Listen, as it happens I have another property with an apartment which has just become vacant." He seemed to consider the matter for a moment, screwing up his face. "The trouble is, it would be a little beyond their means at the present rent."

"Do you really need the rent?" I said, looking at him pleadingly. "Couldn't you lower it a little? For the sake of the children?"

In the end he agreed, and I said a silent but joyful prayer of thanks. By now it was very late, and after giving him the most fervent kiss I could muster, I said goodbye and we left. The following Sunday Saturninus told me how Gargilianus had offered him the vacant apartment at the same rent as he had been paying before.

"But it's a much better place," he told me. "You're a wonder, my lady. I don't know how I can pay you back for this favour."

"Don't even think such a thought," I said. "Really, the joy on your face when I first saw you this afternoon was payment enough. I really mean that."

Needless to say, Saturninus never again referred to my

being one of the aristocracy, and indeed he sometimes treated me with such respect and deference that I felt quite embarrassed. He was my brother, and I was his sister, and I made every effort to try to get him to behave that way with me.

*

It was a Tuesday evening when we gathered together at the bishop's house to hear Tertullian, the speaker from Carthage, who had come to visit the church. The arrangements were similar to a Sunday meeting. We began with a meal, and when it was over and we had washed our hands and said prayers, Optatus stood and introduced Tertullian to the church. He was a tall man, in his forties I judged, with greying curly hair. By the very manner in which he stood I could tell that he was a skilled orator.

"Brothers and sisters in the Lord," he began, in a deep resonant voice, which demonstrated years of training and experience as an orator, "I bring you warm greetings from the saints in Carthage."

As Optatus had hoped, no-one was absent for this meeting and the dining room was unusually full. I was sitting with Felicitas on one end of a bench. At this point I was totally distracted from what the visitor was saying by Saturus who came over and squeezed onto the end of the bench beside me. He leaned over and whispered to me: "You don't mind if I sit here do you?"

"Of course not." The truth was, however, that I felt extremely uncomfortable. I had been doing quite well in trying not to pay him too much attention over the last few weeks, but now here I was in very close proximity to him and quite unable to get away. Should I just relax and enjoy the experience? I felt awful at the thought of doing such a thing. So I settled down to try to concentrate with all my heart and mind on what Tertullian was saying.

The topic which he was speaking about, however, did not give me much relief from discomfort. It only meant that it was coming from a different source. He was addressing us on the subject of persecution, reminding us of a number of Christians who had died for their faith not that long ago. After he had paid tribute to their courage and faithfulness, he launched into a witty and at times caustic attack on those who had perpetrated these acts of persecution. By this he meant the civil authorities and members of the public who had played a part by denouncing people who were known to be Christians. As one acquainted with the law, he assured us, he regarded these acts as illegal and totally unjust. Christians, he said, were not criminals. On the contrary, they were usually the most law-abiding and useful citizens.

All this was encouraging and fascinating for me. I tried to store up some of his arguments in my mind as ammunition, as it were, with which to defend myself against my father's angry attacks. However, our speaker spent a relatively short time addressing these matters. Then he moved on to argue that all these acts of violence against the church should actually be a cause for rejoicing amongst us. God deliberately allowed them to come upon us, he said, so that the church would be purified and strengthened. Moreover, how many of those who came to believe in Jesus did so because of the steadfast testimony of martyrs? I wondered about this, but then he challenged the assembled company directly. It turned out that a large number of those present had indeed been greatly influenced by witnessing the public execution of Christians who had died bravely for what they believed in.

When Tertullian had finished speaking, the bishop asked everyone to stand and join together in the singing of a psalm. I became acutely aware once more of the presence of Saturus at my side. To take my mind off this I fixed my gaze on the cross on the wall. There was one here in the dining room, just as there was in the *exedra* where we had our catechismal classes. It was while we were singing and my eyes were focused on the cross that I was suddenly overwhelmed by a strange and terrifying experience.

The first thing I noticed was that the singing around me seemed to be fading, and was gradually replaced by a great rushing sound. The lamps in the room also seemed to grow dimmer, but the cross began to shine with a brilliant white light.

Then it was no longer a cross, but the figure of a man, his arms outstretched. The brightest light seemed to be coming from his face, which was so radiant that at first I could not look at it.

"Perpetua," the man said, and it seemed as if the rushing sound was actually his voice. At this point I tried to look at his face, and discovered that I could now make out his features. It was no surprise to me that the face was entirely familiar. It was the face which I had seen before and had been completely unable to forget. The same look of indescribable love was still there, as if nothing had changed in the slightest since the last time he had appeared to me.

"What is it, my lord?" I managed to say, although it was hardly more than a whisper.

"Tell them that they are my bride, Perpetua. I am bringing them to perfection for the great wedding feast of the lamb. These trials that will come upon you all are my winnowing fork, to separate the chaff from the wheat. They are my refiner's fire, to separate the dross from the gold. They will come from within as well as from without. Tell them I love them, Perpetua. I will never leave you or forsake you."

At this the figure disappeared, and was replaced once more by the shining cross. The rushing sound faded, and I gradually became aware once more of the psalm that was being sung around me. Then I felt my legs weakening, and I sat down heavily on the bench, steadying myself with my hands. Saturus turned to look at me in concern.

"Are you all right, Perpetua?" he asked, bending over to speak in my ear. I could say nothing, however. I was sobbing uncontrollably, as I saw once again in my mind's eye the radiant beauty of the man's face, and the love that seemed to stream from it in an unending flood.

The singing ended, and the bishop closed the meeting with a prayer and a blessing. In the meantime, I managed to compose myself after a fashion, so that I was ready when Saturus repeated his question.

"My lady, what happened to you?"

"I – I saw him again," I said, and the tears once more rose to my eyes.

"You mean while we were singing?"

"Yes – I saw Jesus while we were singing, and he spoke to me again."

"Come on," he said, helping me to my feet. "Let's go and speak to the bishop about it."

Optatus was speaking with Tertullian when we approached. He introduced both of us to the visitor.

"This is Saturus, one of our deacons and teachers," he said, "and this is Vibia Perpetua, who has recently been enrolled as a catechumen."

"My brother, my sister, I am honoured to meet you," he said.

I felt suddenly small and insignificant, being introduced to this distinguished man. I was someone who had only recently joined the church. How could I have the presumption to speak to the bishop about an experience I had had during the meeting? But then I seemed to hear the words repeated in my mind: "Tell them."

"Perpetua was telling me about something which happened during the meeting," Saturus was saying to Optatus, "and I thought it best for you to hear about it as well."

So there I was, with three sets of distinguished eyes on me, waiting for me to explain what had happened. Well, he had told me to tell them, so what else could I do?

"I believe the Lord Jesus appeared to me again. He – he gave me a message."

"A message?" asked Optatus. "For whom?"

I was slightly flustered at this question.

"He just said 'them' – 'tell them'. I think he meant the church."

I was feeling rather nervous, and was still recovering from the shock of the experience. Optatus obviously noticed this, and invited me to come and sit down in the reception room. He asked Tertullian and Saturus to come with us. Once the four of us were settled, the bishop said:

"Now my sister, please take your time and recount to us exactly what happened. If the Lord has indeed spoken to the church through you, we must test what you say for its validity and then make sure that the message is conveyed in a suitable fashion."

So I told them about my experience as best I could, although words failed me as I tried to describe the radiant face that I had now seen for the second time. I repeated the words exactly as they had been spoken to me. When I had finished, the three men sat in silence for a few moments, during which I wondered if they were going to declare me a heretic or a madwoman. Tertullian was the first to speak.

"My sister," he said, "you are greatly privileged to be given this gift of communicating so directly with the Lord himself. I know of others who have had such experiences, but they are not many. The vision as you describe seems to me entirely valid and trustworthy." Here he turned to the bishop. "I suggest that you pray for discernment during the next few days, and if it seems good to you, our sister should be given the opportunity of conveying this message to the church on the Lord's Day."

"I will certainly do that," said Optatus. "It is of course, quite unusual for one so young in the faith to be entrusted with such a message. Let us pray that if it is not from the Lord, he will make that clear to us."

"You said 'again'," said Tertullian to me. "The Lord Jesus appeared to you again. This is not the first time, then?"

"Before I joined the church he appeared to me once in a dream. In fact, that is really why I came at first."

"Indeed?" said the rhetorician. "I will give you one piece of advice, my sister."

"What is that, sir?" I asked.

"Write it down," he said. "Anything that happens to you, or that the Lord communicates to you for others – always write it down as soon as possible. Then it will not be lost as your memory fades, and others can have that much more confidence in what you pass on to them."

I promised I would do this, resolving to write down an account of what I had experienced that evening as soon as I got home.

"You say Jesus warned us about trials coming from within, as well as from without," said Saturus. "Do you have any idea what he meant by that?"

The first thing that entered my mind was the struggle I had

been going through myself that evening when Saturus had sat down next to me. I couldn't very well tell him about that, though. I thought then of Aspasius, and of how he had spoken to me about the bishop. That subject too seemed fraught with difficulty, however, so I decided to plead ignorance.

"I really don't know," I said. "He did not specify any particular kind of trials."

"Come," said Optatus, "I think we have troubled our sister enough. Let us return to the company."

Felicitas and Revocatus were evidently burning with curiosity about what had been going on. I suggested that we left immediately, so that I could talk with them when we were on our own. As we walked home, I described the vision I had had, what Jesus had said to me, and what Tertullian and the bishop had said about it. I tried to explain it all as matter-of-factly as I could, but I was aware even as I spoke that the whole thing sounded quite out of this world. By the time I was finished my two slaves were looking at me in awe.

"Please don't gape at me like that," I said. "It makes me feel uncomfortable."

"Sorry, my lady," said Felicitas. "It's just – well, you've seen the Lord. That's like one of the apostles or something."

"Oh don't be ridiculous, Felicitas. It's only in dreams and visions."

"But don't you feel very privileged?" she pressed me. I thought about this.

"Well, I suppose so. But on the other hand, something inside me wishes it was someone else who had been given this privilege."

"I think that's wrong, my lady," said Felicitas, and I was surprised at her boldness. I glanced at her and saw that there was even a hint of reproach in her eyes. But the question was still there in my mind, 'Why me?'

"What do you think, Revocatus," I asked. He had been unusually quiet.

"I don't mind if it's you or someone else. But all this scares me."

"How do you mean?" I asked him.

"Whoever the message comes through, it scares me that Jesus is warning us about having to go through trials. He didn't just say one trial – he said lots. And all different kinds. Doesn't that scare you?"

While I considered this, Felicitas spoke up before me: "Well, of course it's scary. But hasn't he promised to always be with us, whatever we have to go through? He'll give us strength and courage."

Felicitas' simple faith never ceased to amaze me.

"I'm scared," I confessed. "I don't want to have to fight a battle. But I don't think we have a choice."

"We can run away," said Revocatus. "There's always a choice."

"But running away means giving in to Satan," I said. "Then you're defeated."

"That's what scares me most," he replied. "What were the words he used to describe the trials, my lady? A winnowing fork, and a refiner's fire. To get rid of the chaff and the dross. And didn't Tertullian say something very like that too? What if I'm just chaff or dross? What if these trials are being sent just to get me out of the church? Or you, or anyone else?"

I had to admit that this was a sobering thought, and I searched for some words with which to encourage him.

"Listen," I said. "We three are fortunate. We have one another – we live together in one household. Let us resolve to pray for one another every day. To pray together, too. To pray that we'll be strong enough to fight whatever battle may come to us. And may Jesus himself give us the strength."

I looked at Revocatus and was surprised to see that there were tears in his eyes. He took my hand in his.

"Thank you, my lady," he whispered. "I want to do that. And I want to fight and win. But I need so much more courage than I feel I have."

I stopped, there in the street, and embraced him. What passers-by might have thought, I don't like to imagine, but I could not help myself. I knew that deep down I shared his anxiety and his doubts.

"Christ give us all more courage," I said.

17

A Family Divided

As soon as we got home I found a sheet of papyrus and a pen and wrote down in as much detail as I could exactly what had happened to me during the meeting, and the words Jesus had spoken to me in the vision. The following Sunday I took this to the bishop's house and let him read it. He suggested that I should simply read this out during the fellowship meal – he would call on me to do so at an appropriate moment. I felt very nervous when the moment came, and I stood up, clutching my piece of papyrus. But the words still echoed in my mind: "Tell them." Urged on by this command, I read out what I had written, and was surprised at how bold my voice sounded, when inside I was quaking with nervousness. When I had finished there was silence in the room, and I felt terribly self-conscious. I sat down, not knowing what else to do. At that moment Aspasius the elder rose and thanked me, then led us all in a prayer for strength and endurance through the trials that were to come. Afterwards a number of people came up to me and thanked me for what I had shared. The attention which my experience seemed to draw made me feel very uncomfortable, but what made it worth it was the conviction that Jesus really had communicated a message to his church, and that he had actually used me to do so.

Despite our fears and the warnings we had received, however, the months that followed seemed peaceful. We continued to attend the catechismal classes, while others continued to join the church, and new classes were started to accommodate them. People came from all different backgrounds

– slaves, freedmen, even one or two more of the aristocracy. There were soldiers, too, and some, such as actors, gladiators and priests, who had to give up their professions as the cost of becoming Christians. Sometimes it seemed as if the whole world was going to follow Jesus, and the thought filled us with joy and excitement. We began to attend the meetings at the cemetery on Sunday mornings as well as the meals at the bishop's house in the evenings. These early morning meetings were held in remembrance of Jesus' death and resurrection. The climax of each meeting was the breaking of bread, the Eucharist, but as unbaptised catechumens we were not yet allowed to stay for that part of the meeting. One Sunday morning, just as we were going to leave, Saturus came up to speak to me.

"I had a very interesting conversation with someone in the forum yesterday," he said, giving me an enigmatic smile.

"What about?" I asked, guessing that he had some gem to share with me.

"About following Jesus. What was particularly interesting was who it was I was speaking with."

"Someone I know?" I asked, mildly curious now.

"It was your mother."

I gaped at him, dumbfounded. I had not seen my mother for a week or so, it was true, but in all the time since the wedding she had never indicated to me that she had any interest in the Christians. Saturus was smiling at the look of consternation on my face, but he waited for me to speak.

"Did she – I mean, was she sympathetic at all?"

"She said she wanted to know about the Christian religion for herself," he said. "I think she was sympathetic, yes."

I was bubbling over with questions now, and couldn't decide which to ask first. I decided to go for something all-encompassing.

"Tell me all about it!" I said. "What was the result?"

"She is not a Christian yet, if that is what you are wondering," he said laughing, "but she may not be far off it."

"That's wonderful!" I exclaimed, and then I began to quiz him about the whole conversation. However, he would not say much about it. Instead he suggested that I go and speak with her myself.

"I asked her why she hadn't spoken with you," he said, "but she said she found it too awkward to bring up the subject. She was waiting for you to talk to her, I think."

At this I felt a stab of guilt. I realised that, to avoid confrontation, I had been deliberately avoiding the topic of my new faith with all of the members of my family. In reality, perhaps it was only my father who was so bitterly opposed to the Christians. At the thought of him, I had another question.

"Does my father know about any of this?" I asked, concerned now for my mother.

"She didn't say," said Saturus. "As I said, I think you should go and speak with her yourself."

I did not need any more persuasion. In fact, there was another matter entirely about which I had been meaning to speak with her. I had had some vague suspicions for a week or two, but now I was almost certain. I wanted to talk with my mother first though, before telling anyone else, even Felicitas or Lupercus. I was almost certain that I was expecting a baby.

As usual, Felicitas, Revocatus and I left the cemetery with the other catechumens before the breaking of the bread, and I told Felicitas that I wanted to go immediately to see my mother. Revocatus returned home, while we two made our way to my father's house. On the way I told Felicitas about my mother's conversation with Saturus. She too was overjoyed at the news, but did not seem too surprised.

"I thought she might join us soon," she said. "I've been praying for her for more than two months now."

I looked at her in astonishment.

"More than two months! You didn't mention it to me."

She shrugged and smiled.

"It was just one of those things I was doing on my own, my lady," she said. "Sometimes there are people or things that I feel I ought to pray for specially."

"Any other things that you'd like to tell me about now?" I asked in mock reproach.

"Your brother Cornelius."

"Cornelius?" I said in surprise. "But not Gaius?"

She looked a little uncomfortable at this.

"Of course, my lady, I've tried to pray for both of them," she said hesitantly. "I thought it wasn't right to pray for just one of them, but – well, Cornelius is the one I really felt I ought to pray for. Do you understand, my lady?"

"I think I do, Felicitas," I replied, "and it gives me great hope for my mother and Cornelius, at least!"

My mother was sitting in the colonnade sewing when we arrived at the house. She rose and embraced me tenderly, and I realised again how I had wronged her by not talking with her sooner.

"I hear you were speaking with Saturus in the forum yesterday," I said when we had settled ourselves. My mother looked a little embarrassed at this.

"My dear, I hope you don't mind," she said.

"Don't mind?" I said, astonished at her reaction. "I was overjoyed, mother. I'm only sorry now that I hadn't spoken with you more myself."

"That's what I meant, dearest," she said. "I know I should really have talked with you, but somehow – well, it was just rather difficult."

"It was my fault, mother," I said. "Please forgive me – I've been avoiding talking to you because... Well, I suppose I was afraid. Afraid of father, really. Does he know anything about this?"

"I don't know how much he suspects. He doesn't know that I went to see Saturus yesterday. But I've tried to speak up for you on several occasions now, when he's been complaining about you. So he knows I don't share his sentiments at all."

I could not keep my next question in for any longer: "Mother – are you going to follow Jesus too?"

There was a long pause during which my mother seemed to be studying her sewing. Finally she spoke.

"I found what Saturus had to say very convincing," she said. "And you – I can see that you have something that I don't have. I don't know if I can explain exactly what it is, but – perhaps you know what I mean?"

"Whatever it is that you mean, mother, I want you to have it too, with all my heart," I said clasping her hands in mine. "Do you know that Felicitas has been praying specially for you for the last two months?"

My mother looked at her in surprise and she blushed, gave a slight bow, but said nothing.

"What about Cornelius?" I went on, to my mother. "And Gaius?"

"I haven't spoken with them about it really," she said, "but I know that Gaius tends to side with your father."

I thought about Felicitas' prayers. It all seemed to make sense in a way. Just then my mother laughed, and I looked at her questioningly.

"It's just something Saturus said to me," she said. "He was trying to explain about starting to follow Jesus. He said it's like being born again. It seemed such a strange notion."

"Oh!" I said, feeling like I'd just received a bucket of cold water in my face. "Mother, there's something else I had to tell you."

Immediately her eyes flitted to my stomach. She was a quick-witted woman. Or perhaps it was just maternal instinct. Now it was my turn to laugh. I put my hands on my stomach.

"I see you've guessed already," I said "although I'm not absolutely sure about it."

I glanced at Felicitas whose eyes were wide with astonishment. I felt a little sorry for her finding out the news in this setting, since I knew that she would feel unable to speak to me as a friend in my mother's presence. Nevertheless I smiled at her to reassure her that we could talk about it later. When I had explained everything to my mother we calculated that the baby would be due the following February. She seemed tremendously excited about the idea of having a grandchild. She had my father called so he could hear the news too. I felt rather apprehensive as he appeared, but he seemed pleased to see me.

"So – how is my wayward daughter?" he said coming up to embrace me.

"As wayward as ever, I'm afraid," I replied.

"Perpetua has some wonderful news, dearest," said my mother.

"Don't tell me," said my father dryly, "she's decided to become a worshipper of Isis."

"Oh, father!" I said laughing. "Nothing like that – I'm going to have a baby."

My father's gruff expression broke into a smile.

"Well," he said, "that is good news. Mind you just make sure it's a boy, my dear. The first one should always be a son."

"I'll see what I can do," I said.

We left soon after this and returned home. Now that my mother and father had heard my news, not to mention Felicitas, I felt rather guilty that Lupercus still knew nothing and I was anxious to tell him. Of course, he too was overjoyed by the news and began to make a great fuss of me. I was scarcely allowed to move for the rest of the day, so that, by the time we left for the catechismal class in the afternoon, I was beginning to wonder if I should have told him at all.

Thankfully this wore off after a few days and he began to treat me more or less normally again. He was away from home more and more these days, however, trying to expand the family olive oil business with contracts in Carthage, and it was at these times that he fretted most. I assured him that I was in good care, with Felicitas on hand if there was any kind of emergency, and my family not far away. Just a few weeks after I had first heard about my mother's interest in the Christians it was a great joy to hear that both she and Cornelius had asked to join a catechismal class. However, a few days after this, my father came to visit us. His manner now was altogether different from when I had told him about the baby. I knew he was angry, but he was trying not to show it, but rather to appear self-controlled and reasonable.

"My daughter," he said to me, "I really think things have gone too far now."

"Father," I replied, "you don't really imagine that I am going to change my mind about following Jesus at this stage do you?"

"Perpetua, my dear," he said, and there was a pleading in his tone, "things are not as they were before. You are soon going to be a mother – does that not mean anything to you?"

"Why , of course it does, father. And I thank God that I am to be privileged with such a gift from him."

"Listen, my daughter, as long as you persist in your

stubbornness, your life is in very grave danger – don't you realise that? And it is not just your own life which you are dicing with, now – have you considered that?"

I sighed. I had indeed considered it, but I had to admit that the possibility of suffering for my faith seemed more remote now. For over a year we had had peace in the church, and some people were beginning to say that the times of persecution were over. So many people were coming into the church now that it seemed much safer than before.

"Father," I said, "I really don't think that the danger is as great as it once was."

At this point my father stood up and clapped his hands together in a mixture of anguish and frustration.

"No!" he said vehemently. "My daughter, that is exactly where you are wrong. Have you not been following court affairs? The emperor is becoming more and more hostile to both Jews and Christians. He has been insulted too often now by these self-styled citizens of God's kingdom who refuse to pay fitting honour to his imperial majesty. Now you know I never liked Severus, and I would never have chosen him for the purple. But emperor he is, and you must understand that he is a powerful and ruthless man, Perpetua. Please believe me, the time is running out for you and your companions. I want you to reconsider – or at least promise me you won't do anything foolish. There are always ways out of difficulty, you know."

I was reminded of the same advice which Gargilianus had offered me, and I realised that it was a very tempting option. The point on which Christians were usually convicted was their refusal to perform the required sacrifice to the spirit of the emperor. The church taught that this amounted to demon worship, and could not be done by a Christian. It was quite likely, however, that a bribe could be offered to some official which would satisfy him, even if the sacrifice had not been offered. I thought about the life that was growing within me. For the sake of a tiny, innocent child would I be willing to compromise my faith with a few gold coins? The choice seemed terrible, for it seemed that I would be tortured by guilt whichever way I chose. I could only pray that any such decision would never be mine to make. However, my father's words of warning seemed all too convincing.

"Father," I said, taking his hand in mine, "I know that this life within me is precious. You must be in no doubt that I believe that with all my heart. But I have given my life to Jesus – it is for him to decide what will happen to me, and to the child within me. I cannot promise you anything."

At this he pulled away from me with a groan. I felt as if I had wounded him with my words, no less than if I had struck him in the face with a rod.

"Please, father," I said, "I don't think we will get anywhere talking about this any further. Perhaps you should leave, now."

He looked into my eyes, as if he were searching for some crumb of meaning that he could understand and take in. But after some moments he turned away in despair and left without another word.

*

It was a strange dream, and although it seemed to me that it was from God, I was not completely sure. I was standing in a forest watching while a woodman swung a large axe at the base of a young oak tree. Over and over again the blade came thudding into the trunk, while chips of wood flew out and scattered about on the ground. At each blow the young tree quivered, and I could almost imagine that I heard a faint cry, like the sigh of the wind in its branches, as if the tree could feel the axe blows and was crying out in pain each time the blade struck home. From up in the branches something tiny fell to the ground at my feet. Stooping down I saw that it was a tiny acorn. I scooped out a hollow in the earth and carefully buried it. Then, as the tree finally came crashing to the ground, I knew that the little acorn was safe. I imagined that in the years to come it would break out of the ground and grow into a great oak tree just like the one it had fallen from. It would be nourished, too from the decaying leaves and branches of the fallen tree around it, for the woodman did not seem to be doing anything with the felled timber. Instead he wiped the sweat from his brow, took a last look at his handiwork, then turned to go. As he turned, to my horror I saw that his face was one that I knew well – it was the face of my father.

I woke up sweating with the images of the dream still crystal clear in my mind. I lay awake, pondering the meaning of the dream. I felt the baby kicking inside me, as I often did during the night. That little child would be safe – surely that was the message of the dream. I caressed my swollen abdomen, and thought again of the little acorn I had buried in the ground. But if the tiny acorn was my child, what was to be my fate? The face of the woodman, my father's face, swam before my eyes in the darkness of the room. Surely he would never do anything that would put my life in danger?

The baby was born later that summer. It was not an easy birth, indeed at times during the struggle I despaired of bringing the child into the world alive at all. But finally, after many hours, it was all over, and the midwife announced to me that it was a boy. The first thing to be done was to take the child and lay him at the feet of his father. I had no fears whatsoever that Lupercus would reject this first child, especially as it was a son, but I did according to custom. Lupercus duly picked up the child in his arms and named him Marcus Gargilianus Lupercus.

It is a difficult thing to explain, but from the moment of his birth I felt an overwhelming love for my son. Suddenly my world was turned upside down, and I could think of nothing else, day and night, than how my child should be cared for. I announced that I would not even have a wet nurse, but would feed him myself, which Lupercus considered bizarre, even perverse. It was not at all the usual custom, but I felt that God had given me such a desire to love and care for my son that I could not hand him over to another to be fed from their breast. Felicitas also thought it strange, but she accepted it. Only a few weeks previously she had confided to me that she herself was expecting a baby too.

"It will be your turn next, then," I told her. "You will see when you have a child of your own."

One result of my new-found obsession with my child was that I found that my feelings for Saturus were much easier to deal with. I still liked him, and enjoyed being in his company, but the struggle was not the same as before. I felt free to be with him now where before I had felt that every moment in his presence I was fighting a battle against my secret desire. I gave thanks, therefore, not only for the gift of my child, but also for relief from one battle that, it seemed, I no longer had to fight.

18

The Edict

I was sitting with Felicitas under the shade of the colonnade, nursing Marcus. Lupercus had been away in Carthage for several days, but was expected back soon. Just then we heard noises from the main entrance, and guessed that he had arrived. These were normally happy times – Lupercus always missed me when he was away, and now he missed his son as well. Conveniently, Marcus seemed to be falling asleep, so, clasping him gently in my arms, I rose and went to meet my husband. He came forward to embrace me, as usual, but I sensed at once that he was troubled about something. Perhaps, I thought, he had had a frustrating time with the merchants he had been to see.

"My dear," he said, "I have some important news which I must tell you about at once."

I looked at him, a little worried now. He had evidently been riding hard, his clothes were dusty and mud-spattered and his face was reddened by the sun and the wind.

"What is it, dearest?" I said. "Please, sit down and rest before anything else."

He sat down heavily on a couch and looked at me. There was fear in his eyes, and I wondered what could have put him in such a state.

"You know, Perpetua, that the emperor is on campaign away in the east, trying to keep the Parthians at bay. Right now, apparently, he is in Jerusalem, or he was several days ago anyway. He has issued an edict, my dear, worded in the strongest terms possible, which strictly forbids anyone from converting either to the Jews or to the Christians. The penalty for disregarding this command will be death."

It took me some moments to take this in. The idea of dying for being a Christian was obviously not new to me, but now it seemed to have leapt from the musty shelves of distant possibility to the stark reality of here and now. Evidently the time of peace which the church had been enjoying was rapidly drawing to a close.

"I came home as soon as I heard about this," Lupercus went on. "I wanted you to have as much warning as possible."

"Thank you," I said. "It will help to be that much more ready."

I saw that he looked slightly puzzled at my response.

"What are you going to do?" he asked.

"Do?" I said. I looked down at the sleeping child in my arms, then I looked back at my husband. "I will pray for strength to fight the battle."

"What battle are you talking about, my dear? You surely don't intend to get yourself arrested under this law, do you? All you need do is to keep your head down for a while. Stop meeting with the Christians. Make the sacrifice to the emperor, or say something that will convince them you're not really a Christian. What is the point of provoking the authorities at such a time as this?"

He gazed into my eyes, as if desperately searching for the response he wished for. I stared back into his dusty, sweat-streaked features, unable to say a word. Marcus wriggled in my arms, and I clutched him close. Finally I turned away.

"I must have some time alone," I said, and with that I left him standing there in the vestibule, helpless.

I went to my room, laid my sleeping son carefully on the bed, then fell on my knees to pray. I did not know what words to say, but I began with the Lord's Prayer, which we normally did at regular prayer times.

"Lead us not into temptation," I whispered, "but deliver us from evil..."

In my mind's eye I could see the face of Lupercus gazing pleadingly into my eyes. That was the temptation I was facing. That was the evil. The world that did not understand, and that screamed at me that I was being a fool. I prayed for Lupercus, and for Marcus, and I prayed for myself. Before long I rose abruptly to my feet and went in search of Felicitas.

She and Revocatus were together in the courtyard, watering the plants that were copiously arranged around the colonnade. Felicitas had overheard my conversation with Lupercus, and would of course have passed on the news to her brother. They both turned to me as I entered the courtyard. In the face of Felicitas I read worry and concern, in that of Revocatus I saw fear.

"Come," I said, "we must go to the bishop's house."

I went back to my room where Marcus still lay sleeping on the bed. I gently lifted him, and in a few minutes we were out of the house and walking along the streets. Out in the warm sunshine, with people passing us who hadn't a care in the world, it all seemed completely unreal. Were our lives really in such danger all of a sudden? I wondered how many others in the town had already heard of the edict. Probably not many, as yet. And would they care at all? I knew some who would. My father, for example. We walked in silence. What was there to say? As we passed through the familiar streets, I had the sensation of being a stranger walking through the streets of a strange town. It was a disturbing feeling – the feeling that suddenly I no longer belonged in the town where I had lived all my life.

We reached the bishop's house and he ushered us in, immediately noticing the troubled looks on our faces.

"What is it, my children?" he asked. We were still standing in the main entrance.

"I see you haven't yet heard the news," I said. "My husband has just returned from Carthage where he heard of an edict issued by the emperor a few days ago in Jerusalem."

"An edict?" asked Optatus. "Concerning what?"

"It is an order of prohibition, strictly forbidding anyone from converting to the Jews or to the Christians – on pain of death."

Optatus said nothing at first as he took this in. Then he spoke.

"That is a new strategy," he said slowly. "He hopes to

stamp us out by targeting new converts. Catechumens, in other words."

He looked from one to another of our faces, evidently wondering how each of us was responding to the news.

"Come," he said, leading the way towards the reception room, "we must talk."

Once we were seated, the bishop looked at us. He seemed hesitant. His gaze rested on the child in my arms.

"So," he said, "what do you intend to do?"

It struck me as ironic that he should ask the same question as my husband. I looked at Felicitas and Revocatus to see if they would respond, but they were looking back at me, obviously waiting for me to speak first.

"Sir," I said, "it seems to me that there is only one choice open to us. We must stand firm in the face of this attack. We must pray for strength. And you must pray for us, too."

"You are a courageous woman," said the bishop. He turned to the others. "You are all of one mind?"

Felicitas nodded. Revocatus did not speak. He looked up into Optatus' eyes.

"I fear that in such circumstances each one must make his own decision," said the bishop.

Revocatus appeared to be wrestling in his mind. He looked at Felicitas, then he looked at me. Finally he spoke, as if forcing the words out almost against his will.

"I too will stand firm," he said.

*

News of the edict soon spread through the town. It was two days later that I received the inevitable visit from my father. I don't think he really had much hope of persuading me, but he wanted to see how I was reacting. The slightest hint of fear or unsteadiness in my temperament would have given him a world of hope. But what was most difficult was the news he brought me of my mother and brother.

"I am glad to report to you," he said, "that they have both decided to stop meeting with the Christians for the time being.

This, it seems to me, is the only rational response in the circumstances. I no longer hold out any hopes of turning you away from the perverse beliefs of the Christians, but surely you must see that to continue meeting with them just now is tantamount to folly of the most obstinate kind."

"I have told you before, father," I replied. "My life is not my own. I will do what the one whom I follow did when he faced arrest and trial."

"What was that?" asked my father, with hopeless resignation in his voice.

"He went willingly."

There was a squeal from Marcus who was lying in a cradle nearby. Hearing this sound, my father pointed a trembling finger at me.

"You are the most heartless of mothers who ever walked this earth!" he said, his eyes blazing with fury. "And the most disloyal and insolent of daughters. I almost wish you were already arrested and languishing in prison, for surely then you would awaken from your pitiful folly and see sense."

With this he turned on his heel and strode out of the house. His last words chilled me to the heart, for I suddenly recalled the face of the woodman in my dream – the face of my father. Did he really believe what he had just said? If so, I realised that I was in even greater danger now. I sensed that he would certainly do all he could to have me arrested if he was convinced that this was a sure way of forcing me to change my mind.

The next day was Sunday, and before the morning meeting at the cemetery Saturus gathered all of us together – Felicitas, Revocatus and I, as well as Saturninus and Secundulus. We all knew about the emperor's edict by that time. Saturus simply wanted to pray for us, which he did, placing his hands on each of our heads in turn and praying for each one individually. Even before he placed his hands on my head, I somehow knew that something would happen. It was not like the first time, however. This time the overwhelming sensation I had was of intense emotion. I felt a tremendous love within me, as if my heart would burst. Love for whom? Strangely, the images of the people who came into my mind were of complete strangers –

rough-looking soldiers, judges, the proconsul, the emperor himself. These were our persecutors, but I realised with a shock that they were also children whom God loved with the same unfathomable love which we ourselves had discovered. I felt a love for these people that seemed utterly incongruous. As Saturus took his hands from my head and turned to Felicitas, kneeling beside me, tears that I could not hold back were already streaming down my cheeks.

"What is it?" whispered Felicitas to me, when Saturus had moved on to Revocatus.

I looked at her, wiping the tears from my face.

"They don't know," I whispered back. "God loves them so much – but they don't know!"

It was not the most lucid of explanations, but Felicitas evidently managed to leap to where I was in my mind and understood immediately.

"You are right, my lady," she replied. "That is the greatest tragedy of all."

When Saturus had finished, Saturninus spoke up. He obviously felt that someone should speak for all of us.

"This business doesn't scare me," he said. "We will win a crown yet. It is a glorious thought that we might be counted worthy to die for our Lord."

I looked at Revocatus to see how he was reacting to these bold words. He saw me looking at him, and smiled.

"You're too full of words, brother," he said to Saturninus. "Are you sure your actions will be as bold?"

"You wait and see," he replied. "Let them put me on a cross, or throw me to the beasts – yes, they can even burn me alive – I promise you I will die rejoicing."

"It is good to be bold," said Saturus, "but Revocatus is right my brother. Words are easier than actions. What we all must do from now on is pray for one another."

"You won't be in any great danger yourself, mind," remarked Saturninus to Saturus. "It seems they're only interested in the new recruits at the moment."

"I don't believe any of us are safe from danger," he replied. "My faith is not in the wording of an edict that seems to let me off for the time being – it is in the God who can save me from death at any time."

It was two weeks later, on a warm September evening, that we were sitting in the lamplit dining room of the bishop's house once more. I had grown to love these fellowship meals, simple though they were, in the cheery setting of the bishop's crowded dining room. I found myself gazing around at the other members of the church, and realised that these were indeed my family now. Some I had not yet got to know very well, some were very new, recently admitted as catechumens and even younger in the faith than we were. It pained me that my mother and brother were not present, but I tried to respect their decision. I did not know it then, but that was the last time I was going to be sitting there, with my new family, in that now familiar room.

During an interval between courses the bishop stood up to make an announcement.

"It will no doubt have come to your attention," he began, in his slow and ponderous voice, "that we are growing in number."

This was true, as was evident by how crowded the room was on Sunday evenings.

"Indeed," he went on, "if all were present – which is not the case this evening –" a hint of reproach here; my mother and brother were not the only members who were more reluctant to meet together in these days of danger – "I am sure that we could not all fit into this room. I am therefore planning to knock down this wall –" he indicated one of the side walls of the dining room – "to join this room with the adjoining one, thus forming a larger space for us to meet in. The builders will be arriving to start work tomorrow morning, but the work is expected to take at least two weeks to complete, and the room will not be usable while it is being done. Regretfully, therefore, I have to announce that we will be unable to gather together next Sunday evening, though of course the morning Eucharist will be celebrated at the cemetery as normal. If anyone has any questions, now is the time to ask them."

There was a buzz of excited conversation at this announcement, and people turned to look at the wall that was to be removed, trying to imagine what the new space would be like. Then Aspasius the elder rose to his feet.

"Our brother Optatus," he said, "has found a solution to the problem of our growing numbers which might at first seem like the only one possible. It is well known, however, that in a larger town such as Carthage, the Christians do not have just one meeting place but several. I wonder if he has given any thought to the possibility of having two meeting places here in Thuburbo Minus."

There was a slight pause here, but Aspasius did not give the bishop long enough to make a reply before he continued with his speech.

"Might I humbly offer the hospitality of my own home as the provision of such a second meeting place. It is true that it is not so large a house as this, and the dining room could not hold quite so many, but it could certainly accommodate the overflow, so to speak. In any case, I would like to offer it as a meeting place for the whole church next Sunday evening, while this room is unavailable – though of course we will be even more cramped than we are now. Nevertheless, it is surely better to meet somewhere than not at all."

The buzz of conversation, which had subsided as soon as Aspasius had begun to speak, now started up again, with a redoubled intensity. Although Aspasius' proposal seemed to make good sense on the face of it, I felt strangely suspicious about it. I could see that what he now so casually referred to as 'the overflow' could quickly become an entirely separate group – composed almost certainly of those church members who were most sympathetic to the teachings of the Phrygians. Perhaps Aspasius was even hoping to be appointed as a second bishop in the town. As it turned out, Optatus seemed to share my suspicions, though he did not voice them explicitly.

"Our brother has made a very generous offer," he began in reply to the elder's speech. "However I feel that to split the church in two would be a grave and dangerous step at this point in time. As we face increasing hostility from those outside, it is a time to stand together, not to divide ourselves into different groups. As to his offer of a meeting place for next week, I am confident that the work will be completed by the following Sunday, and that only one week will be missed. As we will be gathering at the cemetery in the morning, we can hardly be charged with failing to meet together. I do not think, therefore, that there is any need for our brother to trouble himself and his household on our behalf."

"I would not see it as a source of trouble," replied Aspasius, "but rather as a blessing on our household. Whatever you say, my brother, the offer still stands. Any who would like to meet together next Sunday evening will be welcome at my house."

I recalled his words to me about those in the church whom he considered to be lacking in zeal. He was probably hoping that such an invitation would sort out the more zealous church members from those whose sincerity he evidently questioned.

"I think that you are acting in rather a divisive way, Aspasius," said the bishop.

"I see nothing wrong with what I am proposing," replied the elder. "The offer stands."

The atmosphere in the room had become suddenly tense. There was a moment's silence and then a rustle of whispers in place of the loud buzz there had been before. The bishop said nothing more, presumably hoping that the best way of dealing with the problem was to act as if it were not an important issue. I sensed, however, that underlying the exchange between the two men, there was a very important issue at stake.

On our way home Revocatus, Felicitas and I discussed whether to go to Aspasius' house the following Sunday. The bishop had informed us that our catechismal class, which took place in the reception room in another part of the house, could continue as normal. Felicitas thought that Aspasius' proposal had seemed reasonable, but we all agreed that he ought to have backed down when the bishop expressed his disapproval. In the end, we decided not to go to the elder's house the following week. Revocatus was sure, however, that there would be a number in the church who would go.

The following Sunday, before we left for the catechismal class, I went to tell Sextus that we would be returning to eat the evening meal at our own house, rather than eating at the bishop's house. Sextus was now our cook, a job he did surprisingly well, and much better than he did most jobs.

"What time will you be returning exactly, my lady?" he asked. I told him, and he promised to have the meal ready soon after that. I still disliked having him in my household and tried to avoid him whenever I could. But surely, I told myself as I turned to go, that was uncharitable.

When we arrived at the bishop's house the first thing Optatus did was to show us the new dining room. It was very dusty and messy, but it was clear that the room would be much more spacious. He was having terracotta tiles placed all around the walls. These had been beautifully produced by Saturus' family pottery. Some showed different scenes illustrating stories from the scriptures, while others were decorated with Christian symbols like the cross, and the chi-rho symbol. Delighted as he was with the work, however, I sensed that the bishop was uneasy, and guessed that it was because of the meeting at Aspasius' house that evening. To put him more at his ease I mentioned to him that we would not be going.

Since there was no hurry to finish, the class went on a little longer than usual. We left the house together when it was already growing dark outside, and the streets were becoming quiet as everyone went home for their meal. The bishop had asked Saturus to stay behind, to discuss with him, I guessed, the problem of how to deal with Aspasius. We had not gone far down the road when there was the sudden clatter of armour and a detachment of soldiers suddenly emerged from the shadows of a temple entrance. This sight was unusual enough, but I soon saw that they were heading in our direction, and my blood froze. 'This is it,' I thought to myself. 'Our time has come.'

The soldiers quickly came up to us and seized us – there was no hope of escaping even if we had wanted to. Their captain then uttered the words which I had been dreading.

"In the name of his imperial majesty, the emperor Septimius Severus, I place you all under arrest on suspicion of fraternising with the sect known as the Christians. Hail Caesar!"

Part Four

THE JOURNEY HOME

19

The Prisoners

"Don't lay a hand on the lady!" Saturninus took a step towards the soldier who was about to bind my wrists, as had already been done to the three men.

"Who's your friend?" the soldier asked me, with a lewd grin. "Got something going with you, has he?"

He gave a crude guffaw, and Saturninus raised his bound hands in a threatening gesture, but was held back by another soldier.

"No, Saturninus," I said, seeing things were about to turn ugly. "Let them bind me if they wish. Otherwise I might be tempted to hit him myself."

The soldiers laughed uproariously at this, but it had the desired effect. Saturninus visibly calmed and stepped back from us.

"As you wish, my lady," he said.

I shot him a brief smile.

"We will all stand trial," I said. "But let it be only on the charge of being Christians. However," I turned back to the soldier, holding out Marcus to him, "you'll have to take the baby."

The soldier looked embarrassed, clearly unsure of how to deal with this. He looked at his superior.

"Let her be," said the captain, gruffly. "She can carry the baby."

Once the others were all bound we set off down the road, and I wondered where they were going to take us. I thought of asking the captain, but decided it might only tempt more mockery. It was with shock and astonishment that I realised after some minutes that we seemed to be heading in the direction of my father's house. A few minutes more and we were there, brought to a halt outside the main entrance. The captain went in and soon reappeared with my father at his side. I caught his eye, expecting a look of dismay on his face, but instead there was something more like grim satisfaction. I realised with horror that he had done exactly what I had feared. He had had us all arrested, in the certainty that it would force me to change my mind. I felt a tremendous pity for him then, for I knew that things were not going to turn out as he planned.

"You can lodge them in here," said my father, leading the way through the vestibule and into a small reception room off it which was hardly ever used. The couches had been removed and replaced with some sleeping mats from the slaves' quarters. There was an old wooden table against one wall, on which were a jug of water and an earthenware cup.

The ropes that had bound the others' wrists were untied, then, after the captain had detailed two of the soldiers to stay on guard outside the door, he left with the rest of them. There was no sign of my father, nor indeed of any of the other members of my family. A hush fell in the room, interrupted only by the sound of Secundulus who was wheezing badly. I realised that we had been marched quite briskly, probably faster than Secundulus was comfortable with, and he was now sitting on one of the mats, rather breathless. I went over and sat beside him.

"Are you all right?" I asked him.

"Don't worry about me, my lady," he replied with a grin. "There'll be worse to come, no doubt."

"What's going to happen to us?" asked Revocatus. No-one had much idea about this.

"All we can say for sure," I said, "is that this is some plan of my father's to force us to deny our faith. How things will turn out, assuming we remain steadfast, only God knows."

We settled down to wait, and it was not long before a slave came bringing some food on a tray. There was bread, cheese and some apples. It was not much but we were hungry. We prayed together before eating, which drew some curious looks from our two guards. There was a murmuring from their direction, then laughter. After we had prayed, however, the atmosphere in the room seemed much more cheerful. When she had had enough to eat Felicitas began to sing a psalm, the words of which seemed suddenly so much more real than when we had sung them together at the bishop's house:

"I love you, O Lord my strength.
The Lord is my rock, my fortress and my deliverer;
My God is my rock, in whom I take refuge.
He is my shield and the horn of my salvation, my stronghold.
I call to the Lord, who is worthy of praise,
And I am saved from my enemies."

It was a long psalm, but Felicitas seemed to know all the verses, and she sang it beautifully. The guards were staring in the doorway, looking a little confused. Perhaps they weren't quite sure if this sort of thing should be allowed.

"It's just like a fellowship meal," said Secundulus. "And I'd rather be here than at Aspasius' house."

"I'll bet he's laid on more than bread and cheese, mind," remarked Saturninus, who had a healthy appetite and was looking wistfully at the now empty tray. We all laughed.

"Here! You in there! Quiet down!" One of the guards had decided enough was enough.

Everyone fell silent. I got up and walked over to him.

"Listen," I said, "you may not realise it, but we are soldiers in here, just like you are."

He looked baffled at this.

"What are you talking about, now?" he asked.

"We are soldiers of Christ, and we are fighting a battle – no, not with swords and spears like you do, but with spiritual weapons. We fight against evil, and against Satan, the prince of evil. When you hear us singing, or joking together, I have just one small request – leave us be. Think of it as barrack-room banter, if you like."

The soldier looked at me as if I was mad, but then he grinned.

"You're a right cocky woman, you are," he said. "On you go then, have your fun. We'll have another song if you like – that was a nice bit of singing from the slave-girl."

So Felicitas sang some more psalms, and the rest of us joined in with those ones that we knew. I urged her not to sing too loudly, though, so as not to draw the unwelcome attention of my father. Whether he didn't hear us, or just decided to ignore us, I don't know, but we had seen nothing of him all evening when I gave Marcus his evening feed and we finally lay down on the mats to sleep.

The others all seemed to sleep well, but I was not used to such a hard bed, and my mind was troubled too, wondering about the inevitable confrontation with my father. I slept fitfully, but mostly lay awake, listening to the peaceful breathing of the others and the occasional whimper from Marcus, lying beside me. The guards had been replaced by two others late in the evening, and they seemed to be awake too, sometimes talking together in low voices. I finally fell asleep for an hour or so, but still woke before the others.

It was the middle of the morning before my father finally appeared. He exchanged some brief words with the guards outside, then came into the room. He looked around the room at us all, then he turned to me.

"So," he said, "how have you enjoyed getting a taste of what our exalted emperor has in store for those who stubbornly persist in calling themselves Christians?"

He spat the word out as if the very utterance of it was sickening to him. I sighed.

"We stand firm in our faith, if that is what you mean," I replied. I took note of the expression on his face as I said these words. He tried to hide it, but I could see a glimmer of doubt and fear beneath his anger.

"Let me explain the situation, my daughter," he said. "You have been arrested under the terms of the recent edict. I have assured the magistrate, under whose orders the arrests have been made, that you will soon see sense and turn away from this foolish course. He himself finds it almost inconceivable that a mother with so young a child should choose to put herself in such a predicament. If you persist in your folly, you will be transferred to the prison in Carthage. There you will await a hearing before the proconsul Minucius Timinianus – a hard man who is known to have a deep dislike for Christians. I do not need to remind you of the penalty for your crime."

"We have committed no crime," I said, looking him steadily in the eye. "However I am afraid, father, that you may regret what you have done."

"Haven't you understood anything?" he exploded. "To be labelled with the very name Christian is a crime!"

"Father," I said, "everything has a name by which it is called." I looked around the room, and my gaze rested on the water-jug. "Do you see that jug, or pitcher on the table?"

"Yes," he replied shortly, in a suspicious tone. "What about it?"

"You call it a jug because that's what it is. It cannot be called a lamp, or a chair, or a snake."

Felicitas giggled, but my father only scowled.

"So too with me," I went on. "I cannot be called other than what I am. And what I am is a Christian. Look -" I indicated each of the others in turn. "A Christian. A Christian. And him – a Christian. And her – a Christian. And me -" I laid my hand on my breast. "A Christian."

Each time I spoke the word my father's rage seemed to increase. As I spoke it for the last time, I wondered if I had pushed him too far. He stepped towards me menacingly, his hands held out towards me like claws. His face was a mask of hatred, and I really thought that he was about to tear my eyes from their sockets, or some such diabolical thing. I did not flinch, however, but stared into his face, pleadingly, praying that he might understand the truth. Just then he stopped in his tracks. His face changed suddenly, becoming like that of one who is worn out and defeated by a struggle that he cannot endure. Then without another word he turned and walked out of the room. We did not see him again for several days.

I found out where he had gone from my mother, who came to speak with us later that day. She seemed very fearful, and explained that he had gone to appeal to the magistrate, to see if we could be released despite our refusal to deny Christ. The magistrate regretfully informed him that news of our arrest had already been sent to Minucius Timinianus, and that it was now too late to go back on it. No doubt the magistrate had sent the message so promptly in the hope of impressing the proconsul with his zeal. In despair, then, my father had left for Carthage, presumably to make an appeal on my behalf to Minucius himself. I wondered if he would have any luck. From his own description of the proconsul, it seemed unlikely.

"Does anyone in the church know what has happened?" I asked my mother.

"I do not know," she replied. "I have heard nothing from them."

"That is my one request, then, mother," I told her. "Please send word and make sure they know what is happening."

She promised to do this, then left, ushered out by the guards who, I understood, were not supposed to allow anyone in to speak with us. They were the ones I had spoken with the night before, however, and they seemed happy to relax the rules a little, as long as my father was away. Food and water were brought to us regularly by slaves, but I saw no more of my mother. I wondered how much news Lupercus had received, and whether there was any possibility of his visiting me. I tried to imagine what his reaction would be to our arrest, but found that I was very unsure of how he would take it. He would be sympathetic, I was fairly sure, but at the same time embarrassed. I felt sorry for him, for he did not deserve this, after the understanding he had shown me. In any case, he never came to see me while we remained in my father's house. In the evening the night guards arrived, to be replaced in the morning by the daytime guards once more.

Later that following morning, it was with great joy that we heard the voices of Saturus and Optatus the bishop outside the room.

"No visitors allowed," said one of the guards. "We have strict orders."

I heard a murmuring, and the chink of coins.

"You're quite right, sir," said the guard, in a friendlier tone, "exceptions can be made in special circumstances. Here – " he looked in the doorway, "you've got visitors."

They came into the room and we all embraced one another warmly. I now noticed that there was also a woman with them, whom I recognised as a deaconess from the church.

"We came as soon as we heard," said Optatus. "The first matter is whether you have any needs. Are you being treated well?"

"Perfectly well," I said. "And now that my father is away it is relatively peaceful as well – for the moment."

"Little Marcus," said Saturus, "is he all right? Do you want someone else to look after him?"

He was lying awake on one of the mats, playing with somebody's sandal. I looked down at him, wondering what to say.

"I would rather keep him with me as long as I can," I replied. "He is happy enough here."

"Then there is another matter, of the gravest importance, which we must attend to," said Optatus.

"What's that?" asked Saturninus.

"I fear that this may be the last opportunity we will have to baptise you," he said. "Once you are taken to the prison in Carthage it will be quite impossible. Of course, even here we will not be able to observe all the usual requirements, but we will do what we can, given the circumstances. Are you all willing to go ahead with this?"

There was a murmuring of agreement. I looked at Revocatus, and was encouraged to see that he was nodding as enthusiastically as anyone. We all knew what this would mean. Having been arrested on suspicion of being Christians, we would now be flagrantly making the final step of our initiation into the faith. It was as if we were anxious to leave no doubt whatever in the minds of the authorities that we were guilty of the charge. Optatus explained to the guards that there was a rite that we needed to observe according to our religion, which would involve using the fountain in the courtyard. They seemed dubious about this, and demanded an additional payment, which Optatus duly produced.

"The first step," he continued, once this was settled, "is your final renunciation of Satan before you go through the waters. I know that he is testing you all in these days, and you must take your stand against him now, both in word, and in the symbol of baptism."

Each of us in turn went through the questions and answers that were familiar to us from other baptisms we had witnessed in the church. Then came a final exorcism, done by Optatus with much pomp and ceremony, and watched with undisguised curiosity by the guards. Saturus then took Felicitas and me to the courtyard, accompanied by the deaconess, a woman named Livia. In the centre of the courtyard was a large fountain, whose basin could just accommodate a person lying down. Saturus called Felicitas forward first and she stepped into the fountain with him, sitting down in the water. Saturus then laid his hands on her head.

"Do you believe in God the Father Almighty?"

"I believe."

Saturus tipped her backwards so that she went right under the water. Some of the water splashed out of the fountain and flowed across the marble flagstones, making the surface perilously slippery. Then he helped her back up to a sitting position.

"Do you believe in Jesus Christ, the Son of God, born of the Holy Spirit and the Virgin Mary, who was crucified in the days of Pontius Pilate, died, rose again from the dead on the third day, ascended into heaven, sat down at the right hand of the Father, and will come again to judge the living and the dead?"

"I believe."

Another splash, and more water on the flagstones.

"Do you believe in the Holy Spirit, in the Holy Church, and in the resurrection of the body?"

"I believe."

A third time Felicitas went under and was raised again. When she had climbed out of the water, Saturus then poured oil over her head from a flask that he had brought with him, and then she went over to the deaconess, Livia, who had a towel for her to dry herself.

Then my turn came. I went forward and stepped into the

water of the fountain. It was November, and the water felt ice-cold. As I sat down I suddenly noticed two faces watching from the doorway of the dining room. It was my mother and Cornelius. My mother's face no longer showed fear – instead she smiled and nodded. I smiled back, overjoyed that they had come to witness this event. As Saturus tipped me back under the water the shock of its icy coldness stabbed through my whole body. Suddenly I was reminded of my first dream, when I had lain in that cold tomb. For a brief moment as I lay there under the water, I felt again the terror of being left there forever, conscious yet unable to move a muscle. Then, just as the hot wind had come rushing through that ice-cold tomb, Saturus' hands heaved me up once more out of the water. I felt a tremendous joy flood through me in that instant – a joy that I was alive, and a great love for the one who had called me to this new life. And I knew then with a dogged certainty that those who wanted us killed could do nothing to our spirits. We were alive now, and even death itself could not touch us.

After this we returned to the reception room where Optatus was waiting with the men. It was their turn now, and Livia remained with us while they all went to the courtyard. After some time they all returned to the room to join us once more. Optatus had already arranged a loaf of bread on the table, along with three cups. The first contained wine, the second water, and the third a pale creamy liquid, which I knew to be a mixture of milk and honey. This was to be our first Eucharist, and these last two cups were always given after baptism.

Optatus first made a lengthy prayer, giving thanks for the great sacrifice made by our Lord Jesus on our behalf, and praying for each of us to be strengthened and filled with his Spirit. After this he broke off a piece of bread for each of us and handed it to us. I took the piece that he gave me. It was just ordinary bread in one sense, the same as we had eaten for breakfast that morning. But in another sense, it was the very flesh of Jesus' body. The wine in the cup on the table, though just the same as any other wine, was, in that other mystical sense, the very blood that he had shed when he was crucified. It was a gruesome thought – reminiscent, I thought to myself, of the stories that Saturus had once heard and believed about Christians eating the flesh of babies. But, as the Lord himself had said to his followers: "Unless you can eat the flesh of the Son of Man and drink his blood, you have no life in you." This bread and wine, therefore, were the life-giving elements that we needed to bring us out of the stone-cold tomb and raise us to new life.

Before we took the wine, Optatus gave us the milk and honey, which represented the abundance of our new life in Christ, and finally the water, which symbolised the inner washing that took place at our baptism. The guards were still watching the whole time, fascinated, as we went through these procedures. The last thing we did was to pray together. It was customary at this point for those who had just gone through baptism to ask God for specific spiritual gifts. Some would ask for the gift of speaking in other tongues, and others for prophecies and visions, or the ability to heal the sick by laying hands on them.

I knew that I had already been blessed with dreams and visions, and I was not sure if it was right to ask for more such blessings. As we stood together, our arms upraised, I prayed silently, "Jesus, you have given me so much – what more can I ask for?"

Then suddenly I knew, as clearly as if at that moment a voice had spoken in my ear. There was one gift that I would need more than any other on the journey that lay ahead of us in the days to come.

"Lord Jesus," I prayed, out loud now, "I ask for nothing else but the strength to endure as you endured, to suffer as you suffered, and to count it a joy to share in your suffering."

When Optatus and Saturus had left, after tears and embraces and farewells, we were left alone once more with our guards. The one I had spoken to on the first night turned to me.

"Now listen here, you," he said, "this never happened, right? Not a word to anyone about it."

I gave him a sly look, then smiled.

"All what never happened?" I said, innocently. "I've really no idea what you're referring to."

He grinned back.

"That's the idea, my lady," he said, and went back out to divide up the morning's takings with his companion.

20

Descent into Hell

Darkness and heat! The overwhelming stench, and bodies everywhere, all around us. I clung to Felicitas and she clung to me. We were both sobbing, trying to glean some comfort from each other. But where could comfort be found in that living hell? If only it were a dream, I thought. If only I could wake up and find myself back in Thuburbo, even as a prisoner in my father's house. Nothing about our situation then had prepared us in the slightest for the conditions here.

I felt something scratching my leg. In the pitch blackness I leaned down to feel what it was. Some kind of creature squirmed away from my grasp, and I let out a shriek.

"What is it?" whispered Felicitas.

"I think it was a rat on my leg."

"Aye, there's plenty of rats to share the lodgings with us," said an unfamiliar voice from close by in the darkness. The speaker cackled horribly.

"Who's that?" I asked uneasily.

"Eutrapelus is the name. We don't get many ladies in here, you know. What're you here for?"

"We're Christians," came the voice of Saturninus out of the darkness a few feet away. "There are five of us."

"I know there's five of you – I counted you when you got thrown in. Wasn't room for one more in here, never mind five."

"Did you hear that, Artaxius? They're Christians!" This was a voice from the other side of the crowded dungeon. "Here! Are you from Carthage?"

"From Thuburbo Minus," I said.

"There's four of us here from the church in Carthage," the voice went on. "We were all arrested two weeks ago."

"Mother Isis preserve us," came another voice. "As if the rats weren't enough! Now we're being infested with Christians!"

Someone near me spat, and I felt the spittle land on my arm. I wondered how the spitter could have aimed so well without being able to see anything.

"That's what we think of Christians here!"

"Here, why don't you go and join your friends over there?" This was Eutrapelus again. "Then you're all in the one place."

This seemed like a good idea. It was a tremendous encouragement to me that there were other Christians already there, and I felt that, in this hell-hole of a prison, to stay together was at least one small thing we could do to try to survive. With great difficulty we all moved ourselves over the bodies that were sitting and lying between where we were and where the voice had come from. Whenever we inadvertently trod on someone we were rewarded with curses and fists striking out at us. Of course, there wasn't room beside the four Christians from Carthage, and nobody wanted to move, so we ended up even more cramped than before. Secundulus was wheezing terribly, and could barely speak. Felicitas, now six months pregnant, said she thought she was going to vomit. This was overheard and greeted by howls of disgust and anger.

"It's filthy enough in here, missy! We don't need anyone puking up to make it worse!"

Almost immediately, there was the sound of retching. This at least had the effect of encouraging some of those nearby to move away, giving us more space. The four from Carthage were named Jocundus, Artaxius, Quintus and Saturninus. We told them briefly how we had been arrested under the edict, detained at my father's house for a week, then transferred here that day.

We were in the holding prison, which was by the governor's residence on the Byrsa Hill in Carthage. My father had utterly failed in his appeal to have us released, and had returned with the magistrate and more soldiers. In despair, with the soldiers waiting at the door to take us away, he had pleaded with us once again to renounce our faith, but we had stood firm. The following morning we had set off from Thuburbo in an enclosed army wagon, to be taken to Carthage.

I had brought Marcus with me in the wagon, but on our arrival at the prison he had been taken from me. I had protested vehemently, but the prison officer told me mockingly that the dungeon where we would be detained was no place for a baby. It was at that moment that the reality of what we were going to have to go through first sank in. He would not say what he was going to do with my child, and I was tortured with worry. I feared for his life – why would they bother to keep him alive, when I myself was facing the death sentence?

The dungeon where we were was underground and had no windows or lights of any kind. It was not very large, but was unbelievably crowded. It was impossible to tell exactly how many people were confined in that space, but the air was almost unbreathable, and the heat was stifling, even though it was winter. We had no idea how long we were going to be kept there. The Christians from Carthage had already been waiting two weeks. We found out from them that no food was provided. Prisoners had to rely on relatives or friends to bring it, and even then they had to pay the guards more than the food was worth in order to be allowed into the dungeon to give it to the prisoners. Two deacons from the church in Carthage had been helping the Christians in this way. They came each morning with food and water, changing the waste bucket that they were using, and bringing news and messages from outside.

To me, the night did not seem very different from the day. The temperature dropped a little, and most people seemed to manage to get some sleep. I barely slept all night, lying awake instead wondering what the guards had done with Marcus. At least the deacons would come in the morning and might be able to find out where he was. They would also be able to send word back to the church in Thuburbo Minus about where we were. As I lay awake on the hard stone floor of the dungeon listening to the intermittent sounds of scuffling around me, and wondering if it was rats or just other prisoners, I began to doubt if I could endure these conditions for very long. Again and again the thought crept into my restless mind – it would be so easy to get out. I would only have to say I was no longer a Christian. It wouldn't have to be true. I could perform the sacrifice to the emperor, just once, to convince them. Then I could be back with Marcus, back in my own home with my husband Lupercus, back in the church, in the new dining room that Optatus had been preparing. I thought of Saturus, saw his face before me in my mind. But then I imagined how he would react when I explained why I had been released. A puzzled frown, a look of wounded love. For now I could see in his face the likeness of that other face. I heard once more the words that Jesus had spoken to me in the vision: "I will never leave you or forsake you." Was that true? Was he really with us here in this awful place? Was he looking after Marcus? Doubts crowded into my mind, and tears rolled down my cheeks. "Where are you, Jesus?" I whispered. But no answer came, and finally I fell into a troubled sleep, my mind still tortured by nightmares that were, if possible, even more horrible than the reality.

I woke early to the sound of Felicitas retching into the waste bucket beside me. I found I was ravenously hungry, having eaten nothing since the previous morning.

"Jocundus? Artaxius?" I said. "Is anyone awake?"

"I am," came the reply from Artaxius.

"When do the deacons come?" I asked.

"Not this early. Maybe in an hour or so."

"Are you all right, Felicitas?" I asked. She seemed to be finished.

"I feel better now, anyway. At least I don't feel hungry right now – I was famished last night."

"Secundulus?"

"I'm here." His voice sounded very weak.

"How are you?" I asked him.

"I – I'm not sure, my sister. I don't know if I'll last very long here. It's – so hard to breathe."

"You shouldn't be here," I told him. "Maybe the deacons will be able to get you moved."

It seemed like hours before the two deacons arrived, but they came eventually. Their names were Tertius and

Pomponius, and they were obviously surprised to find us there along with the others. Pomponius left immediately to fetch more food and water, and a second bucket. They had brought some bread and stew, and we shared this out among the nine of us in the meantime. Before we ate we all prayed the Lord's Prayer together, and gave thanks to God for providing us with food. I could not eat a thing, however, before asking Tertius the deacon about my son. He was rather astonished that they should have arrested me when I was nursing a baby, but as soon as he heard my story he went to ask the guard what had been done with him. He soon returned with the news that Marcus was in another part of the prison, and had been put in the care of a young slave-girl. He had not been allowed to see him, so he could give me no more information. This gave me some measure of relief, although it did not sound overly comforting. I could imagine that the slave-girl might not know the first thing about caring for a child, and I feared that he would not be feeding at all while he was separated from me.

By this time Pomponius had returned with extra food, and we all prayed together once more. The two deacons assured us that they would send word of our plight to the church in Thuburbo, and that they would inform the church in Carthage too. Many people would be praying for us, they told us, and I found some encouragement in this. There was news from Rome that some Christians there had been arrested too. We imagined that there were probably others, scattered around the empire, languishing like us in other dark and filthy prisons. All of us were waiting to go on trial for the crime that we so readily confessed to – that of bearing the name Christians.

Tertius and Pomponius were very concerned about Secundulus' state of health. They spoke to the chief officer about him, but were told that there was nowhere else for him to go.

"There is nothing to do but pray," the deacons told us, as they prepared to leave us once more. The guards had opened the door, letting in the pale light from the stairs outside, and were hurrying them to leave. Once they had gone we were plunged into pitch blackness once again.

"You need to offer them some ready cash, that's what you need," came the distinctive voice of Eutrapelus.

"What do you mean?" asked Saturninus.

"They let you out for a bit – up to the courtyard – if you shake enough gold under their noses."

"You might have mentioned that while our friends were still with us," I told him, angrily. "We haven't got anything with us here, have we? Secundulus may not live much longer if he is kept in here."

"How long are you expecting to live anyway?" he asked with a cruel laugh. "Better to die in here than get burned alive in the forum."

I wanted to lash out and hit him for these barbarous words, but he was too far away, and anyway I realised that what he was saying was true. If Secundulus did not live long enough to face trial and execution, he would still have died a martyr for the faith. Nevertheless, the thought of bribing the guards had given me fresh hope that I might be able to see Marcus for a short time and see that he was being properly cared for.

Somehow we got through the long dark hours of that day and the following night. During the night Secundulus had several severe fits of coughing and I feared that we were going to lose him, but each time he pulled through. I slept a little better than the previous night, more from exhaustion than anything else. I was less worried too now, having hope that Marcus was still alive. Morning came and so did Tertius and Pomponius with our breakfast. We talked to them about bribing the guards, and they immediately went and offered them all that they had with them, for which the soldiers grudgingly allowed them to take Secundulus up to the courtyard for an hour or so. The rest of us stayed in the dungeon, and my hopes of seeing Marcus were dashed once again.

When they brought him back he seemed much better, almost back to normal, and quite cheerful.

"It's like heaven up there, after being down here," he told us.

"Don't worry – we'll get you all up there tomorrow I hope," said Pomponius. "It's going to be an expensive business, but I'm sure we'll manage it."

"I could happily strangle those guards," said Saturninus. "They're nothing but dogs!"

"In between praying for them, I hope," I said, laughing at him.

"I'm sorry, my lady, but I find that very difficult."

"Haven't you read the story of the jailer in Philippi who was put in charge of the apostles Paul and Silas? He became a Christian didn't he? Even soldiers can turn and follow Jesus."

"I'll pray for that, but I don't have much faith," he said.

Secundulus' health quickly deteriorated again after he had been brought back down to the dungeon, but he seemed to have an inner strength that kept him going despite the weakness of his body. Revocatus meanwhile was going through a struggle of his own, wrestling with a different sort of weakness.

"My lady," he told me, "I wanted you to know. Ever since we were thrown in here I've been thinking about how to get let out. Whatever they want me to do, I really think I'd be ready to do it if only it would mean escape from this terrible place. I know it's wrong – but I'm so scared of what they'll do to us."

"You're not the only one," I said. "I lay awake all the first night thinking the same thing."

"You, my lady?" he asked in astonishment. "But you're so brave. All of you are. I thought it was only me who was afraid."

"Don't be ridiculous," I told him. "Anyone would be scared down here. This is the battle that we have to fight – the battle against temptation. And we're fighting it together – don't let Satan tell you anything different."

In the darkness I felt his hand on my arm. There was a pause, then he spoke again, in a whisper:

"Thank you, my lady."

The next morning Pomponius and Tertius arrived with enough money to buy us all several hours up in the courtyard. We ate our breakfast there together, and then, joy of joys, I heard the approaching cry of a baby. I looked up and saw a young girl coming into the courtyard carrying Marcus in her arms. He was obviously far from happy, and his cries were weak, not at all like the full-throated yelling I was used to hearing when he was unhappy.

"He hasn't fed at all since you arrived," she told me.

I took him in my arms, and was shocked at how much weight he appeared to have lost in those few days. I immediately settled down to feed him, and he sucked ravenously. I wondered what on earth I was going to do with him. If only they would let me have him with me in the dungeon.

It was possible for us to wash ourselves and our clothes, and we all did so. Felicitas in particular was relieved to be able to clean herself up properly at last. She seemed, if anything though, the most cheerful of all of us.

"What makes you so happy?" I asked her as we knelt together at a basin, scrubbing our tunics.

"We are following in his footsteps," she told me, her eyes shining. "I know it's horrible here, my lady, but I keep on telling myself – we are privileged to be able to suffer for the sake of Jesus."

"Keep telling the rest of us, too," I told her. "I know it's true, but I find it easy to forget. And then there is Marcus – that's the hardest thing for me. I only wish I could have him with me."

She put her hand on her own swollen abdomen.

"My lady," she said, in a more anxious tone now, "is it true that they won't execute a woman who is pregnant?"

"That is true," I said. It was the first time the thought had occurred to me. "It's against the law."

"It's right, of course," she said. "They couldn't execute a baby, but if the rest of you die together, I don't want to be left behind."

"That's what will happen, nevertheless," I said, appalled at the thought. "Unless we have to wait a very long time for our trial, and that would be equally awful, in this hell-hole."

Just then I heard a familiar voice calling my name.

"Vibia! My dearest!" I looked up to see my mother hastening across the prison courtyard from the entrance. Then I saw that my brother Cornelius was coming up behind her. I rushed over to meet them.

"Vibia!" said my mother, embracing me with tears in her eyes, "we could stand it no longer, worrying about you. How are they treating you?"

Suddenly, as I stood there in my mother's embrace, still clutching Marcus in my arms, the awfulness of our situation overwhelmed me, and my eyes flooded with tears.

"It's terrible, mother," I sobbed. "It's so dark down there, and there are so many people together in a tiny dungeon. And they won't let me have Marcus with me."

My mother looked into my eyes, and the tears were streaming down her cheeks too. And yet I saw something beneath her anguish which gave me encouragement. I saw that now she believed in what we were doing, too.

"But this is where we are meant to be," I told her. "Do you believe that, mother?"

I watched the signs of an inner struggle on her face. Finally she turned away, unable to look at me as she gave her reply.

"Yes, my dearest – I believe that, too."

"And you, Cornelius," I said, turning to him. "Do you believe it?"

"I – I don't know, Vibia," he said, hesitantly. "It seems so awful. How could God want such a thing?"

"But don't you see?" I said. "The church will only be strong if we stand firm in the face of such trials. It is Satan who wants to destroy the church. It is he who wants us to give in."

As I spoke I found that a feeling of strength and power flowed through me. In that brief moment I could almost say, like Felicitas, that I felt privileged to be going through this ordeal.

"I don't know, my sister," he said again. "You must pray for me."

"And you must pray for me," I replied. "For all of us."

"Right, that's enough!" came a harsh cry from one of the guards. "You've been up here long enough. It's time you went back down where you belong."

My mother began to weep once more. I gave Marcus into her arms.

"You must look after him, mother," I said. I had no idea how this might turn out, but at least it would relieve me of a great deal of anxiety. Clearly he could not remain in the prison. I tore myself away from them. As I walked towards the doorway leading to the stairs down to the dungeon, a black depression seemed to engulf me. My feet felt like lead, and each step seemed to take an immense effort. Once we were back down in the stifling heat and darkness of the dungeon I lay down, exhausted. I wanted only to sleep. To forget where I was and what we were going through. To forget the anguish and suffering of my mother and brother, not to mention my father. To forget that Felicitas was going to have a baby and that Secundulus could scarcely breathe. In a few moments I had my wish, and was sleeping a sleep of oblivion.

*

I do not know exactly how long we were kept in that terrible dungeon. Days passed, and then weeks. It may even have been months. Each day was a struggle to survive. Tertius and Pomponius came every morning, and sometimes we were allowed up to the courtyard. My mother and Cornelius were staying with friends in Carthage so as to be near us, and they came most days too. Secundulus lived for about two weeks more, but then one night, while he was having a terrible fit of coughing we heard a sudden horrible gurgling sound, and he fell silent.

"He's gone," whispered Saturninus, who had been holding him in his arms. It was a blow to the rest of us in one way, but we rejoiced that he had gone home ahead of us. He had suffered far more than any of us, and it was a relief to know that, for him, the battle was over at last. We summoned the guards and they took his body away. The following day some believers from the church in Carthage came and collected it.

It was not an uncommon occurrence for a prisoner to die in those atrocious conditions. We all suffered from ill health, and Quintus, one of the four from Carthage, also died while he was still there awaiting trial. The other three were taken away to their hearing one day not long after. They all stood firm, Tertius and Pomponius told us, and were sentenced to be burned at the stake. We never saw them again in this life.

For me I think the worst thing was to be separated from

Marcus. I missed him terribly during those days. Of course, I saw him whenever my mother came to visit, but then she had to take him from me again when she left. I kept begging the guards to be allowed to keep him with me. Perhaps they tired of listening to my pleas, or perhaps the chief officer had a change of mind, but one day they suddenly announced to me that I could keep him. I was overjoyed. I made my way down the stairs to the dungeon once more, but this time with little Marcus in my arms. Suddenly the whole ordeal seemed bearable, indeed, I could say, almost a pleasure. Marcus took a little while to adjust to life in the dark, but I knew that he was happy with me, too. And yet doubts still crept into my mind as a held him in my arms down in that dark hole. Often the question came back to haunt me: "What am I doing to my child?"

It was some time after this that the letter arrived for me, delivered by my mother.

"Who is it from?" I asked, overwhelmed by curiosity.

"From your husband," she replied.

Impatiently, I tore open the seal and unrolled the letter. It was not long, written in Lupercus' own neat hand.

'Marcus Lupercus, to my dearest wife Perpetua,' he wrote, 'please forgive me for not coming to you in person. Some may say that I was a fool to marry you, knowing full well that things might turn out this way. I know that what I am going through will seem to you a mere trifle compared with your own suffering, but you must remember that I did not choose this path, except in so far as I chose you as my wife. Ever since your arrest I have found it increasingly difficult to deal with colleagues and business contacts both in Thuburbo Minus and in Carthage, where, as you know, I have been trying to win a number of new contracts. Everyone seems to know about you, and I need not tell you that the affair is generally regarded very unfavourably. I have therefore had to choose between staying here in Africa, and living with the stigma of my position, whilst watching the family business slowly disintegrate before my eyes, or moving away somewhere else completely and starting again with a clean slate. Without troubling you with the details, I have chosen the latter, and even now I am about to take ship for Italy, where I pray that the gods might grant me a turn in my fortunes once again. It is not a decision in which I take pride, but I feel driven by necessity. The one thing I must stress to you is that I do not regret taking you as my wife, and I treasure the memories of the times we had together. Farewell my dearest. I have never ceased to love you with all my heart.'

I sat there for a long while after reading it, the tears rolling down my cheeks. My mother sat with me, her arm around me, but she said nothing. I realised that I still did not love Lupercus, but nevertheless I felt betrayed.

"He didn't even wait till the hearing," was all I said.

*

One day my mother and brother came with some news which seemed to offer us an unexpected hope.

"It has just been announced in the forum," said Cornelius. "The proconsul died last night."

I considered this for some moments, trying to work out the consequences. It was under the authority of the proconsul, Minucius Timinianus, that we had been arrested, and it was before him that we were waiting to stand trial. Suddenly it seemed that there was a very real possibility that we might be freed instead. If the proconsul's successor was a tolerant man, with a lenient attitude to Christians, he would probably not have us killed.

"Who is to succeed him?" I asked.

"The procurator, Publius Hilarianus," said my mother. The name was familiar to me, but I knew nothing about him.

"What is he like?" I pressed her.

"Well, he is ambitious. An efficient administrator. And very religious, they say." That was not good news.

"My dear sister," said Cornelius, "I don't think I can stand waiting any longer to know what is going to happen to you. I have an idea. Have you not had dreams and visions in the past in which God has revealed things to you? Perhaps you could pray for some vision or sign now, by which we would know whether you are to be condemned or freed."

I considered this for some moments. Could I really pray for such a thing? Something inside me seemed to leap at the thought, and I knew that this was exactly what I should do. Perhaps it would encourage Cornelius if God spoke directly to me confirming our fate.

"I will do what you have suggested," I told him. "Come back tomorrow and I will let you know what answer I have been given."

I told the others about Cornelius' request and we all prayed fervently that God would speak to me that night. It was with something of a sense of excitement, therefore, that I lay down to sleep that evening on the floor of the dungeon.

21

Ascent into Heaven

I was standing in a desolate place, hemmed in by the dark walls of enormous cliffs. Before me there was a ladder made of bronze, stretching up as far as the eye could see, as if it reached to the very heavens. It seemed to offer the only way out of that place. Despite its immense height it was exceedingly narrow. Certainly only one person could climb it at a time, and anyone who wished to had two other perils to face in doing so. The first was the fact that there were a great many blades and weapons attached to the sides of the ladder, impeding the progress of the climber. It seemed to me that these weapons were razor-sharp, and that even to brush against one of them might result in a dreadful wound. With great care, however, one might pass between them unscathed. The second peril was even more terrifying. At the foot of the ladder, guarding it, so to speak, against any who might try to begin its ascent, was a huge and horrible dragon. It was at that very moment staring out at me with unveiled malice in its fiery red eyes. One of its front claws twitched menacingly, as if itching to get at me and begin to tear at my flesh. Its jaws opened a crack and I glimpsed a row of fearsome teeth. It seemed to be daring me to approach, mocking me if I was even thinking of trying to ascend the ladder. I stood rooted to the spot, unable to move from sheer terror.

Then I looked up once more at the ladder and noticed for the first time that there was a figure already climbing it, rung by rung, carefully twisting between the hideous weapons. At that moment he stopped and turned to look down at me, and I saw that it was Saturus. At the sight of him I gasped. How he had got there, I could not imagine.

"Perpetua!" he called to me, and his voice was filled with excitement, not at all fearful.

"Wait!" I cried back. "I'm coming up as well!"

"I'm waiting," he replied, "but take care of that dragon. Don't let it bite you!"

Suddenly I knew that the dragon had no power whatsoever to stop me. The sight of Saturus already climbing the ladder had given me a renewed confidence, and the dragon's claws and teeth, the razor-sharp weapons, and the immense height of the ladder, held no more terror for me.

"He will not harm me," I said, "in the name of Jesus!"

As I uttered this name, a strange thing happened. I saw the dragon flinch. It was still looking at me, but instead of malice I now saw fear in its eyes. I began to walk towards the foot of the ladder. The creature evidently knew that it had to try to stop me, but it was clearly terrified of me now. Slowly, hesitantly, it began to thrust its horrible head out from underneath the ladder.

"In the name of Jesus!" I repeated in a loud voice, having seen that the very sound of that name seemed to torture the dragon. I then stepped right on the dragon's head, using it as the first rung of the ladder. As I began to climb there was a horrible hissing and gurgling sound from below me. I looked down to see the dragon squirming away into the shadows of the cliff, its head bruised terribly where I had stood on it.

Now I had to pay attention to the dangers on either side of me. As I climbed each rung I had to watch carefully that I did not accidentally touch the swords, knives, spikes and hooks that protruded into my path. It was a slow and painstaking task, but Saturus was still above me, waiting, and shouting down words of encouragement. Looking down I now saw that the others were climbing up below me – Felicitas, Revocatus and Saturninus. In turn I shouted down to encourage them as they climbed.

At last I was just below Saturus, and I found that he himself was at the very top of the ladder. It seemed that the ladder had not been as tall as it had looked from the ground. He climbed over the top and I quickly followed, anxious to see what kind of a place we had arrived at.

We were in a garden the like of which I had never even dreamed of before in my life. The first thing that struck me was the vastness of the place. There were tall stately trees and beautiful shrubs, but they were planted at wide intervals, so that one could see for miles in every direction. Then there were the flowers. These were of a beauty and variety unsurpassed by anything I had seen on earth. I suppose it was from the flowers that the beautiful scent that filled the air was rising, too. And everywhere there were birds flying in the air. The sunlight was intense, but of a quality that did not seem harsh, but rather made everything in its light seem more alive.

I became aware that there was a huge crowd of people nearby, stretching into the distance, and the crowd parted as we walked towards them. Then I saw a figure sitting at the centre of the crowd. He was very tall, and he was dressed as a shepherd. The simple clothes that he wore were in stark contrast to the radiant white garments worn by all of those standing around him. Close by him were a number of sheep, and I now saw that he was sitting milking one of them. It was at that moment that he looked up from his task, and I first caught sight of his face.

That face that I knew so well, now! But this time it seemed as if I was really meeting him, not just seeing him in a vision. There was still that look of indescribable love in his eyes. He gazed at me, and I sensed that he was looking right into my heart, to see every secret thought. For a moment I was afraid of what he might see, and I had an impulse to turn away and hide, but I knew that this would be futile, and that, in any case, there was no need. The look of love never once faded from his eyes as he gazed at me, and into me.

"I am glad you have come, my child," he said to me. "You dealt well with the dragon."

I thought back to the moment of terror I had first experienced at the foot of the ladder. What if I had never begun to climb, out of fear of the dragon? The awfulness of this thought appalled me.

"Come," said the shepherd, beckoning me towards him.

I walked up to him, my heart racing with wonder and joy. He had a ladle, with which he now spooned up some of the milk he had been drawing, and offered it to me. I held out my cupped hands and he poured the warm liquid into them. I raised my hands to my lips and drank. The taste was sweet, and seemed strangely familiar, but I could not say what it was it reminded me of. As I swallowed it, the voices of all that vast crowd who were standing around us were raised in a single word: "Amen!" I knew with a deep feeling of joy and peace that I had come home.

But just then that moment of bliss was snatched from me, and I woke from my dream to find myself lying on the hard stone floor of the dark dungeon. Marcus was lying wrapped up beside me, and had begun to cry for milk. I could still taste the milk that I had just received in my dream, that sweet honey taste. And then I remembered where I had tasted it before. It was the milk and honey mixture that we had received at our baptism.

*

"Well, it seems clear enough," said Felicitas. "From what your mother told us about Hilarianus, I don't think we were really expecting to be freed now anyway."

We were all up in the courtyard, enjoying the cool fresh air for a while. My mother and brother were with us, and I had just recounted my dream to them all. My younger brother Cornelius, the one who had asked for the vision, was not saying anything. I put my arm around him.

"You mustn't worry," I told him. "We know now that we are in God's hands."

"In God's hands or not – I almost feel like we have lost you already."

"I know it is hard to think that we will soon be parted," I told him, "but we are all on the same journey – we are all going home. We are going to get there before you, it seems, but there is cause for rejoicing in that, as well as for grief at the parting. And if you had seen that garden, and spoken with the Shepherd

219

– really, I wish I had never woken up."

"Poor little Marcus," said my mother, cradling him in her arms.

"One day he will hear the story for himself," I said, "and I pray that he will understand."

This thought triggered a memory for me – a memory of something that the rhetorician Tertullian had said to me.

"Papyrus and a pen!" I said. "Can you bring me some? I want to write it down."

"That's an excellent idea," said Pomponius. "We'll bring you some tomorrow."

"Are you going to write down everything?" asked Felicitas, with excitement in her eyes.

"Everything?" I asked, rather puzzled. "Everything in the dream, yes, of course."

"No, no!" she said. "I mean everything! Everything that's happened to us up till now. My lady, you must. If only for little Marcus."

I paused for a moment to consider this, and the more I thought about it, the more I became convinced that it was what I must do.

"Yes," I said, after some moments, "you are right, Felicitas. I am going to write down everything. The whole story from when we were arrested."

"There's one thing I don't understand," said Saturninus, who had evidently been deep in thought up till that moment. We all looked at him. "Saturus went up the ladder ahead of you. Does that mean he's going die somehow even before we are?"

This had puzzled me as well, but I hadn't given it much thought until then.

"Perhaps it's just because he was our teacher," I suggested. "He led us all, in a way."

As it turned out, however, there was more to it than that. The following day Pomponius brought me some sheets of papyrus, a pen and some ink, as he had promised. I began to write down the account of all that had happened to us, but there was not time to complete it while we were in the courtyard that day. He offered to keep it safe for me, but I told him I wanted to keep it with me. Somehow, those sheets of papyrus seemed very precious to me, and even though I could not even see them in the darkness of the dungeon, they were a comfort to me.

Now that Secundulus was gone it was not so urgent for us to have time out of the dungeon every day and sometimes we went a day or two without leaving our dark cell. The next time we were up in the courtyard I was sitting with my pen and papyrus, continuing my account, when suddenly I heard a familiar, but altogether unexpected voice.

"Perpetua! Felicitas!" I looked up in amazement to see Saturus coming over towards us.

I could not help myself. I jumped up and rushed over to embrace him.

"Saturus!" I said. "You have come to visit us!"

"No, Perpetua," he replied. "It is not a visit. I should have come long before now if it were just a visit I was going to make."

"What do you mean?" I asked, completely baffled by his reply.

"I am sorry it has taken me so long to do what I knew I should do," he said, "but here I am now. I have come to join you."

"Come to join us?" I said, astonished. "You mean they arrested you as well?"

"Not exactly," he said, with a smile. "I simply paid a visit to the governor, Hilarianus and told him that it was I who had induced you all to become Christians. I promised him that if he didn't put me in prison with you I would continue to seek more converts as long as I remained at liberty to do so."

I gaped at him.

"You gave yourself up?"

"Perpetua – you must realise that ever since the day you were arrested I have felt guilty about remaining free myself. You were much more than just disciples to me. You were like my own children. Every day since they took you away you have haunted my thoughts, and every night I would lie awake for hours wondering what was happening to you."

"And yet – you never came to see us." I was not reproachful, but puzzled.

"No – because I knew deep down that simply to visit you was not enough. I sensed the Lord calling me to come to be with you in prison. To walk the journey with you to the very end. But I am not the world's most courageous person, Perpetua." He laughed. "I'm afraid it took me longer than it should have to obey his call."

I looked at him in wonder.

"You are wrong," I told him. "You have done a very courageous thing. And anyway, you're in plenty of time. As you can see, we're still enjoying the hospitality of the holding prison. We haven't even had our hearing yet."

"What's this?" he asked, suddenly noticing that I had been writing.

I explained to him what I was doing, and told him all about the dream. The fact that he had been the first to climb the ladder now seemed to make much more sense, and it was obviously a tremendous encouragement to him.

"You see, Perpetua," he said smiling, "far from being so surprised, you should have been expecting me!"

*

A few days later Pomponius and Tertius brought us news of what we had all been waiting for. We had become the talk of the town, it seemed, especially after the Christians from Carthage had been publicly burned in the forum, and the rumour was that our hearing was coming up soon. A massive crowd had gathered to witness the trial of the others, and the deacons were sure that even more people would come to watch ours. Some would come to jeer and gloat over the suffering of the hated Christians. Many others would come out of curiosity, to try to understand what made us so stubborn in our refusal to bow before the might of Rome – what made us willing to face death rather than make one small sacrifice. It had become common knowledge, too, that I had a baby with me, and that Felicitas was pregnant. These facts seemed to make us something of a novelty, even for condemned Christians. It was easy to forget the outside world, shut in between the four walls of the prison, but we were reminded now that life was going on out there, and that we ourselves had become a centre of attention in the city of Carthage.

Saturus had also brought news of the church in Thuburbo Minus, but it was not very encouraging. Optatus had completed the work on his new dining room, and the church was meeting there. Relations between him and Aspasius, however, had deteriorated since our arrest. A number of church members had continued to meet at Aspasius' house even after Optatus' dining room was ready. Although it was still supposedly one church there were two distinct factions, those who remained loyal to the bishop, and those who were now openly questioning his authority and who favoured his replacement by Aspasius. Both factions spoke highly of us – they were already referring to us as 'the martyrs' – and both claimed that, had we still been there, we would have sided with their camp.

It was that same day that my father came to the prison. When I first caught sight of him across the prison courtyard, my first reflex was to feel anger that he should still be trying to persuade me. Then I took a closer look at him, and saw that he had aged noticeably since our arrest. The look on his face was not that of anger, but rather he looked worn and haggard. In fact, he looked a broken man, and I found that thought shocking. I realised that he was now filled with remorse for his own actions, but what shook me most was that remorse seemed to have driven out all trace of the indignation and anger which had inspired those actions.

"Perpetua," he said, and his voice was the voice of love that I had heard so seldom these past years, and yet now it was tortured with anguish, even guilt. "My daughter, I am sorry."

I held him in an embrace, but I could say nothing.

"Daughter," he said, "if you will accept that I should still call you that, after what I have done – have pity on me. I did what I did out of love for you – you must understand that. Just as I have done everything out of love for you. Just as I lavished everything on you, yes, favouring you above your brothers – I admit it. Just as I allowed you your heart's desire, to study under Sosigenes. Just as I have striven through all the years of your short life up till now to show that I loved you. Even this was done out of love – you must believe me."

"Father," I said, but with great effort, "I do believe you. I know that you never understood the depth of the love that holds me to Jesus Christ my saviour. And, ignorant of that, you have committed what is, in your eyes, a terrible mistake. But I do not count it a mistake, father. God's hand is in all this, of that I am convinced. All will happen as he wills, for we are in his hands."

At this my father lurched to his knees, as if in pain, and took my hands in his to kiss them, with tears running down his cheeks.

"My lady," he said, no longer addressing me as his daughter, "I appeal to you as that which I brought you up to be – a respectable married woman, of good character and noble family. Do not abandon us to be the reproach of those we once counted as friends and peers. Think of your brothers, think of your mother and your aunt. Or, if you no longer care about us, at least think of your child. How will he be able to live once you are gone? Give up your pride! You are destroying all of us! If anything happens to you, our family will become nothing – all that has been passed down to us by our ancestors will be thrown away, as onto a rubbish heap. Don't you realise that?"

"You speak for our whole family," I replied, "but in truth this is not the way things are. I know that mother and Cornelius do not think this way, in any case. It is only you who do not understand, father, and I wish with all my heart that you did, for it tortures me to see you thus."

"Then I am a fool," he said, looking up into my eyes with a pitiful expression on his face, "for I understand nothing."

And with that he got up from where he had been kneeling and left without another word. I stood staring after him numbly for several minutes. I felt utterly drained. Felicitas, who had been standing close by the whole time holding Marcus, now came over and took my arm. We stood there silent for some time, and her presence was a comfort to me. Then she spoke.

"We are all being wounded in the battle, my lady," she said, "but I fear that so far you have taken the most blows."

Just then there was a harsh cry, and the guards were upon us, ushering us all back down into the dungeon.

It was only a few days after that that our waiting finally ended. We were once more in the courtyard, on a dull winter's morning, eating the breakfast that Tertius and Pomponius had brought us when suddenly a detachment of soldiers marched in and came crashing to a halt in the middle of the courtyard. The chief prison officer appeared, and saluted their captain.

"Hail Caesar!" he said.

"Hail Caesar!" came the reply. "I am here on the orders of his excellency, Governor Hilarianus. The prisoners from Thuburbo Minus who are charged with conversion to Christianity are to be brought to their hearing immediately."

22

The Healing of Hope

They would not allow me to take Marcus with me. I had to leave him once more in the care of the slave-girl at the prison, which made me very anxious about him. We were then led out of the prison and we entered the forum. People began to stare at us, and then we heard them talking excitedly to one another. One phrase was repeated over and over: "The Christians! It's the Christians!" In this way the news that our hearing was imminent spread like wildfire around the neighbourhood of the forum, and a huge crowd began to gather.

A makeshift podium had been set up in front of the basilica on one side of the forum. On the podium was an ornate chair, with a prisoner's dock facing it. The dock was a simple wooden platform, with a rope around it. This was where we were led, and it soon became the focus of attention for the crowds of people who were now flocking to witness the trial. Soon Hilarianus the governor appeared, and mounted the podium with great pomp, along with several other officials. After he had sat down on the chair, one of the officials began to read from a scroll. Each of us was named, and it was announced that we had been arrested under the recent edict on suspicion of having converted to Christianity. The official finished reading, handed the scroll to Hilarianus, and stepped to one side. By now the crowd had begun to quieten down, in anticipation of what was going to happen. The governor remained seated in silence for some moments, studying the scroll. A hush fell, and then he spoke.

"Marcus Saturus."

Saturus stepped forward and stood in the prisoner's dock.

"I order you to make the sacrifice to the genius of their divine excellencies Lucius Septimius Severus and his son, Marcus Aurelius Antoninus."

"It is the decree of the one true God," replied Saturus, slowly and deliberately, "that we should sacrifice to him alone, rather than to idols."

The governor shifted restlessly on his chair, and there was a ripple of excitement through the crowd.

"Are you a Christian?" asked Hilarianus.

"I am."

"I need not remind you of the sentence which you risk by your obstinacy, young man," went on Hilarianus. "Sacrifice, and you will be deemed worthy of life."

"I will not," replied Saturus.

"Perhaps you would like some time to reconsider."

"It is a straightforward matter. There is no need to reconsider."

By now a few in the crowd had begun to call out, "Burn them!" and such things. The governor sighed and motioned with his hand. One of the soldiers stepped up to the dock and led Saturus down. One by one the others were called up, and each in turn gave the governor the same reply. They would not sacrifice because they were Christians. As each was led down again I became more and more nervous, wondering if I would be next. In fact, I was called last of all.

"Vibia Perpetua," called Hilarianus, and I stepped forward, my heart beating with apprehension. Just then, a movement to one side of the podium caught my eye. Looking across I saw my father coming towards me, holding Marcus in his arms. He strode up to the dock, seized me by the arm, while still holding my baby with his other arm, and pulled me down from the platform. An excited buzz arose from the watching crowd, and two soldiers stepped forward to restrain my father, but Hilarianus motioned for them to step back.

"My daughter, please!" hissed my father. "Perform the sacrifice – have pity on your baby!"

"Yes, indeed," said Hilarianus, obviously still hoping that I might be turned from the reckless course which the others had taken by the drama of this interruption. "Have pity on your father's grey head. Have pity on your infant son. Offer the sacrifice for the welfare of the emperors."

"I will not," I replied.

"Are you a Christian?"

"Yes, I am."

At this point my father broke down in tears and threw himself on me, begging me to change my mind.

"Enough!" said the governor, evidently tiring of the whole affair. But my father was in such a state by now that he could not let me go. When he would not be persuaded by words the governor ordered him to be beaten. I stood watching in agony of spirit as Marcus was taken from him and he was thrown to the ground and struck with a rod. At each blow I winced, feeling the pain as if I myself were suffering the beating. The crowd were jeering and calling out once again for our death. My father was pulled to his feet and led away, and Hilarianus then passed sentence. We waited anxiously to hear what our fate was to be. One fear we had was that I, and perhaps Saturus, might be given a more lenient sentence because of our higher social rank. But we were all given the same sentence.

"In view of your self-confessed guilt, of which those present are witnesses, you are all condemned to be exposed to the beasts," said Hilarianus, and he sounded almost indifferent by this stage. "This will take place at the games to be held in honour of his imperial majesty Geta Caesar on the occasion of his birthday. Hail Caesar."

At this the soldiers who had brought us there came to attention and saluted. Then we were led away, back to the prison, amid the jeers and catcalls of the crowd. Geta Caesar was Septimius Severus' younger son. I was not sure when his birthday was, but it was evidently approaching. I caught Felicitas' eye and she smiled at me.

"We've done it, my lady," she said, her eyes shining. "We didn't give in!"

She took Revocatus' hand in hers. He was looking proud and happy. He too smiled at me. As for Saturninus, he began to call out to the crowd, warning them of God's judgement if they were ready to gloat over our deaths. Only Saturus seemed more subdued, and I moved closer to him.

"Are you all right?" I asked him. He looked into my eyes, and I saw in his face not fear, but sadness and love.

"I am happy to be condemned for following Jesus," he replied. "But I feel pity for those who have condemned us. They are the ones who are really the condemned prisoners. Prisoners of sin and darkness, awaiting the reward for their deeds, which is eternal destruction. The tragedy is that they could be set free any time they wanted, if only they knew it. I was praying that some at least of those present might be moved by what they have witnessed to turn away from their own reckless course and find salvation in Jesus."

I glanced around at the jeering mob, searching for a face that might be showing some evidence of such a sentiment. At that moment I noticed a familiar face, someone who was certainly not jeering. It was the deacon Pomponius.

"We are praying for you!" he called, above the noise of the crowd.

"Pomponius!" I called back. "Can you fetch Marcus? He is with my father."

He nodded, and disappeared into the crowd.

We did not see him again until the next morning. We had been taken back to the holding prison, although we were told that we would later be transferred to the military prison to await the day of the games. That night I missed Marcus terribly and lay awake worrying about him. He had grown used to being with me in the prison, dark and horrible though it was, and he was also accustomed to me feeding him. Of course, I was suffering in this respect as well, for the feeding had stopped so suddenly that my breasts had become swollen and painful.

In the morning Pomponius arrived with some discouraging news. My father had flatly refused to allow Marcus to be taken back to the prison.

"How is he?" I asked in concern, remembering the condition he had been in when he had been left with the slave-girl. "Is he feeding at all?"

"He was feeding when I went there," replied Pomponius. "He was being given some porridge. They say he does not seem to have desire for milk any longer."

I wondered how this could be, but at the same time the thought occurred to me that this was perhaps the moment for me to let him go. It had to happen sooner or later, I knew, but up till then I had been putting it off, holding on to him for as long as I could. Now, however, I sensed that the time had come. I found this almost unbearably painful. I had my papyrus and pen with me, and I now took these, went and sat down a little distance from the others and began to write some more of my account. As I wrote, I imagined my son in a few years' time, having begun to learn his letters, sitting reading the words I had written. In this way I could communicate my thoughts and feelings to him, despite the fact that I might never see him again.

Later that day I realised that my breasts were no longer swollen or painful, but seemed to have returned to normal. This I took as further confirmation – Marcus' place was no longer with me. And yet, in my heart an empty space was left, which I knew could never be filled. I grieved for him, as if he had died.

Several days went by and still we remained waiting in the holding prison. We had ascertained that Geta Caesar's birthday was on the 7th March, less than three weeks away. We spent a great deal of time praying together. One day while we were praying I suddenly found myself calling out involuntarily:

"Dinocrates!" There was a pause while the others waited for me to go on.

"I'm sorry," I said, feeling rather foolish, and very bewildered, "The word just came out – I don't know why."

Of the others, only Saturninus did not know who Dinocrates was, so I briefly explained to him.

"I think there is still pain in your heart at that loss," said Saturus. "It is the Parentalia just now, you know."

I thought back to the day when Felicitas and I had been returning from Dinocrates' grave and had met Saturus in the street. I thought back, too, to the last days of Dinocrates' young life, and the awful pain and suffering he had gone through. I realised that, having searched for so long for an answer to why he should have suffered so much and died so young, I had still not found one. If only he had lived, I thought, he would have heard about Jesus too. And somehow I knew that he would have chosen to follow him as well, along with my mother, Cornelius and me. At that moment, a glimmer of hope flickered in my mind, and I felt an overwhelming urge to pray for him. I remembered the question I had asked Saturus that day – can Dinocrates be rescued? He had not said yes or no, but now I felt a strange hope within me, and I began to pray, fervently, in words that were not my own but seemed to come through me rather than from within me.

*

In the distance I could see a dark opening, like the mouth of a cave. There seemed to be a large number of people inside in the darkness. Just then a small figure emerged from the opening, and I realised with a shock that it was my little brother, Dinocrates. The sight of him brought back horrific memories of his last days, for his face was still half eaten away by the awful wound he had had when he died. He looked horribly pale and dirty as well, dressed in filthy rags, and he seemed very hot. The dark hole that he had come out of was evidently not unlike our own prison cell. He wanted something to drink, and I now noticed for the first time that there was a raised basin of water just near him. My heart went out to him, and I wanted to go and help him, but between us there was a great abyss. I watched as he approached the basin, but soon realised that he was too small to be able to reach the rim. He tried to heave himself up to the height of the rim, but in vain. At that moment he looked across in my direction. He could evidently see me, and looked at me with pleading in his grotesquely disfigured face, but, as I stood watching him from across the abyss, there was nothing I could do to help him.

At that moment I woke up. It was a disturbing dream, with nothing in it of the hope and encouragement I had found in other dreams. I did not tell the others about it, but I wrote it down – for Marcus, I told myself. I resolved, however, to keep on praying for Dinocrates, and this I did faithfully every day, often with tears running down my cheeks. I felt that this was a task I had been given, something I had to complete before the day of the games.

It was only a few days later that we were finally transferred to the military prison. For this we were all shackled together and led out to be escorted once more by a detachment of soldiers. As we stood there in the sunlight, waiting to be led away, I gave thanks that we had seen the last of that horrible dungeon. Pomponius had assured us that, though the day of our death was fast approaching, we could nevertheless look forward to somewhat better conditions in the military prison.

Standing there in the courtyard I suddenly found myself drifting into a kind of trance. The courtyard around me faded away and I seemed to be standing in the same place as I had been in my dream of Dinocrates. My little brother was still there, but what a change had come over him! He was now clean and dressed in a smart white tunic, he did not seem to be hot or thirsty any more, and on his face where the wound had been eating away at his flesh, there was now only a faint scar. Moreover, the pool from which he had been unable to drink before was now much lower. In fact its rim was now only at the height of his waist, and he could drink from it as much as he pleased. I also noticed that there was a small bowl, suspended, as it were, above the basin. This bowl was made of gold, and it was also full of water. Dinocrates now took it in his hands and began to drink from it. He drank and drank, and yet the bowl remained full, despite the fact that he ought to have emptied it several times over. At last he had drunk enough, and he sat down on the ground. I saw that he had his wooden building blocks with him there, and he now took them and began to play with them. I laughed out loud at this. Here was the Dinocrates that I wanted to remember, before he had ever fallen ill. I could see that he was building something with the bricks, but I could not make out what it was. Just then I came to, still laughing with joy. I became aware that the others were giving me curious looks.

"What is it, my lady?" asked Felicitas. I was not sure what to say.

"I was just rejoicing," I said, "at our victory over death."

At that point the captain of our escort barked an order, and we were marched out of the prison gates into the streets of the city.

The military prison was on the outskirts of the city, not far from the amphitheatre. By this time we were getting used to being led around as prisoners, and having to endure the stares and mockery of the crowds. Nevertheless, it was a painful process making our way slowly through the city streets, and it seemed to take an eternity to get to our destination. On our arrival at the military prison we were put together into a cell which was separated from a corridor by bars. It offered little in the way of comfort, but there were three barred windows in the wall opposite the corridor, letting in light and air. This made it seem positively luxurious compared with the loathsome dungeon where we had languished for so long in the holding prison. In addition we were actually given a little food each day, though it was not really adequate to live on. One evening, soon after we had arrived there, an important looking officer came along and stopped in the corridor outside our cell. He was a man of about fifty, with a rugged, though not unpleasant face.

"You," he said, addressing Saturus through the bars, "over here."

Saturus got up, and went over to where the officer stood. The soldier looked at him for some time without saying anything, while Saturus stared back uneasily.

"Don't I know you from somewhere?" the soldier asked eventually.

Saturus looked at him in bewilderment, then suddenly a flicker of recognition appeared in his eyes.

"You're not... You weren't on board the *Poseidon*, were you?"

The man clapped his hands together and nodded his head with satisfaction.

"I knew it," he said. "As soon as I set eyes on you I thought there was something familiar about you. You're the one that had the dream – or was it your friend?"

The rest of us could only stare in amazement. We all knew

the story of how Saturus and his friend Matthias had been warned in a dream that the *Poseidon* was going to sink and had escaped in time, but who this soldier was we had no idea.

"It was my friend who had the dream," replied Saturus, "and I now thank God for saving our lives by sending him that dream. Nor was that the last time that God saved my life, in order that I might live long enough for my stubborn heart to give in and turn to him."

"You were on board the ship then, sir?" I asked, unable to contain my curiosity any longer. "But I heard that every passenger and crew member perished when the ship went down."

"I was at the port doing guard duty on board when your friend asked to disembark," he said. "I'm sure I'd have forgotten the incident long ago if it weren't for what happened to the ship." He turned back to Saturus. "So – you're a Christian. You didn't mention that at the time."

"I was not a Christian then, though my companion was."

The officer looked at him thoughtfully, then his gaze rested on each of us in turn.

"Christians, eh? And you're all to die on Caesar's birthday." He paused and looked away, then turned back to us. "My name is Appius Pudens," he said, "and I'm adjutant in charge of this prison. If there's anything you need, let me know."

With that he turned and strode off down the corridor, leaving us all staring after him in astonishment.

23

Comfort in Adversity

Up till that point Tertius and Pomponius had been allowed to deliver food for us, but had not been allowed to visit us. Bribery did not seem to be an option at this establishment, but the conditions were so much more tolerable than in the holding prison that this didn't seem to be much of a hardship. The next day, however, the prison adjutant, Pudens, came to see us once again with the two deacons at his heels.

"Some visitors to see you," he said briefly, with the hint of a smile. He unlocked the door and allowed them in, then left, without even bothering to lock the door again. The deacons had brought food and drink, as usual, but they also had something else. Pomponius was carrying a written scroll which he handed to Saturus.

"This is from Tertullian, for all of you," he said. With great curiosity, Saturus unrolled it, and began to read out loud.

"To the martyrs," he read. He glanced around at us, with a surprised smile on his face. "Blessed martyrs designate – along with the provision which our lady mother the church from her bountiful breasts, and each brother out of his private means, makes for your bodily wants in the prison, accept also from me some contribution to your spiritual sustenance. For it is not good that the flesh be feasted and the spirit starve. On the contrary, if that which is weak is being cared for, it is only right that that which is still weaker should not be neglected."

Tertullian, the rhetorician and writer, had actually written something especially for us. I do not think we had fully realised before then quite what celebrities we had become in the church in Carthage. The letter itself was quite long and was of tremendous encouragement to all of us. The prison was the devil's house, Tertullian wrote, but he urged us to take the opportunity while we were there of doing battle against him, particularly by keeping that unity and love amongst us that was such a powerful weapon against him. We had been cut off from the world by our imprisonment, he went on, but that was no great loss when one considered how much of the world was filled with the works of Satan. We had to endure hardship, it was true, but this could be likened to the discipline of a soldier preparing for battle or an athlete training for a great contest. He acknowledged that it was a fearsome trial that had been set before us, to face the wild beasts in the amphitheatre, but he urged us to set our minds on the heavenly glory and divine reward which would be ours if we stood firm to the end. Recalling examples of those in history who had endured as much for mere earthly glory, he exhorted us to be all the more courageous, given the surpassing greatness of our own hope.

When Saturus had finished reading, he rolled up the scroll again.

"I trust we may be allowed to keep this treasure with us," he said to the deacons.

"Why, of course," replied Tertius. "The letter was written for you."

During the days that followed we received a number of other visitors. My mother and brother came often, and so did others from the church in Carthage. On several occasions we were even allowed to eat a fellowship meal together with our visitors, for which we were allowed the use of the soldiers' mess hall. The adjutant Pudens continued to show us favour. One day he came to our cell alone, let himself in, and sat down among us.

"There is something I wanted to talk to you about," he said. He paused, staring at the stone floor, as if trying to find the right words. "You are not the first to come here to await death in the amphitheatre. I am well used to having such prisoners here – common criminals, thieves, murderers, rebels and the like. For the most part, I have to say, they are pitiful specimens of humanity, though I don't blame them in the slightest for their despair. I've often wondered what I myself would turn out to be if I were put in their situation. But you – you are different." He looked around at us. "I can't describe what it is, exactly – a sort of inner power, perhaps. Here you are, shut up in prison, waiting to die in the arena, but I do not see any hint of defeat in your spirit. On the contrary, I see victory. I do not understand what it is you have. But I know that it's because you are Christians."

"You speak the truth, sir," said Saturus. "We are only ordinary men and women, and in ourselves we are no better than any common criminal who has been here before us. But we have within us the Holy Spirit, the Spirit of Jesus Christ himself, and that is what you have seen. And that Spirit is the gift that he gives freely to those who choose to follow him."

At that point, Pudens seemed to be seized by a violent emotion, and he turned and spoke to Saturus with urgency in his voice.

"In that case, I want to follow him too! Tell me what I must do."

"Turn away from your sins," replied Saturus. "They are only a prison in which you are living. Then accept the freedom which Jesus Christ offers you if you will follow him."

I believe that, there and then, in that bare prison cell, the life of that prison adjutant was changed for ever. He whose job was to keep prisoners locked up, was himself delivered from his own prison cell, and walked out into the freedom of following Jesus. We all gathered round to pray for him, and urged him to speak to the deacons as soon as possible. Then he left us, filled with joy.

"You see," I said to Saturninus, recalling his lack of faith, "even prison officers have souls that can be rescued."

That night we sang hymns together in our cell, something we had not done since we had left my father's house in Thuburbo Minus. We too were filled with joy, and we poured forth praises to God. We were in the devil's house, as Tertullian had described it, but I sensed that we were trampling on the devil's head, just as I had trampled on the head of the dragon in my dream.

The next day, however, brought discouragement on two fronts. Firstly my father came to see me. It was the last time I would ever see him, and perhaps the most painful. There seemed little left within him of the man I had once known and respected as my father. Indeed I began to fear even for his sanity. Had the whole affair actually driven him out of his mind? As he threw himself on the floor and tore the hairs from his beard in anguish at the sight of me, I could only stare back in horror. He was cursing himself and saying things that would move a heart of stone to pity for him. I knelt down beside him and put my arm around him.

"I love you, father," I said to him. "I have always loved you. But you must go now."

I helped him to his feet, calling for a guard to let him out. He staggered out, like a man twenty years older than he really was, grey-haired and haggard.

"Goodbye, father," I said, with tears in my eyes. He looked back at me, but it seemed that the man who was looking at me was a complete stranger. He said nothing, but simply turned and left. If anything, I felt the loss of my father more deeply even than the loss of my son. I could communicate with Marcus through my writing, and had a measure of confidence that he would understand, and support me, as it were, in what I had done. But I felt that there was a yawning abyss between my father and me, across which neither of us could communicate with the other.

The second discouragement that came that day was an order from Pudens' superior, the military tribune. Apparently, word had reached him that we were being treated with unaccustomed favour, and he had heard rumours, too, about Christians employing sorcery to escape from prison. He therefore ordered that we receive no more visitors, and be kept permanently chained up in our cell. Pudens explained all this to us, and said that, reluctant though he was, he saw no alternative but to comply. He was a soldier under orders, and he dared not disobey. We reassured him that we would be all right, and would certainly not blame him, but it was hard to face such conditions once more, after having been allowed so much freedom.

A few days after this the tribune arrived at the prison in person, and came to inspect us, to check, I suppose, that Pudens was faithfully carrying out his orders, and to reassure himself that we were being held securely. As he stood outside our cell regarding our chains with grim satisfaction, I got to my feet and stepped towards him, although I could not go far, being chained to the wall.

"Might I have a word with you, sir?" I asked. I had had enough of these harsh conditions, and I had a plan which I thought was at least worth a try. The tribune looked slightly taken aback.

"What is it?" he asked in an irritated tone.

"You are aware, I am sure," I said, "that we are being kept here in preparation for the games on Caesar's birthday. Naturally, we count this a great privilege, I do not need to tell you that." The tribune snorted. "That marks us out, of course, as the most distinguished of all the condemned prisoners being held here."

"Just get to the point," said the tribune, shortly. I looked down at my filthy tattered clothes, ran my hand through my unkempt hair, and indicated the others, all in a similar state of neglect. We all looked pale, thin and sickly.

"I put it to you that you might be running a risk, having us appear like this at the games, which are supposed to be in honour of his imperial majesty. On the other hand, it might be to your credit if we came forth to fight the beasts in a cleaner and healthier condition. I do not doubt that you maintain the highest standards among the troops who serve under you. But we, warriors appointed to fight on the emperor's great day, might cause some to question that, should we seem to have been allowed to lapse into indiscipline and squalor whilst in your keeping."

The tribune said nothing at first, but his face reddened perceptibly. It was not clear whether this was out of anger or embarrassment. Probably there was a bit of both. Finally he gave his reply.

"Very well," he said, through gritted teeth. "I will speak to the adjutant."

Soon afterwards, Pudens came to see us, with amazement on his face.

"What on earth did you say to him?" he asked us.

"It was the noble Perpetua who must take the credit," said Saturus. "She has the makings of an orator."

Thus our chains were removed once more, and we were once again allowed visitors, and many other favours besides. Each day we were allowed to go and wash ourselves, and were brought fresh clothes regularly. The tribune never came back, as far as I know.

Meanwhile, Pudens had spoken to the deacons, and was now meeting with the church. We asked him if anyone outside the church knew of this, but he told us he was trying to keep it secret. There was, of course, no question in the current climate that he would be able to keep his post in the army if his conversion was discovered. Most likely he would immediately be arrested, just as we had been, and would be condemned to die in his turn. We therefore had sympathy with him, and we prayed with him on several occasions.

*

The memories of my dreams were a source of strength to me during those days, and I often read over the accounts I had written. I was secretly hoping that I would be granted just one more dream before the day of the games, but I said nothing about this to the others.

One morning Saturus shook me awake.

"Perpetua," he was saying, "wake up, my sister."

I look at him, bleary-eyed, and could see immediately that something had happened, by the look of joy on his face. I sat up.

"What is it?" I asked.

"I need a sheet of papyrus, and your pen," he said, excitedly. "I've been given a dream!"

"You?" I said. He had caught me off guard, newly awoken from sleep, and I confess that my instinctive reaction to this news was grossly uncharitable. I had begun to take it for granted that it was I who had the dreams, and recounted them to others.

The thought that someone else, even if it was Saturus, might be given a dream awakened an intense jealousy within me. Now he was looking at me, evidently trying to read some meaning into the single word I had uttered. Almost immediately I began to feel guilty. What had I ever done to deserve to be singled out as the only one who should receive dreams from the Lord?

"That's wonderful," I said, though I still did not feel any excitement about it inside. "What was it about?"

"I dreamed we had died," he said, "and we were taken to heaven by angels. You were there at my side, Perpetua, and the others were with us."

"What was it like?" I asked, my curiosity now getting the better of my pride. And the fact that I had been in the dream made it a little easier to take. By now the others had also gathered around to listen.

"It was like a huge garden," said Saturus. "There were rose bushes, and the most amazing flowers all around. There were tall trees, like cypresses, with leaves that were constantly falling to the ground. There was a wonderful smell, too. You felt as though breathing the air actually gave you nourishment, that you might not have to ever eat or drink if you could just breathe in that air."

"Did you meet anyone there?" asked Revocatus.

"There were angels," said Saturus. "They wanted to treat us with great honour and respect, which I found rather embarrassing, since they themselves looked so radiant and beautiful. We also met four people that I didn't recognise. You others did, however. They were the four from Carthage, Jucundus, Saturninus, and Artaxius, who were burnt alive, and Quintus who died while he was still with you in prison. Then one of the angels took us to meet the Lord."

"You met the Lord?" said Felicitas, with a gasp. I was trying hard to be happy for Saturus, but there was still that niggling wounded pride in me, especially when I saw Felicitas' excited face.

"We were taken into this enclosed place – the walls were bright, and... I don't know how to describe them – as if they were made of light itself. That's where we met the Lord. He was sitting on a throne, and all around him were crowds of angels chanting together, over and over: 'Holy, holy, holy!'"

"What did he look like?" asked Felicitas.

"He looked like an old man – at least he had white hair, but when you looked at his face, it was young, the face of a youth. And there was such love in his face – I know that Perpetua has tried to describe the face that she has seen, but I could never imagine it properly myself. You felt that he knew you completely, everything about you, which of course is mostly pretty bad, and yet he still loved you completely, as if you were as perfect and lovely as he was. We were lifted up by angels so that we could kiss him, and he welcomed us home.

"There were some people standing on either side of him – I think they were elders. They said to us: 'Go out and enjoy yourselves.' So we came out of the gates again, but just as we did so -" Saturus paused, and the joyful look on his face changed to one of pain and anxiety. "This was the awful part," he said.

"What happened?" said Saturninus, with impatience. "What bad thing could possibly have happened there?"

"Well, just outside the gate we saw the bishop Optatus standing a little way away on one side and Aspasius the elder a little way away on the other. I could see that they weren't speaking to one another, and they were both very sad. They came up to us, and threw themselves at our feet, begging us to make peace between them. We said to them: 'What are you doing falling at our feet?'

"It was terrible to see them like that, in that otherwise blissful place. We lifted them to their feet and took them over to sit down under a rose arbour, and we spoke with them, trying to see what the problem was between them. But some of the angels came and began to lead them away. 'These ones have come here to find rest,' they told them. 'You must settle your quarrels among yourselves.' They seemed to blame the bishop for allowing his church to become so divided."

"It's awful," said Felicitas, "but it's exactly like we knew was happening in the church in Thuburbo Minus. Oh, why can't they live together in peace?"

"It is pride that is the root of such things," I said, thoughtfully. The others looked at me, sensing that I had something on my mind that had made me say that. "I fear we are all in danger of falling into that trap."

"Well, the angels wouldn't allow them to trouble us, in any case. We were told to rest and enjoy ourselves. These problems were no longer ours, they said. And anyway, it was difficult to feel sad or worried in that place. It was so beautiful. Besides, there were lots of other brothers and sisters there who had died, like we had. And we knew that there would no longer be any divisions or quarrels between us there. We were all one family, and we had come home."

At that point Saturus stopped. He was staring up at the window with a faraway look in his eyes.

"What happened next?" asked Felicitas, eagerly. He looked down from the window.

"That's all," he said. "That's when I woke up."

We all sat in silence for some moments, contemplating the images that Saturus had just been describing. It was now only four days until the day of the games. In four days, I thought to myself, we'll be there. And what will it matter then who was given a dream and who wasn't? Then it will be real for all of us.

"Here," I said with a smile, handing Saturus a sheet of papyrus and my pen, "Write it all down now."

So he began to write, but just then, Felicitas interrupted once more.

"I was there with you, wasn't I?" she asked him.

"You were," he replied.

We had been getting increasingly worried about Felicitas, who was now in her eighth month, and had grown quite large. Pudens had confirmed that she would certainly not be taken away to die until she had given birth, but that the rest of us would fight at the games as previously ordered. She was miserable at the thought of being left behind and then, once the baby was born, being killed alongside some common criminals somewhere. But now Saturus' dream had obviously reawakened a hope in her.

"Perhaps the baby will come before the day of the games after all," she said. And yet, there was no sign that such a premature delivery was imminent.

Two days passed, and still there was no sign of anything. I decided I had had enough of waiting.

"Listen," I said to the others, "it is now or never for Felicitas' child. I believe that only a miracle can bring about the birth at this stage. But is our God not a God of miracles? Let's all pray together now for this thing, and let's not stop praying until we have an answer."

The others all agreed, and so right away Felicitas knelt down in the middle of the cell, and the rest of us stood around her, and laid our hands on her.

"Wait," I said, suddenly convinced that our prayer was certainly going to be answered. I went across to the bars and called a guard over, saying that we wished to speak to Pudens the adjutant. When he came, I explained to him what we were going to do.

"I am convinced that the Lord is going to answer," I said, "so can you have a midwife called to the prison? Who knows – by the time she gets here her services may already be required!"

"Yes of course, my lady," said Pudens, and hurried off without a moment's hesitation.

And with that, I returned to join the others, and we began to pray as we had never prayed together before.

24

The Last Days

There was blood everywhere, but we had done it. The living proof was the tiny form that lay kicking and screaming in the hands of the midwife. The contractions had started almost as soon as we stopped praying, and even I had been caught off guard by the rapidity of the answer to our prayers. Not that there had been anything particularly miraculous about the delivery once it had been set in motion. It was long and hard, as we should have expected with such a premature birth, and more than once I was fearful that, far from being left to die after the rest of us, Felicitas was in danger of dying two days before us.

Pudens had posted a guard outside the cell with instructions to fetch anything that the midwife needed, and although he was of some use once or twice during the long and arduous delivery, for most of the time I wished he wasn't there. He seemed to treat the whole thing as a spectacle put on for his entertainment, and it was when Felicitas seemed in most pain that he seemed to relish the spectacle the most. Preparation, I reflected, for what we would all be going through in the arena in two days time.

"Doesn't seem to be able to stand much pain, does she?" he commented idly, after one particularly difficult moment. He gave a contemptuous laugh. "Obviously didn't think of that when she signed up for the amphitheatre games, eh?"

Felicitas gave him a withering look, but when she spoke her voice was quiet and controlled.

"I'm going through this on my own," she said, "and I willingly accept it for the sake of the child within me. But in the amphitheatre I know that I won't be suffering on my own.

There is another who lives within me who will suffer with me then, and it will be a joy to suffer for his sake. So do not think that I would shrink back now, having failed to count the cost."

Thankfully it was soon after that that the baby finally emerged, and the worst of the ordeal was over. It was a little girl. What her chances of survival were I didn't think too hard about, but the midwife seemed optimistic.

"She's a healthy little thing," she said. "If she's well cared for there's no reason why she shouldn't pull through."

But the end of that story, I thought to myself, we shall never know. Later Pomponius and Tertius visited and Felicitas gave the child into their care. She had deliberately forced herself to try not to become attached to her, knowing that it would only make things more difficult.

"Don't worry," said Pomponius. "I'm sure she'll be well cared for. We'll find one of the sisters who will be more than willing to take her as her own – particularly in view of who her mother is."

*

I was lying awake in our cell when suddenly I heard a violent knocking echoing along the corridor. Someone was at the door of the prison, and was calling me. I got up, and found that the cell door was not locked. This did not strike me as strange, and I gradually became aware as I walked through the prison towards the main gate, past sleeping guards, that I was in fact dreaming once more.

It was Pomponius who was at the door of the prison, and I unlocked the gate and went out to join him. We were not in the city of Carthage, however, but in a desolate country. The only signs of human habitation were the prison, which soon melted into the shadows behind us, and, up ahead, the enormous shape of the amphitheatre, which loomed larger and larger as we approached it. We were both hurrying, as if eager to get there, and when we arrived we were out of breath.

Pomponius seemed to know exactly where to go. He led me through dark corridors beneath the terraces, where the faint noise of the crowds above us could just be heard. Then we emerged into the arena, with the roar of the crowd all around us. The deacon took me to the centre of the arena, and left me there.

"Don't worry," he said before leaving. "You are not alone. We are praying for you."

I was waiting for the beasts to be set loose, wondering what creatures I was going to face, but then, to my surprise, a man emerged – the proud figure of an Egyptian wrestler. I was not going to fight the beasts at all, but rather, it was to be a wrestling match. This seemed bizarre, for it was unheard of for women to compete in such a contest. However, in the almost casual way that reality shifts in the dream world, I suddenly became aware that my body was not in fact that of a woman, but that of a man. Just then my seconds appeared, stripped off my clothes, and began to rub me with oil in preparation for the fight. Meanwhile, the Egyptian, a menacing brute, was rolling himself in the dust. If it was not a beast I was to fight, nevertheless my opponent seemed scarcely human.

At that point the master of the games appeared. He was no ordinary man, but a giant. His head was higher than the top of the amphitheatre. He held the rod of his office in one hand, and a living branch with golden apples growing from it in the other.

"The rules of the fight are these," he announced. "If the Egyptian wins, he will kill her with the sword, but if she defeats him, she will win this branch."

With that, he withdrew, and the two of us approached each other. In a moment of panic, I realised I had no idea what to do in such a contest. But then, as he sprang at me, my instincts took over, and I found that, for one thing, I seemed to be immensely strong. My opponent was also strong, however, and for some time we wrestled together, neither able to get a proper grip on the other, but always twisting and writhing out of each other's grasp. The Egyptian seemed to be trying desperately to get a hold of my feet, but every time he got close to doing so, I used my feet to strike out at his face. The contest continued like this for some time, both of us becoming more and more desperate in our attempts to overpower the other.

Then all at once I realised that I had another tremendous advantage. I could float in the air, defying the very laws of gravity, and I began to do so, pummelling my opponent merci-lessly, with my feet completely off the ground. He was so taken aback by this that he began to retreat in confusion. I saw my opportunity and made a swift lunge at his head, grasping it in my arms, with my hands locked together behind it. In this way I brought him down to land on his face in the dust of the arena floor. Then I stood over him, with one foot placed squarely on his head. I had won. The crowd were cheering wildly, and the master of the games reappeared. Now, however, he was of a more normal size. From somewhere, there was the sound of psalms being sung – it was my assistants. I walked up to the master of the games, and then I recognised his face for the first time – it was none other than Jesus himself. He handed me the branch, kissed me, and said "Peace be with you, my daughter." Overjoyed, I turned and headed towards the Gate of Life. But before I reached it I had woken up.

My first thought on waking was of tremendous gratitude. I had felt so guilty about my pride and jealousy that I had given up hope of being given any more dreams. I realised again, however, that these dreams were not some kind of a reward for my own goodness, but simply a gift freely given by the Lord to one who deserved nothing.

My next thought was to work out the meaning of the dream. The Egyptian was Satan himself – that at least seemed clear to me. And therefore the message was that it was not just wild beasts we would be fighting the following day, but the devil himself. I also knew that we could be confident of victory. We would die, but our very deaths would be the victory by which we would defeat Satan. Much as he might wish us to suffer, he would far rather we relent, even at this stage, offer the sacrifice, curse Jesus and thus return to being his slaves and prisoners once more. But I had crushed his head, and not for the first time either, and I knew that in reality, that is precisely what I would be doing once more, even as I faced the terrors of the amphitheatre.

One by one the others woke, Felicitas last of all, having been exhausted after her long ordeal of the previous day. And so we began the last day of our lives. What is it like, to know that you have only one more day to live? For me, it was strangely peaceful. After breakfast I wrote down my dream, and then told it to the others. We talked together, and prayed together. We were all at peace. We knew that the struggle was nearly over. For it had been a struggle, for each of us. We all knew how desperately easy it would be to give up the fight, even now. A few words to the guard, a message to the governor, one small sacrifice. And then freedom – of a sort. But each of us, too, knew how high the stakes were, and how much we would lose if we bought our freedom in this way. And somehow we had found the strength each day to carry on the fight. So now the end was in sight. Tomorrow, the struggle would be over at last.

We had one last request to put to Pudens, and it was Saturus who spoke to him when he came to see us that morning.

"What are the arrangements for the *cena libera* this evening?" he asked the adjutant.

"You are to eat here, in the prison," he replied. "Normally we use the mess hall. The public will be allowed in, of course."

This was only what we expected. The *cena libera*, or free banquet, was the traditional last meal of those who were going to fight in the amphitheatre on the following day, and the public were allowed in to watch. The thought of going through such a performance was unpleasant to say the least.

"We have been discussing it," went on Saturus, "and we would like to hold it as a fellowship meal. At least then those who come to gloat over us will not be able to accuse us of gluttony or drunkenness."

"That," said Pudens, "is an excellent idea."

*

So that is what we did. When evening came we were taken up to the mess hall, and we sat around a table. Food and wine were brought to us, and though it was the best meal we had had for months, it was a moderate affair. Normally the *cena libera* was celebrated as an orgy of eating and drinking. For many participants their only hope of getting to sleep that night would be by drinking themselves unconscious. We, however, ate and drank as if it were a normal evening meal. We began with prayers, and in between courses we sang hymns and psalms, and read from the scriptures. Pudens had arranged for some books to be brought from the church.

Even before we began there were people there who had come to watch. They seemed surprised at the small amount of food and drink that was being set before us, and some began to jeer and mock us. Others, however, remained silent, and watched and listened with curiosity. Those who were not church members or catechumens, would normally have no opportunity of witnessing a Christian fellowship meal, so our public version of it was a rare event. Saturus took the chance to speak to the onlookers.

"See," he said, "this is what we have been condemned for. We are Christians – we meet together peacefully to eat a meal. We sing songs of praise and thanks to God, and we pray together. Now you can see for yourselves what dangerous criminals you are dealing with."

"Scum!" cried one of those watching, "You deserve nothing but death – you are traitors and sorcerers! The world will be a better place once you are gone."

"Look at the dogs!" said another. "Even the sight of them makes me sick!"

"Why come to see us, then?" asked Saturus. "Won't it be enough to watch us die tomorrow? If you can't stand the sight of us, you don't need to stay."

"Gah!" came the reply. "Thinks he's clever, that one does."

"You should be grateful of the company," said another, but in a less contemptuous tone. "We've come to enjoy the meal with you."

"That's kind," replied Saturus, "but we cannot count you as our friends who will turn into our enemies tomorrow. And I hope you are taking a careful note of what we look like, for you may see us again one day. Not in this world, it's true, but in the world to come, when you stand before the judgement seat of God. What will you say then, when the Judge of the World confronts you with our innocent blood?"

At this, some continued to mock us and insult us, but others seemed genuinely taken aback by these words. Evidently they were beginning to question all that was commonly said about Christians, and to wonder just how much of it was true. I was praying that some among them might even believe because of what they saw and heard.

And then, at last, it was all over. The members of the public were ushered out, and we were taken back to our cell for the night. I lay awake for a while, staring out through the barred windows at the starlit sky outside. I thought back over my life, picturing all the people I had known. I thought of Dinocrates, and of my other brothers Gaius and Cornelius. I thought of my father, and my mother. I thought of little Marcus, now in my mother's care. Some memories were happy, others were painful, but the memory of Marcus, his tiny body clutched against my own, was the most painful of all. I remembered my lessons with Sosigenes, and I thought of Lupercus and his family. Where were they now, I wondered? I thought of Felicitas and Revocatus, and then I remembered Secundulus, and how he had suffered. Then I recalled how I had first gone with Felicitas to meet Saturus. I glanced over to where he lay, apparently sleeping peacefully, and I laughed quietly as I remembered the struggles I had gone through with my feelings for him. But he was not sleeping, and he opened his eyes and looked over in my direction at the sound of my laughter.

"What is it, sister?" he asked in a whisper. I felt an instinctive knot of fear in my stomach at the thought of him discovering what I had been laughing at. But then I felt a great desire to tell him. I realised that no ill could come of it now, and it seemed suddenly important that he should know, before we died together.

I rose quietly and went across to the corner of the cell furthest from the other sleeping forms.

"Come and I'll tell you," I said in a low voice, sitting down. When he had got up too, and come across to sit down beside me, I wondered what on earth I should say. He waited patiently as I sat silent for some moments.

"Saturus," I said at last, "I have a confession to make."

"If there is something on your conscience," he replied, "it is good for you to be rid of the burden before tomorrow."

"I don't know if it's on my conscience now," I said, "but it was once."

In the dim light I could see he looked intrigued, but he said nothing, waiting for me to continue.

"It... it concerns you," I said, getting the words out with some effort. "It concerns my feelings for you."

"My lady," he said, sounding rather bewildered, "I don't understand what you mean."

"Saturus, I loved you." There. It was out. Saturus said nothing, and I felt terribly embarrassed, wondering if I had done the right thing at all. "I loved you in a way I never should have," I went on. "I was a married woman, and you were not my husband. But I never loved my husband – I only ever loved you. I struggled so hard – do you remember the first time I came to the catechismal class? You were teaching about the wife of noble character. Didn't you think it strange that I said nothing all through the lesson?"

"I – I don't remember," said Saturus in a faltering voice. There was a pause, then a sound came from Saturus which might have been a laugh, though it almost sounded more like a sob.

"My lady," he said, clutching my arm. Then he pulled away again. "My sister – why did you marry him? I mean, if you didn't love him?"

"It was my father," I said. "He and Lupercus' father were old friends. They'd always wanted us to get married."

"But you weren't obliged to accept that, surely?"

"We had a deal, Lupercus and I. My father would never have allowed me to come to the catechismal classes, but Lupercus offered me the freedom to come – in return for being his wife. Oh, he loved me – there was never any question of that."

Saturus was silent for a long time. I didn't know what to say, so I remained silent too. Finally he spoke.

"I know how he felt," he said. "I too would have given anything to have you as my wife."

At first the meaning of these words did not sink in. I thought he was simply being polite, offering an idle compliment. But then the earnestness of his tone and the utter sincerity of what he had said came home to me.

"You mean you... But..." I was completely lost for words.

"Yes," he said, "we didn't know it, but we were both keeping the same secret from each other. I loved you, Perpetua. I loved you almost from the first time we met."

"But – why didn't you say anything?" Suddenly a vision flashed through my mind of how things might have happened. Saturus and I could have been married, no matter what my family said. It wasn't as if I had pandered to their wishes in any other way, I told myself with grim humour.

"You forget, my sister, that when I first met you – and began to love you – you were not a Christian. I was waiting to see if you were really going to follow Jesus. Otherwise you could never have been my wife. And then I didn't see you for several months. When at last I saw you again, and found that you had decided to join us, you were already married."

I sat in stunned silence at the realisation of what had happened. Suddenly Saturus laughed.

"The wife of noble character – that was just coincidence. Of course, I never knew you were going to be there that Sunday. But when you came, and I saw you once more, married now – it was very painful."

Gently, I took his arm.

"I'm sorry," I said, simply.

"No," he answered, "don't be sorry. I don't think it was ever meant to be. It was just part of the struggle. Just one incident in the battle. I only wish Lupercus had joined us too, that's all."

"Perhaps he will, yet," I said. "I find my faith has grown these last months. I can believe such things now, though I would not have done before."

"Perpetua," he said, taking my hand in his and giving it a gentle squeeze. "Thank you."

I wanted to take him in my arms, but with a great effort of will I held myself back. Instead I squeezed his hand in return.

"Good night," I said, and we both went quietly back to our beds.

For a while I still lay awake, looking out at the stars once more, my mind turning over and over what might have been. But soon I drifted off into a peaceful, dreamless sleep.

25

Weaponless Warriors

I'd never had anything against killing, in itself. It was my job, you might say. I couldn't have spent a lifetime in the army if I were the squeamish type. And yes, I've done my fair share of it over the years. I fought with the Legion in the mountains of the west not too many years ago, putting down the barbarian uprisings there. And in my younger days I campaigned in Germany with the emperor himself. But killing a man in battle who is coming against you armed, and who has chosen to risk his life in what he considers a worthwhile cause is one thing. Leading a group of unarmed prisoners to the amphitheatre to be ripped to pieces by wild animals as a form of entertainment for the masses is another. It had never seemed to me a particularly noble task for a soldier in the Army of Imperial Rome. It seemed particularly ignoble when the prisoners included two women, one of whom had just given birth to a child a month premature. Add to this the fact that the charges on which the prisoners had been found guilty, I myself was now guilty of as well, and the whole thing took on a nightmarish quality.

These then were the thoughts that were going through my mind that morning, as I accompanied the five to their death in the arena. In the few weeks I had had them under my charge in the military prison in Carthage they had become my friends – no, more than that, my brothers and sisters. I owed them so much, I felt that nothing I could do would be adequate to repay them. For they had shown me, even unwittingly, the very Gate of Life, the way out of my prison, and I had stepped through it, to share with them the joy, the peace, and the freedom that they themselves had found.

And now I was leading them to their death. That was how I was repaying them. And yet that procession, from the prison to the games, seemed more like a triumphal march for them than the last steps of a group of condemned criminals. I was watching them out of the corner of my eye. Their heads were held high, and their faces seemed to shine. I knew why, of course. It was not the terror of the arena that they were thinking of, but the images of what lay beyond. They had shared with me dreams that they had had, in which they had seen just a glimpse of the joy that awaited them on the other side of death. And I knew, too, that they regarded themselves as soldiers in the thick of battle, but that their victory was certain. I knew that feeling myself. To be marching towards the enemy, and to know that the outcome is in no doubt whatever, as long as each man does his duty and stands firm.

It was only this aspect of the matter that enabled me to keep going that morning, for their air of joy and triumph was infectious. I shared in it, however ironic that might seem. And as we marched through the narrow crowded streets, the people stared. There wasn't much jeering, less than was usual in the case of a troop of condemned prisoners being led to their execution. It was more a matter of curious, even bewildered, stares. They couldn't understand, these common people, the citizens of Carthage, how a group who were about to die could appear so triumphant. And so they stared, and wondered. Many of them were making their way, along with us, towards the amphitheatre. They wanted to be there for the kill, to see if these strange aberrations of humanity would be as brave once in the arena as they appeared to be as they passed through the streets to get there. And the prisoners were not ashamed to return their stares. Perpetua in particular I noticed, looking every inch the noblewoman, despite her months of imprisonment, walking along calmly as if she were out for a morning stroll, and defying the watching crowds with her dignified gaze.

At the gates of the amphitheatre we encountered our first taste of battle, so to speak. The organiser of the games was there in person, along with several other officials, including my direct superior, the military tribune. The organiser of the games had prepared a set of clothes for the prisoners to wear. He had thought it would be amusing for them to be dressed in robes like priests of Saturn and priestesses of Ceres. It would be a sort of sign that their stand as Christians and their refusal to participate in pagan religion had ultimately been crushed and defeated.

The prisoners looked at the garments. They had reluctantly begun to put them on when Perpetua spoke up. She was holding up the robe that she had been given, in a way that suggested that it might carry some unmentionable disease within its folds, and she was looking at it with revulsion.

"I cannot wear this," she said, simply.

"Sorry, lady, you haven't got any choice," replied the games organiser, with a sneer. "You seem to forget that you're a condemned criminal. It's my business to keep the crowds in there happy, and I've chosen these outfits in order to do that."

Perpetua turned to him with a bold and fiery look in her eyes.

"We have been condemned for exercising our freedom," she said, "for refusing to bow to the dictates of an unjust edict which condemns the innocent. We have gladly accepted death as the price of that freedom. How dare you now try to take that dearly bought freedom away from us again?"

The man was so stunned by the ferocity with which these words were delivered that he could find nothing to say in reply. I looked at the military tribune, who was clearly uncomfortable at this development, but who now took the opportunity of exercising his authority.

"The lady speaks the truth," he announced. "They shall appear in the clothes they have on now."

"But..." began the organiser, but he was silenced by an impatient gesture from the tribune.

"These prisoners are my responsibility, not yours," he snapped. "I have made my decision."

And so we continued on our way, into the gate of the amphitheatre, and were soon swallowed up within the dark labyrinth of passageways beneath the terraces, making our way to the arena entrance from which the prisoners were to emerge. Once we had arrived there was no delay, for they were actually waiting for us, and the five were immediately sent out into the arena.

The moment they appeared there was a tremendous roar from the watching mob. They strode over towards the podium where the governor Hilarianus was seated, the one who had sentenced them to death at these games. They appeared defiant as they stood before him, and Saturus was evidently trying to say something to him, but his voice was drowned by the noise of the crowd. Nevertheless, he used gestures and signs to convey his meaning. Pointing at Hilarianus and then himself, he then pointed up to heaven and then at Hilarianus.

"You have condemned us," he was saying, "but God himself will condemn you if you do not turn to him and repent."

It was clear to all those watching what was meant, and for such an act of defiance and provocation the crowd wanted an immediate punishment.

"Scourge them!" the cry went up. "Scourge them!"

Hilarianus, always one to play to the crowds, quickly ordered that this be done, and a troop of gladiators was sent out. There is a low platform towards one end of the arena, with stocks for prisoners to be chained up for various purposes. The five were led up onto this platform, bound ready in a line, and then duly scourged, all five together, while the crowd bayed and cheered as their blood began to flow. I could not watch this, but turned away.

"God forgive them," I prayed under my breath, "and forgive me too, for bringing them to this."

After this they were unbound and brought back to the gateway, in preparation for their encounter with the beasts. Through the pain, however, I could see that their spirits had not been broken by this initial ordeal.

"Christ Jesus suffered in this way for us," said Saturus. "It is our privilege now to suffer for him."

I will not describe every detail of the events of that morning. Even if I could organise the jumbled images which lie scattered about in my memory like the tattered fragments of a nightmare remembered on waking, it would be too painful to go through it so systematically. For others in the church who witnessed the contest, the saintly bearing of the martyrs throughout was, no doubt, a tremendous inspiration and encouragement. For me, however, all such thoughts were tainted by the guilty knowledge that I myself had played a part in inflicting this torture upon them.

It was Saturninus and Revocatus who first faced the beasts, being paired at the start with a leopard. The creature drew blood with its claws, but did not attack them in earnest, so that after a time it was withdrawn. The two were then placed in the stocks on the platform where they were left to the attentions of a bear. This creature did far more damage than the leopard, and left them badly mauled, though still alive.

Saturus, meanwhile, escaped lightly. He was initially matched with a wild boar, being chained together with it by a young gladiator. But the animal showed no interest in the Christian whom it was supposed to be attacking, turning instead on the gladiator and goring him horribly. I heard that the man actually died from his wounds some days later. Saturus, on the other hand, was merely dragged along the ground for a few paces, his dignity suffering more than anything. Then, when he had been placed in the stocks to await the bear, that creature refused even to come out of its cage, so that Saturus was still unhurt, apart from the scourging, when he returned to the gateway.

I should mention that these trials closely matched what the prisoners themselves had wished for. Saturus, the oldest and wisest among them, had expressed his desire to be finished off quickly by one bite of a leopard's jaws. His greatest fear was to be slowly ripped apart by a bear, that most gruesome of deaths in the arena. Saturninus and Revocatus had both argued, on the other hand, that the greater their suffering on the day, the greater the reward that would await them beyond death. Accordingly they had vowed not to shrink from any trial, however terrible, that was put before them.

However, it is the contest of the two women, who were to be pitted against a mad heifer, which remains most clearly etched on my mind. The actual contest was preceded by an episode the like of which I have never witnessed before or since in the amphitheatre. The women were stripped naked for the fight, placed in nets, and then led out into the arena. At this point the mood of the crowd seemed to shift. Gladiators, wild animals, and even unarmed men were one thing to watch. This however, suddenly seemed to have crossed an unspoken boundary into unacceptable barbarism. The two must have appeared so utterly defenceless as to cause offence to the crowd at being presented with such a spectacle. Felicitas, fresh from childbirth, actually had milk dripping from her breasts. They stood there in the middle of the arena, motionless, while the noise of the crowd gradually ebbed away to an uneasy silence. Hilarianus, seeing that things were not going according to plan, quickly gave an order that they be taken away, dressed, and then brought back.

This done, they then faced the heifer. The crowd seemed to be happier with them clothed. Not that this made any sense, for they were still two defenceless young women, barely out of adolescence, innocent of any crime, who were about to be torn to pieces by wild beasts, whether they were clothed or not. It was as if their clothes somehow had the effect of veiling the stark truth of the matter, which had been too painfully obvious when they were presented naked.

Even when they had been tossed by the heifer, and Perpetua lay on the ground wounded, with her tunic ripped at the side, she made an almost absurd effort to pull the tear closed, so as not to expose her naked thigh. Her hair too had become dishevelled in the fight, and she now asked for a hairpin to pin it back up. I believe she had noticed the unease with which the crowd had greeted the sight of two young women being sent out to face the beasts, and she was exploiting this weak point up to the hilt. The longer she could maintain the impression of an upright and modest young noblewoman, the more shame would be felt by the watching mob, whether it was openly expressed or not.

Felicitas meanwhile had fallen and been trampled by the beast and was struggling to rise again. Perpetua now saw this and hurried over to her. She helped her to her feet, and the two stood together, defiant in their blood-soaked clothes. To those who had come to the terraces that day to be entertained, this sight was apparently too much to take and cries of "Leave them be!" and "Call off the beast!" could be heard. The crowd seemed to have had their fill of torturing defenceless young women, and the heifer was taken away, while the two made their way towards the Gate of Life. Once again the course of the morning's programme seemed to have taken a strange turn. As they stumbled over towards the gateway the crowd was subdued, and while they were still some way away from it I was amazed to hear the sound of soft singing on the air. Perpetua and Felicitas had raised their voices together in a psalm as they staggered across the arena. The sound was so out of place there, and so unexpected, that it had an almost dreamlike quality. As they passed closer to us I could make out the words:

> *"Therefore my heart is glad and my tongue rejoices;*
> *my body also will rest secure,*
> *Because you will not abandon me to the grave,*
> *nor will you let your Holy One see decay.*
> *You have made known to me the path of life;*
> *you will fill me with joy in your presence,*
> *with eternal pleasures at your right hand."*

By now they had reached the gateway, and they stopped singing. Perpetua suddenly looked around her, like someone who had been asleep or in a trance. She didn't seem to know where she was. I later heard what she had said when she got there.

"Well then," she asked, "when are we to be thrown to that heifer or whatever it's to be?"

I have seen men wounded in battle who behaved in a similar way. Terribly wounded, they nevertheless seemed not to suffer the pain and were completely unaware of what had happened to them. A number of people whom I recognised as catechumens from the church in Carthage had by this time congregated around them. One had brought clean water and cloths, and they now did what they could to attend to the wounds of the prisoners.

Meanwhile, Saturus, still relatively unhurt was at the

entrance gate with me.

"The Lord has spared me up till now, just as I asked," he told me. "You can be confident that soon it will all be over in an instant – see, I am to face the leopard now. One bite and I will be gone from this world."

With that, he was led out to meet the creature, but it did not happen quite as he had predicted. The leopard did indeed attack him with a single bite, but it did not kill him. It did however draw a spectacular amount of blood. In an instant he was drenched scarlet from head to foot. I knew that with such rapid loss of blood he would not live long. The leopard, a creature which, I must say, seemed easily satisfied, left him alone after that, and he managed to stagger back towards me. This was the kind of thing the crowd loved, and they roared out "*Salvum lotum*! *Salvum lotum*! Well washed!" It was the traditional greeting used when someone has just been to the baths. I could not help thinking that they were right, though they meant it only as a crude joke. What a washing that was, to be drenched like that in the blood of martyrdom.

"So – I am not quite gone," he gasped, as he approached me. I could only stare at him in horror. "No," he continued, evidently seeing the expression on my face, "you must not be discouraged by these things. They should rather strengthen you. And now – goodbye... Remember me, and keep the faith."

"I will always remember you, my brother," I said, with tears in my eyes. "Only tell me that you forgive me for what I have done."

"God has forgiven you," he said weakly, but with a solemn look in his eyes, "and so do I. Here – give me that ring."

He indicated a gold ring I was wearing. I took it off and handed it to him. He dipped it in the wound from which his blood was still flowing copiously, then handed it back to me.

"I forgive you, my brother," he repeated. "Remember me."

I took the ring without a word – I could say nothing – then he turned to stagger back out into the arena. After only a few steps, however, he collapsed unconscious, and the blood continued to seep into the sand around him. The mangled bodies of Saturninus and Revocatus had already been thrown into the Porta Libitinensis, though they were not yet dead, and Saturus' body was now dragged over and left beside them. It was almost all over now, but the crowd had one more request. They wanted to see each one killed out in the open by a gladiator's sword. No doubt there was some superstition behind this, based on stories of Christians being spirited back to life. The four who were still conscious came out of their own accord when they heard this, carrying the limp body of Saturus between them. A young gladiator was then sent to finish them off. As he passed his sword across the throat of each one they died in silence. All, that is, except Perpetua. As she knelt last of all before the gladiator and lifted her head to bare her neck I could see her gazing sternly into his face, defiant to the last.

The man looked petrified. His hand trembled as he tried to strike her, and instead of cutting the artery the sword merely cut into bone. Perpetua screamed and clutched at her shoulder. Then she took hold of the young man's sword hand and guided it to her own throat. In stark terror he pulled the sword across her neck and she slumped to the ground.

*

At that moment something snapped inside me. I looked down at the blood-stained ring that I still held in my left hand, which I had not yet replaced on my finger. For a moment it seemed that I was holding in my hand the very blood of Christ himself, and I suddenly knew that he was calling me to follow him more closely than I had done up till then. He was calling me to fight for him, but not with sword and shield as I had been trained to do. I was to fight in the way that I had just seen those five weaponless warriors fight in the arena that morning. For I saw now what a victory they had won. I knew that many who had witnessed the spectacle could not possibly have done so and remained unmoved.

The might of Rome had drawn itself up against five defenceless prisoners, and the truth was that it had been defeated. I saw now with startling clarity that the greatest threat to the empire was not the raging hordes of barbarians who were constantly being kept at bay on its far-flung borders. The empire and all it stood for – its values, its gods and its traditions – were being threatened by a small but faithful band of warriors who fought with no weapons other than their own innocence and their blood shed barbarously by those who knew in their hearts that their victims were indeed innocent.

I turned and walked away. My responsibilities as prison adjutant were not over, for I was supposed to take charge of disposing of the prisoners' bodies, but I knew that those from the church who were there would gladly see to that. I paid no heed to the military tribune who called after me: "Where are you going?"

I made my way through the labyrinth of passageways, drawing my sword as I went. The passageways were almost deserted and those few gladiators and assistants whom I passed paid me no attention. No-one was following me. Then, as I emerged into the bright noonday sun outside I stopped and breathed deeply, looking up into the sky. Having made my decision, I felt more peaceful than I had ever felt before. The sword I had been holding clattered to the ground at my side. I had no more need of such weapons. As I walked off down the street I lifted the heavy crested helmet from my head and threw it aside as well. I was free at last, to serve my new master.

HISTORICAL NOTE

This book is based on the true story of the martyrs from Thuburbo Minus who died in Carthage on 7th March 203. Almost all of what we know of them is to be found in the *Passio Sanctarum Perpetuae et Felicitatis* or "The Passion of Saints Perpetua and Felicitas". This is an astonishing document, universally regarded as genuine, and a jewel among early Christian writings. The bulk of it consists of a prison diary written by Perpetua herself. Since this novel has been based so closely on this document it seems crucial to make clear to the reader exactly which elements are historical and which are fiction.

The document covers the period from the arrest of the five catechumens up until the day of their martyrdom, a description of which has been added by an eye-witness. Thus Part 4 of the novel closely follows the events described in the *Passio*. Most of the rest of the novel is fiction, being an attempt to construct a plausible background to the later events. Very little is revealed in the *Passio* about the life of any of the martyrs up until the moment of their arrest, with the exception of the detail that Perpetua had a younger brother named Dinocrates who died of a facial cancer at the age of seven. Of the story related in Part 4 of the novel most is more or less historical, with the exception of a few key elements which should be noted.

Firstly the relationship between Perpetua and Saturus is entirely fictitious, suggested only by the detail that each appeared prominently at least once in the dreams of the other, whereas none of the other martyrs are mentioned by name in the dream descriptions at all.

Secondly, Perpetua's husband remains an enigma with

regard to the historical record. Perpetua is described at the beginning of the *Passio* as being "respectably married" and having a child at the breast. Subsequently she herself makes mention of her son, her father and mother, her brothers and even her aunt, but never once does she mention her husband. The character of Lupercus is also, therefore, completely fictitious. To what extent my description of the events suggests a plausible explanation for Perpetua's deafening silence on the subject of her own husband is up to the reader to judge.

As far as the dreams are concerned it should be noted that all those described after the time of the arrest are based on the dream narratives in the *Passio*, whereas all dreams and visions before that are fictitious. Perpetua is however mentioned as having had a number of such experiences at some time before she was arrested.

One other point to note is that the prison adjutant, Pudens, is a historical character, and he really did become a Christian while the martyrs were in his care. His earlier encounter with Saturus is, however, fictitious. It is interesting to note that the church calendar of Carthage, at a later date, makes mention of the martyrdom of a soldier named Pudens on the 3rd day of the Calends of May. It is tempting to believe that this was the very same one who is mentioned in the *Passio*.

The works of Tertullian are, of course, invaluable in researching the life of the church in Africa during this period. It is not certain whether his treatise *Ad Martyras* or "To the Martyrs", which appears in Chapter 23, was really addressed to this particular group of martyrs but it seems to me highly likely, given that in it, for example, he specifically addresses the women of the group.

That the martyrs were actually from Thuburbo Minus (modern day Tebourba) is not mentioned in the original Latin document, and this has led some to question this detail, and to assume that they were simply from Carthage, as the original *Passio* would lead one to believe. However, a slightly later Greek translation mentions that they were arrested in Thuburbo Minus, and the tradition has certainly been preserved by the church down to the present day that this was their home town.

It is difficult to see how this could have happened, given the dominance of the church in Carthage, if it were not true.

Unlike many impressive and well-preserved Roman sites in Tunisia, Thuburbo Minus has received little attention. Most of the remains have been built over, although one area has been preserved in the hope that it will be excavated in the future, and the site of the amphitheatre, described in Chapter 1, is clearly visible. However most of the details in the novel concerning the layout of the town are invented. It is to be hoped that, one day, excavations will shed more light on this important Roman colony, and even perhaps on the lives of Perpetua and her fellow martyrs.